Irish

Fairy Legends and Traditions

SIENA

This edition published and distributed by Parragon, 1998

Parragon
13 Whiteladies Road
Clifton
Bristol
BS8 1PB

ISBN 0 75252 676 6

Cover illustration courtesy of the Bridgeman Art Library

A copy of the British Library Cataloguing-in-Publication Data
is available from the British Library.

Printed and bound in the EC

PREFACE.

THE erudite Lessing styles a preface " the history of a book." Now, though there can be no necessity for a preface in that sense of the word to the reprint of a work of mere whim, which has been nearly ten years before the public, yet a few words are requisite to prevent the present condensed and revised edition from being considered an abridgment.

However compact may be the mode of printing adopted, the act of compressing into one volume the three in which the " Fairy Legends" originally appeared, involved to a certain extent the necessity of selection, perhaps the most difficult of all tasks judiciously to perform; but the following statement will show the system proceeded on.

Forty tales descriptive of Irish superstitions now appear instead of fifty. All superfluous annotations have been struck out, and a brief summary at the end of each section substituted, explanatory of the classification adopted, and in which a few additional notes have been introduced, as well as upon the text. It is therefore hoped that this curtailment will be regarded as an essential improvement; some useless repetition in the tales being thereby avoided, and much irrelevant matter in the notes dispensed with, although nothing which illustrates in the slightest degree the popular Fairy Creed of Ireland has been sacrificed. At the same time, the omission of a portion of the ten immaterial tales will sufficiently answer doubts idly raised as to the question of authorship.

CONTENTS.

Page

The Merrow.

The Dullahan.

The Fir Darrig.

Treasure Legends.

Rocks and Stones.

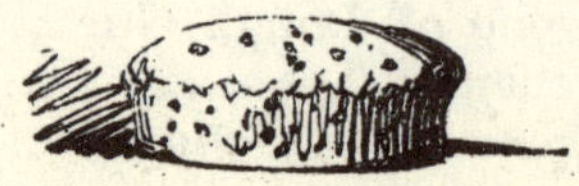

TO THE

DOWAGER LADY CHATTERTON,

CASTLE MAHON.

Thee, Lady, would I lead through Fairy-land
  (Whence cold and doubting reasoners are exiled),
  A land of dreams, with air-built castles piled;
The moonlight Shefros there, in merry band
With artful Cluricaune, should ready stand
  To welcome thee—Imagination's child!
  Till on thy ear would burst so sadly wild
The Banshee's shriek, who points with wither'd hand.
In the dim twilight should the Phooka come,
  Whose dusky form fades in the sunny light,
  That opens clear calm Lakes upon thy sight,
Where blessed spirits dwell in endless bloom.
I know thee, Lady—thou wilt not deride
Such Fairy Scenes.—Then onward with thy Guide.

T. Crofton Croker.

The Wood Engravings after Designs by Mr. Brooke, R. H. A.
Mr. M'Clise, and the Author.

FAIRY LEGENDS.

THE SHEFRO.

———————————————"Fairy Elves
Whose midnight revels, by a forest side
Or fountain, some belated peasant sees,
Or dreams he sees, while over-head the Moon
Sits arbitress, and nearer to the earth
Wheels her pale course."——

MILTON.

LEGENDS OF THE SHEFRO.

THE

LEGEND OF KNOCKSHEOGOWNA.

I.

IN Tipperary is one of the most singularly shaped hills in the world. It has got a peak at the top like a conical nightcap thrown carelessly over your head as you awake in the morning. On the very point is built a sort of lodge, where in the summer the lady who built it and her friends used to go on parties of pleasure; but that was long after the days of the fairies, and it is, I believe, now deserted.

But before lodge was built, or acre sown, there was close to the head of this hill a large pasturage, where a herdsman spent his days and nights among the herd. The spot had been an old fairy ground, and the good people were angry that the scene of their light and airy gambols should be trampled by the rude hoofs of bulls and cows. The lowing of the cattle sounded sad in their ears, and the chief of the fairies of the hill determined in person to drive away the new comers; and the way she thought of was this. When the harvest nights came on, and the moon shone bright and brilliant over the hill, and the cattle were lying down hushed and quiet, and the herdsman, wrapt in his mantle, was musing with his heart gladdened by the glorious company of the stars twinkling above him, she would come and dance before him, — now in one shape — now in another, — but all ugly and frightful to behold. One time she would be a great horse, with the wings of an eagle, and a tail like a dragon, hissing loud and spitting fire. Then in a moment she would change into a little man lame of a leg, with a bull's head, and a lambent flame playing round it. Then into a great ape, with duck's feet and a turkey-cock's tail. But I should be all day about it were I to tell you all the shapes she took. And then she would roar, or neigh, or hiss, or bellow, or howl, or hoot, as never yet was roaring, neighing, hissing, bellowing, howling, or hooting, heard in this world before or since. The poor herdsman would cover his face, and call on all the saints for help, but it was no use. With one puff of her breath she would blow away the fold of his great coat, let him hold it never so tightly over his eyes, and not a saint in heaven paid him the slightest attention. And to make matters worse, he never could stir; no, nor even shut his eyes, but there was obliged to stay, held by what power he knew not, gazing at these terrible sights until the hair of his head would lift his hat half a foot over his crown, and his teeth would be ready to fall out from chattering. But the cattle would scamper about mad, as if they were bitten by the fly; and this would last until the sun rose over the hill.

The poor cattle from want of rest were pining away, and food did them no good; besides, they met with accidents without end.   Never a night passed that some of them did not fall into a pit, and get maimed, or may be, killed. Some would tumble into a river and be drowned: in a word, there seemed never to be an end of the accidents. But what made the matter worse, there could not be a herdsman got to tend the cattle by night. One visit from the fairy drove the stoutest-hearted almost mad. The owner of the ground did not know what to do. He offered double, treble, quadruple wages, but not a man could be found for the sake of money to go through the horror of facing the fairy. She rejoiced at the successful issue of her project, and continued her pranks. The herd gradually thinning, and no man daring to remain on the ground, the fairies came back in numbers, and gambolled as merrily as before, quaffing dew-drops from acorns, and spreading their feast on the heads of capacious mushrooms.

What was to be done? the puzzled farmer thought in vain. He found that his substance was daily diminishing, his people terrified, and his rent-day coming round. It is no wonder that he looked gloomy, and walked mournfully down the road. Now in that part of the world dwelt a man of the name of Larry Hoolahan, who played on the pipes better than any other player within fifteen parishes. A roving dashing blade was Larry, and feared nothing. Give him plenty of liquor, and he would defy the devil. He would face a mad bull, or fight single-handed against a fair. In one of his gloomy walks the farmer met him, and on Larry's asking the cause of his down looks, he told him all his misfortunes. " If that is all ails you," said Larry, " make your mind easy. Were there as many fairies on Knocksheogowna as there are potato blossoms in Eliogurty, I would face them. It would be a queer thing, indeed, if I, who never was afraid of a proper man, should turn my back upon a brat of a fairy not the bigness of one's thumb." " Larry," said the farmer, " do not talk so bold, for you know not who is hearing you; but, if you make your words good, and watch my herds for a week on the top of the mountain, your hand shall be free of my dish till the sun has burnt itself down to the bigness of a farthing rushlight."

The bargain was struck, and Larry went to the hill-top, when the moon began to peep over the brow. He had been regaled at the farmer's house, and was bold with the extract of barley-corn. So he took his seat on a big stone under a hollow of the hill, with his back to the wind, and pulled out his pipes. He had not played long when the voice of the fairies was heard upon the blast, like a slow stream of music. Presently they burst out into a loud laugh, and Larry could plainly hear one say, " What! another man upon the fairies' ring? Go to him, queen, and make him repent his rashness;" and they flew away. Larry felt them pass by his face as they flew like a swarm of midges; and, looking up hastily, he saw between the moon and him a great black cat, standing on the very tip of its claws, with its back up, and mewing with the voice of a water-mill.

Presently it swelled up towards the sky, and, turning round on its left hind leg, whirled till it fell to the ground, from which it started up in the shape of a salmon, with a cravat round its neck, and a pair of new top boots. " Go on, jewel," said Larry; " if you dance, I'll pipe ;" and he struck up. So she turned into this, and that, and the other, but still Larry played on, as he well knew how. At last she lost patience, as ladies will do when you do not mind their scolding, and changed herself into a calf, milk-white as the cream of Cork, and with eyes as mild as those of the girl I love. She came up gentle and fawning, in hopes to throw him off his guard by quietness, and then to work him some wrong. But Larry was not so deceived; for when she came up, he, dropping his pipes, leaped upon her back.

Now from the top of Knocksheogowna, as you look westward to the broad Atlantic, you will see the Shannon, queen of rivers, " spreading like a sea," and running on in gentle course to mingle with the ocean through the fair city of Limerick. It on this night shone under the moon, and looked beautiful from the distant hill. Fifty boats were gliding up and down on the sweet current, and the song of the fishermen rose gaily from the shore. Larry, as I said before, leaped upon the back of the fairy, and she, rejoiced at the opportunity, sprung from the hill-top, and bounded clear, at one jump, over the Shannon, flowing as it was just ten miles from the mountain's base. It was done in a second, and when she alighted on the distant bank, kicking up her heels, she flung Larry on the soft turf. No sooner was he thus planted, than he looked her straight in the face, and scratching his head, cried out, " By my word, well done ! that was not a bad leap *for a calf !*"

She looked at him for a moment, and then assumed her own shape. " Laurence," said she, " you are a bold fellow ; will you come back the way you went ?"   " And that's what I will," said he, " if you let me."   So changing to a calf again, again Larry got on her back, and at another bound they were again upon the top of Knocksheogowna. The fairy once more resuming her figure, addressed him : " You have shown so much courage, Laurence," said she, " that while you keep herds on this hill you never shall be molested by me or mine.   The day dawns, go down to the farmer, and tell him this ; and if any thing I can do may be of service to you, ask and you shall have it." She vanished accordingly ; and kept her word in never visiting the hill during Larry's life : but he never troubled her with requests.   He piped and drank at the farmer's expense, and roosted in his chimney corner, occasionally casting an eye to the flock.   He died at last, and is buried in a green valley of pleasant Tipperary : but whether the fairies returned to the hill of Knocksheogowna[1] after his death is more than I can say.

---

[1] Knocksheogowna signifies " *The Hill of the Fairy Calf.*"

THE

LEGEND OF KNOCKFIERNA.[1]

II.

IT is a very good thing not to be any way in dread of the fairies, for without doubt they have then less power over a person; but to make too free with them, or to disbelieve in them altogether, is as foolish a thing as man, woman, or child can do.

It has been truly said, that "good manners are no burthen," and that "civility costs nothing;" but there are some people foolhardy enough to disregard doing a civil thing, which, whatever they may think, can never harm themselves or any one else, and who at the same time will go out of their way for a bit of mischief, which never

---

[1] " Called by the people of the country 'Knock Dhoinn Firinne,' the mountain of Donn of Truth. This mountain is very high, and may be seen for several miles round; and when people are desirous to know whether or not any day will rain, they look at the top of Knock Firinn, and if they see a vapour or mist there, they immediately conclude that rain will soon follow, believing that Donn (the lord or chief) of that mountain and his aërial assistants are collecting the clouds, and that he holds them there for some short time, to warn the people of the approaching rain.   As the appearance of mist on that mountain in the morning is considered an infallible sign that, that day will be rainy, Donn is called 'Donn Firinne,' Donn of Truth."—MR. EDWARD O'REILLY.

can serve them; but sooner or later they will come to know better, as you shall hear of Carroll O'Daly, a strapping young fellow up out of Connaught, whom they used to call, in his own country, " Devil Daly."

Carroll O'Daly used to go roving about from one place to another, and the fear of nothing stopped him; he would as soon pass an old churchyard or a regular fairy ground, at any hour of the night, as go from one room into another without ever making the sign of the cross, or saying, " Good luck attend you, gentlemen."

It so happened that he was once journeying, in the county of Limerick, towards " the Balbec of Ireland," the venerable town of Kilmallock; and just at the foot of Knockfierna he overtook a respectable-looking man jogging along upon a white pony. The night was coming on, and they rode side by side for some time, without much conversation passing between them, further than saluting each other very kindly; at last, Carroll O'Daly asked his companion how far he was going?

" Not far your way," said the farmer, for such his appearance bespoke him; " I'm only going to the top of this hill here."

" And what might take you there," said O'Daly, " at this time of the night?"

" Why then," replied the farmer, " if you want to know; 'tis the *good people*."

" The fairies, you mean," said O'Daly.

" Whist! whist!" said his fellow-traveller, " or you may be sorry for it;" and he turned his pony off the road they were going towards a little path which led up the side of the mountain, wishing Carroll O'Daly good night and a safe journey.

"That fellow," thought Carroll, "is about no good this blessed night, and I would have no fear of swearing wrong if I took my Bible oath, that it is something else beside the fairies, or the good people, as he calls them, that is taking him up the mountain at this hour. The fairies!" he repeated, "is it for a well-shaped man like him to be going after little chaps like the fairies! to be sure some say there are such things, and more say not; but I know this, that never afraid would I be of a dozen of them, ay, of two dozen, for that matter, if they are no bigger than what I hear tell of."

Carroll O'Daly, whilst these thoughts were passing in his mind, had fixed his eyes steadfastly on the mountain, behind which the full moon was rising majestically. Upon an elevated point that appeared darkly against the moon's disk, he beheld the figure of a man leading a pony, and he had no doubt it was that of the farmer with whom he had just parted company.

A sudden resolve to follow flashed across the mind of O'Daly with the speed of lightning: both his courage and curiosity had been worked up by his cogitations to a pitch of chivalry; and, muttering "Here's after you, old boy!" he dismounted from his horse, bound him to an old thorn tree, and then commenced vigorously ascending the mountain.

Following as well as he could the direction taken by the figures of the man and pony, he pursued his way, occasionally guided by their partial appearance : and, after toiling nearly three hours over a rugged and sometimes swampy path, came to a green spot on the top of the mountain, where he saw the white pony at full liberty grazing as quietly as may be. O'Daly looked around for the rider, but he was nowhere to be seen ; he, however, soon discovered close to where the pony stood an opening in the mountain like the mouth of a pit, and he remembered having heard, when a child, many a tale about the " Poul-duve," or Black Hole of Knockfierna ; how it was the entrance to the fairy castle which was within the mountain; and how a man whose name was Ahern, a land-surveyor in that part of the country, had once attempted to fathom it with a line, and had been drawn down into it and was never again heard of ; with many other tales of the like nature.

" But," thought O'Daly, " these are old woman's stories ; and since I've come up so far, I'll just knock at the castle door and see if the fairies are at home."

No sooner said than done ; for, seizing a large stone, as big, ay, bigger than his two hands, he flung it with all his strength down into the Poul-duve of Knockfierna. He heard it bounding and tumbling about from one rock to another with a terrible noise, and he leant his head over to try and hear when it would reach the bottom, — and what should the very stone he had thrown in do but come up again with as much force as it had gone down, and gave him such a blow full in the face, that it sent him rolling down the side of Knockfierna, head over heels, tumbling from one crag to another, much faster than he came up. And in the morning Carroll O'Daly was found lying beside his horse; the bridge of his nose broken, which disfigured him for life; his head all cut and bruised, and both his eyes closed up, and as black as if Sir Daniel Donnelly had painted them for him.

Carroll O'Daly was never bold again in riding alone near the haunts of the fairies after dusk; but small blame to him for that; and if ever he happened to be benighted in a lonesome place, he would make the best of his way to his journey's end, without asking questions, or turning to the right or to the left, to seek after the good people, or any who kept company with them.

THE

LEGEND OF KNOCKGRAFTON.

III.

THERE was once a poor man who lived in the fertile glen of Aherlow, at the foot of the gloomy Galtee mountains, and he had a great hump on his back: he looked just as if his body had been rolled up and placed upon his shoulders; and his head was pressed down with the weight so much, that his chin, when he was sitting, used to rest upon his knees for support. The country people were rather shy of meeting him in any lonesome place, for though, poor creature, he was as harmless and as inoffensive as a new-born infant, yet his deformity was so great, that he scarcely appeared to be a human being, and some ill-minded persons had set strange stories about him afloat. He was said to have a great knowledge of herbs and charms; but certain it was that he had a mighty skilful hand in plaiting straw and rushes into hats and baskets, which was the way he made his livelihood.

Lusmore, for that was the nickname put upon him by reason of his always wearing a sprig of the fairy cap, or lusmore[1], in his little straw hat, would ever get a higher penny for his plaited work than any one else, and perhaps that was the reason why some one, out of envy, had circulated

---

[1] Literally, the great herb—*Digitalis purpurea*.

the strange stories about him. Be that as it may, it happened that he was returning one evening from the pretty town of Cahir towards Cappagh, and as little Lusmore walked very slowly, on account of the great hump upon his back, it was quite dark when he came to the old moat of Knockgrafton, which stood on the right hand side of his road. Tired and weary was he, and noways comfortable in his own mind at thinking how much farther he had to travel, and that he should be walking all the night; so he sat down under the moat to rest himself, and began looking mournfully enough upon the moon, which,

> " Rising in clouded majesty, at length,
> Apparent Queen, unveil'd her peerless light,
> And o'er the dark her silver mantle threw."

Presently there rose a wild strain of unearthly melody upon the ear of little Lusmore; he listened, and he thought that he had never heard such ravishing music before. It was like the sound of many voices, each mingling and blending with the other so strangely, that they seemed to be one, though all singing different strains, and the words of the song were these: —

Da Luan, Da Mort, Da Luan, Da Mort, Da Luan, Da Mort, when there would be a moment's pause, and then the round of melody went on again.

Lusmore listened attentively, scarcely drawing his breath, lest he might lose the slightest note. He now plainly perceived that the singing was within the moat, and, though at first it had charmed him so much, he began to get tired of hearing the same round sung over and over so often without any change; so availing himself of the pause when the *Da Luan, Da Mort*, had been sung three times, he took up the tune and raised it with the words *augus Da Cadine*, and then went on singing with the voices inside of the moat, *Da Luan, Da Mort*, finishing the melody, when the pause again came, with *augus Da Cadine*.[1]

[1] Correctly written, *Dia Luain, Dia Mairt, agus Dia Ceadaoine*, i. e. Monday, Tuesday, and Wednesday.

The fairies within Knockgrafton, for the song was a fairy melody, when they heard this addition to their tune, were so much delighted, that with instant resolve it was determined to bring the mortal among them, whose musical skill so far exceeded theirs, and little Lusmore was conveyed into their company with the eddying speed of a whirlwind.

Glorious to behold was the sight that burst upon him as he came down through the moat, twirling round and round and round with the lightness of a straw, to the sweetest music that kept time to his motion. The greatest honour was then paid him, for he was put up above all the musicians, and he had servants 'tending upon him, and every thing to his heart's content, and a hearty welcome to all; and in short he was made as much of as if he had been the first man in the land.

Presently Lusmore saw a great consultation going forward among the fairies, and, notwithstanding all their civility, he felt very much frightened, until one, stepping out from the rest, came up to him, and said,—

> " Lusmore! Lusmore!
> Doubt not, nor deplore,
> For the hump which you bore
> On your back is no more!—
> Look down on the floor,
> And view it, Lusmore!"

When these words were said, poor little Lusmore felt himself so light, and so happy, that he thought he could have bounded at one jump over the moon, like the cow in the history of the cat and the fiddle; and he saw, with inexpressible pleasure, his hump tumble down upon the ground from his shoulders. He then tried to lift up his head, and he did so with becoming caution, fearing that he might knock it against the ceiling of the grand hall, where he was; he looked round and round again with the greatest wonder and delight upon every thing, which appeared more and more beautiful; and, overpowered at beholding such a resplendent scene, his head grew dizzy, and his eyesight became dim. At last he fell into a sound sleep, and when he awoke, he found that it was broad daylight, the sun shining brightly, the birds singing sweet; and that he was lying just at the foot of the moat of Knockgrafton, with the cows and sheep grazing peaceably round about him. The first thing Lusmore did, after saying his prayers, was to put his hand behind to feel for his hump, but no sign of one was there on his back, and he looked at himself with great pride, for he had now become a well-shaped dapper little fellow; and more than that, he found himself in a full suit of new clothes, which he concluded the fairies had made for him.

Towards Cappagh he went, stepping out as lightly, and springing up at every step as if he had been all his life a dancing-master. Not a creature who met Lusmore knew him without his hump, and he had great work to persuade every one that he was the same man—in truth he was not, so far as outward appearance went.

Of course it was not long before the story of Lusmore's hump got about, and a great wonder was made of it.   Through the country, for miles round, it was the talk of every one, high and low.

One morning as Lusmore was sitting contented enough at his cabin-door, up came an old woman to him, and asked if he could direct her to Cappagh?

"I need give you no directions, my good woman," said Lusmore, "for this is Cappagh; and who do you want here?"

"I have come," said the woman, "out of Decie's country, in the county of Waterford, looking after one Lusmore, who, I have heard tell, had his hump taken off by the fairies: for there is a son of a gossip of mine has got a hump on him that will be his death; and may be, if he could use the same charm as Lusmore, the hump may be taken off him.   And now I have told you the reason of my coming so far: 't is to find out about this charm, if I can."

Lusmore, who was ever a good-natured little fellow, told the woman all the particulars, how he had raised the tune for the fairies at Knockgrafton, how his hump had been removed from his shoulders, and how he had got a new suit of clothes into the bargain.

The woman thanked him very much, and then went away quite happy and easy in her own mind. When she came back to her gossip's house, in the county Waterford, she told her every thing that Lusmore had said, and they put the little hump-backed man, who was a peevish and cunning creature from his birth, upon a car, and took him all the way across the country.   It was a long journey, but they did not care for that, so the hump was taken from off him; and they brought him, just at nightfall, and left him under the old moat of Knockgrafton.

Jack Madden, for that was the humpy man's name, had not been sitting there long when he heard the tune going on within the moat much sweeter than before; for the fairies were singing it the way Lusmore had settled their music for them, and the song was going on: *Da Luan, Da Mort, Da Luan, Da Mort, Da Luan, Da Mort, augus Da Cadine*, without ever stopping. Jack Madden, who was in a great hurry to get quit of his hump, never thought of waiting until the fairies had done, or watching for a fit opportunity to raise the tune higher again than Lusmore had: so having heard them sing it over seven times without stopping, out he bawls, never minding the time, or the humour of the tune, or how he could bring his words in properly, *augus Da Cadine, augus Da Hena*[1], thinking that if one day was good, two were better; and that, if Lusmore had one new suit of clothes given to him, he should have two.

No sooner had the words passed his lips than he was taken up and whisked into the moat with prodigious force; and the fairies came crowding round about him with great anger, screeching and screaming, and roaring out, "who spoiled our tune? who spoiled our tune?" and one stepped up to him above all the rest, and said—

---

[1] And Wednesday and Thursday

> " Jack Madden ! Jack Madden !
>   Your words came so bad in
>   The tune we feel glad in ; —
>   This castle you 're had in,
>   That your life we may sadden :
>   Here 's two humps for Jack Madden ! "

And twenty of the strongest fairies brought Lusmore's hump and put it down upon poor Jack's back, over his own, where it became fixed as firmly as if it was nailed on with twelvepenny nails, by the best carpenter that ever drove one. Out of their castle they then kicked him, and in the morning when Jack Madden's mother and her gossip came to look after their little man, they found him half dead, lying at the foot of the moat, with the other hump upon his back. Well to be sure, how they did look at each other ! but they were afraid to say any thing, lest a hump might be put upon their own shoulders: home they brought the unlucky Jack Madden with them, as downcast in their hearts and their looks as ever two gossips were; and what through the weight of his other hump, and the long journey, he died soon after, leaving, they say, his heavy curse to any one who would go to listen to fairy tunes again.

THE PRIEST'S SUPPER.

IV.

IT is said by those who ought to understand such things, that the good people, or the fairies, are some of the angels who were turned out of heaven, and who landed on their feet in this world, while the rest of their companions, who had more sin to sink them, went down further to a worse place.   Be this as it may, there was a merry troop of the fairies, dancing and playing all manner of wild pranks on a bright moonlight evening towards the end of September.   The scene of their merriment was not far distant from Inchegeela, in the west of the county Cork — a poor village, although it had a barrack for soldiers; but great mountains and barren rocks, like those round about it, are enough to strike poverty into any place : however, as the fairies can have every thing they want for wishing, poverty does not trouble them much, and all their care is to seek out unfrequented nooks and places where it is not likely any one will come to spoil their sport.

On a nice green sod by the river's side were the little fellows dancing in a ring as gaily as may be, with their red caps wagging about at every bound in the moonshine; and so light were these bounds, that the lobes of dew, although they trembled under their feet, were not disturbed by their capering.   Thus did they carry on their gambols, spinning round and round, and twirling and bobbing, and diving and going through all manner of figures, until one of them chirped out,

> " Cease, cease, with your drumming,
> Here's an end to our mumming,
> By my smell
> I can tell
> A priest this way is coming!"

And away every one of the fairies scampered off as hard as they could, concealing themselves under the green leaves of the lusmore, where, if their little red caps should happen to peep out, they would only look like its crimson bells; and more hid themselves in the hollow of stones, or at the shady side of brambles, and others under the bank of the river, and in holes and crannies of one kind or another.

The fairy speaker was not mistaken; for along the road, which was within view of the river, came Father Horrigan on his pony, thinking to himself that as it was so late he would make an end of his journey at the first cabin he came to. According to this determination, he stopped at the dwelling of Dermod Leary, lifted the latch, and entered with " My blessing on all here."

I need not say that Father Horrigan was a welcome guest wherever he went, for no man was more pious or better beloved in the country. Now it was a great trouble to Dermod that he had nothing to offer his reverence for supper as a relish to the potatoes which " the old woman," for so Dermod called his wife, though she was not much past twenty, had down boiling in the pot over the fire; he thought of the net which he had set in the river, but as it had been there only a short time, the chances were against his finding a fish in it. "No matter," thought Dermod, "there can be no harm in stepping down to try, and may be as I want the fish for the priest's supper that one will be there before me."

Down to the river side went Dermod, and he found in the net as fine a salmon as ever jumped in the bright waters of "the spreading Lee;" but as he was going to take it out, the net was pulled from him, he could not tell how or by whom, and away got the salmon, and went swimming along with the current as gaily as if nothing had happened.

Dermod looked sorrowfully at the wake which the fish had left upon the water, shining like a line of silver in the moonlight, and then, with an angry motion of his right hand, and a stamp of his foot, gave vent to his feelings by muttering, "May bitter bad luck attend you night and day for a blackguard schemer of a salmon, wherever you go! You ought to be ashamed of yourself, if there's any shame in you, to give me the slip after this fashion! And I'm clear in my own mind you'll come to no good, for some kind of evil thing or other helped you — did I not feel it pull the net against me as strong as the devil himself?"

"That's not true for you," said one of the little fairies, who had scampered off at the approach of the priest, coming up to Dermod Leary, with a whole throng of companions at his heels;

" there was only a dozen and a half of us pulling against you."

Dermod gazed on the tiny speaker with wonder, who continued, " Make yourself noways uneasy about the priest's supper; for if you will go back and ask him one question from us, there will be as fine a supper as ever was put on a table spread out before him in less than no time."

" I'll have nothing at all to do with you," replied Dermod, in a tone of determination; and after a pause he added, " I'm much obliged to you for your offer, sir, but I know better than to sell myself to you or the like of you for a supper; and more than that, I know Father Horrigan has more regard for my soul than to wish me to pledge it for ever, out of regard to any thing you could put before him—so there's an end of the matter."

The little speaker, with a pertinacity not to be repulsed by Dermod's manner, continued, " Will you ask the priest one civil question for us ?"

Dermod considered for some time, and he was right in doing so, but he thought that no one could come to harm out of asking a civil question. " I see no objection to do that same, gentlemen," said Dermod; " but I will have nothing in life to do with your supper,—mind that."

" Then," said the little speaking fairy, whilst the rest came crowding after him from all parts, " go and ask Father Horrigan to tell us whether our souls will be saved at the last day, like the souls of good Christians; and if you wish us well, bring back word what he says without delay."

Away went Dermod to his cabin, where he

found the potatoes thrown out on the table, and his good woman handing the biggest of them all, a beautiful laughing red apple, smoking like a hard-ridden horse on a frosty night, over to Father Horrigan.

" Please your reverence," said Dermod, after some hesitation, " may I make bold to ask your honour one question ? "

" What may that be ? " said Father Horrigan.

" Why, then, begging your reverence's pardon for my freedom, it is, If the souls of the good people are to be saved at the last day ? "

" Who bid you ask me that question, Leary ? " said the priest, fixing his eyes upon him very sternly, which Dermod could not stand before at all.

" I 'll tell no lies about the matter, and nothing in life but the truth," said Dermod. " It was the good people themselves who sent me to ask the question, and there they are in thousands down on the bank of the river waiting for me to go back with the answer."

" Go back by all means," said the priest, " and tell them, if they want to know, to come here to me themselves, and I 'll answer that or any other question they are pleased to ask with the greatest pleasure in life."

Dermod accordingly returned to the fairies, who came swarming round about him to hear what the priest had said in reply ; and Dermod spoke out among them like a bold man as he was : but when they heard that they must go to the priest, away they fled, some here and more there ; and some this way and more that, whisking by poor Dermod so fast and in such numbers, that he was quite bewildered.

When he came to himself, which was not for a long time, back he went to his cabin and ate his dry potatoes along with Father Horrigan, who made quite light of the thing ; but Dermod could not help thinking it a mighty hard case that his reverence, whose words had the power to banish the fairies at such a rate, should have no sort of relish to his supper, and that the fine salmon he had in the net should have been got away from him in such a manner.

THE

BREWERY OF EGG-SHELLS.

V.

It may be considered impertinent were I to explain what is meant by a changeling: both Shakspeare and Spenser have already done so, and who is there unacquainted with the Midsummer Night's Dream[1] and the Fairy Queen?[2]

Now Mrs. Sullivan fancied that her youngest child had been changed by " fairies theft," to use Spenser's words, and certainly appearances warranted such a conclusion; for in one night her healthy, blue-eyed boy had become shrivelled up into almost nothing, and never ceased squalling and crying. This naturally made poor Mrs. Sullivan very unhappy; and all the neighbours, by way of comforting her, said, that her own child was, beyond any kind of doubt, with the good people, and that one of themselves had been put in his place.

Mrs. Sullivan of course could not disbelieve what every one told her, but she did not wish to hurt the thing; for although its face was so withered, and its body wasted away to a mere skeleton, it had still a strong resemblance to her own boy: she therefore could not find it in her heart to roast it alive on the griddle, or to burn its nose off with the red hot tongs, or to throw it

---

[1] Act ii. sc. 1. [2] Book 1. canto 10.

out in the snow on the road side, notwithstanding these, and several like proceedings, were strongly recommended to her for the recovery of her child.

One day who should Mrs. Sullivan meet but a cunning woman, well known about the country by the name of Ellen Leah (or Grey Ellen). She had the gift, however she got it, of telling where the dead were, and what was good for the rest of their souls; and could charm away warts and wens, and do a great many wonderful things of the same nature.

" You're in grief this morning, Mrs. Sullivan," were the first words of Ellen Leah to her.

" You may say that, Ellen," said Mrs. Sullivan, " and good cause I have to be in grief, for there was my own fine child whipped off from me out of his cradle, without as much as by your leave, or ask your pardon, and an ugly dony bit of a shrivelled up fairy put in his place; no wonder then that you see me in grief, Ellen."

" Small blame to you, Mrs. Sullivan," said Ellen Leah; " but are you sure 't is a fairy?"

" Sure!" echoed Mrs. Sullivan, " sure enough am I to my sorrow, and can I doubt my own two eyes? Every mother's soul must feel for me!"

" Will you take an old woman's advice?" said Ellen Leah, fixing her wild and mysterious gaze upon the unhappy mother; and, after a pause, she added, " but may be you'll call it foolish?"

" Can you get me back my child, — my own child, Ellen?" said Mrs. Sullivan with great energy.

" If you do as I bid you," returned Ellen Leah,

" you'll know."   Mrs. Sullivan was silent in expectation, and Ellen continued, " Put down the big pot, full of water, on the fire, and make it boil like mad; then get a dozen new laid eggs, break them, and keep the shells, but throw away the rest; when that is done, put the shells in the pot of boiling water, and you will soon know whether it is your own boy or a fairy. If you find that it is a fairy in the cradle, take the red hot poker and cram it down his ugly throat, and you will not have much trouble with him after that, I promise you."

Home went Mrs. Sullivan, and did as Ellen Leah desired. She put the pot on the fire, and plenty of turf under it, and set the water boiling at such a rate, that if ever water was red hot — it surely was.

The child was lying for a wonder quite easy and quiet in the cradle, every now and then cocking his eye, that would twinkle as keen as a star in a frosty night, over at the great fire, and the big pot upon it; and he looked on with great attention at Mrs. Sullivan breaking the eggs, and putting down the egg-shells to boil. At last he asked, with the voice of a very old man, " What are you doing, mammy?"

Mrs. Sullivan's heart, as she said herself, was up in her mouth ready to choke her, at hearing the child speak. But she contrived to put the poker in the fire, and to answer without making any wonder at the words, " I'm brewing, *a vick*," (my son.)

" And what are you brewing, mammy?" said the little imp, whose supernatural gift of speech now proved beyond question that he was a fairy substitute.

"I wish the poker was red," thought Mrs. Sullivan; but it was a large one, and took a long time heating: so she determined to keep him in talk until the poker was in a proper state to thrust down his throat, and therefore repeated the question.

"Is it what I'm brewing, *a vick*," said she, "you want to know?"

"Yes, mammy: what are you brewing?" returned the fairy.

"Egg-shells, *a vick*," said Mrs. Sullivan.

"Oh!" shrieked the imp, starting up in the cradle, and clapping his hands together, "I'm fifteen hundred years in the world, and I never saw a brewery of egg-shells before!" The poker was by this time quite red, and Mrs. Sullivan seizing it, ran furiously towards the cradle; but somehow or other her foot slipped, and she fell flat on the floor, and the poker flew out of her hand to the other end of the house. However, she got up, without much loss of time, and went to the cradle intending to pitch the wicked thing that was in it into the pot of boiling water, when there she saw her own child in a sweet sleep, one of his soft round arms rested upon the pillow — his features were as placid as if their repose had never been disturbed, save the rosy mouth which moved with a gentle and regular breathing.

Who can tell the feelings of a mother when she looks upon her sleeping child? Why should I, therefore, endeavour to describe those of Mrs. Sullivan at again beholding her long lost boy?

The fountain of her heart overflowed with the excess of joy — and she wept ! — tears trickled silently down her cheeks, nor did she strive to check them — they were tears not of sorrow, but of happiness.

LEGEND OF BOTTLE HILL.

VI.

"Come, listen to a tale of times of old,
    Come listen to me——"

IT was in the good days, when the little people most impudently called fairies, were more frequently seen than they are in these unbelieving times, that a farmer, named Mick Purcell, rented a few acres of barren ground in the neighbourhood of the once celebrated preceptory of Mourne, situated about three miles from Mallow, and thirteen from "the beautiful city called Cork." Mick had a wife and family: they all did what they could, and that was but little, for the poor man had no child grown up big enough to help him in his work: and all the poor woman could do was to mind the children, and to milk the one cow, and to boil the potatoes, and carry the eggs to market to Mallow; but with all they could do, 't was hard enough on them to pay the rent. Well, they did manage it for a good while; but at last came a bad year, and the little grain of oats was all spoiled, and the chickens died of the pip, and the pig got the measles, — *she* was sold in Mallow and brought almost nothing; and poor Mick found that he hadn't enough to half pay his rent, and two gales were due.

"Why, then, Molly," says he, "what 'll we do?"

" Wisha, then, mavournene, what would you do but take the cow to the fair of Cork ·and sell her," says she ; " and Monday is fair day, and so you must go to-morrow, that the poor beast may be rested *again* the fair."

" And what 'll we do when she's gone ?" says Mick, sorrowfully.

" Never a know I know, Mick ; but sure God won't leave us without Him, Mick; and you know how good He was to us when poor little Billy was sick, and we had nothing at all for him to take, that good doctor gentleman at Ballydahin come riding and asking for a drink of milk ; and how he gave us two shillings ; and how he sent the things and bottles for the child, and gave me my breakfast when I went over to ask a question, so he did ; and how he came to see Billy, and never left off his goodness till he was quite well ?"

" Oh ! you are always that way, Molly, and I believe you are right after all, so I won't be sorry for selling the cow ; but I'll go to-morrow, and you must put a needle and thread through my coat, for you know 't is ripped under the arm."

Molly told him he should have every thing right ; and about twelve o'clock next day he left her, getting a charge not to sell his cow except for the highest penny. Mick promised to mind it, and went his way along the road. He drove his cow slowly through the little stream which crosses it, and runs by the old walls of Mourne. As he passed he glanced his eye upon the towers and one of the old elder trees, which were only then little bits of switches.

" Oh, then, if I only had half the money that's

buried in you, 't isn't driving this poor cow I'd be now! Why, then, isn't it too bad that it should be there covered over with earth, and many a one besides me wanting? Well, if it's God's will, I'll have some money myself coming back."

So saying, he moved on after his beast; 'twas a fine day, and the sun shone brightly on the walls of the old abbey as he passed under them; he then crossed an extensive mountain tract, and and after six long miles he came to the top of that hill—Bottle Hill 't is called now, but that was not the name of it then, and just there a man overtook him. "Good morrow," says he. "Good morrow, kindly," says Mick, looking at the stranger, who was a little man, you'd almost call him a dwarf, only he wasn't quite so little neither: he had a bit of an old, wrinkled, yellow face, for all the world like a dried cauliflower, only he had a sharp little nose, and red eyes, and white hair, and his lips were not red, but all his face was one colour, and his eyes never were quiet, but looking at every thing, and although they were red, they made Mick feel quite cold when he looked at them. In truth he did not much like the little man's company; and he couldn't see one bit of his legs, nor his body; for, though the day was warm, he was all wrapped up in a big great-coat. Mick drove his cow something faster, but the little man kept up with him. Mick didn't know how he walked, for he was almost afraid to look at him, and to cross himself, for fear the old man would be angry. Yet he thought his fellow-traveller did not seem to walk like other men, nor to put one foot before the other, but to glide over the rough road, and rough enough it was, like a shadow, without noise and without effort. Mick's heart trembled within him, and he said a prayer to himself, wishing he hadn't come out that day, or that he was on Fair-Hill, or that he hadn't the cow to mind, that he might run away from the bad thing — when, in the midst of his fears, he was again addressed by his companion.

"Where are you going with the cow, honest man?"

"To the fair of Cork then," says Mick, trembling at the shrill and piercing tones of the voice.

"Are you going to sell her?" said the stranger.

"Why, then, what else am I going for but to sell her?"

"Will you sell her to me?"

Mick started — he was afraid to have any thing to do with the little man, and he was more afraid to say no.

"What'll you give for her?" at last says he.

"I'll tell you what, I'll give you this bottle," said the little one, pulling a bottle from under his coat.

Mick looked at him and the bottle, and, in spite of his terror, he could not help bursting into a loud fit of laughter.

"Laugh if you will," said the little man, "but I tell you this bottle is better for you than all the money you will get for the cow in Cork — ay, than ten thousand times as much."

Mick laughed again. "Why then," says he, "do you think I am such a fool as to give my good cow for a bottle — and an empty one, too? indeed, then, I won't."

" You had better give me the cow, and take the bottle — you'll not be sorry for it."

" Why, then, and what would Molly say? I'd never hear the end of it; and how would I pay the rent? and what would we all do without a penny of money?"

" I tell you this bottle is better to you than money; take it, and give me the cow. I ask you for the last time, Mick Purcell."

Mick started.

" How does he know my name?" thought he.

The stranger proceeded: " Mick Purcell, I know you, and I have a regard for you; therefore do as I warn you, or you may be sorry for it. How do you know but your cow will die before you get to Cork?"

Mick was going to say " God forbid!" but the little man went on (and he was too attentive to say any thing to stop him; for Mick was a very civil man, and he knew better than to interrupt a gentleman, and that's what many people, that hold their heads higher, don't mind now).

" And how do you know but there will be much cattle at the fair, and you will get a bad price, or may be you might be robbed when you are coming home? but what need I talk more to you, when you are determined to throw away your luck, Mick Purcell."

" Oh! no, I would not throw away my luck, sir," said Mick; " and if I was sure the bottle was as good as you say, though I never liked an empty bottle, although I had drank what was in it, I'd give you the cow in the name ———"

" Never mind names," said the stranger, " but

give me the cow; I would not tell you a lie. Here, take the bottle, and when you go home do what I direct exactly."

Mick hesitated.

"Well then, good bye, I can stay no longer: once more, take it, and be rich; refuse it and beg for your life, and see your children in poverty, and your wife dying for want: that will happen to you, Mick Purcell!" said the little man with a malicious grin, which made him look ten times more ugly than ever.

"May be, 'tis true," said Mick, still hesitating: he did not know what to do — he could hardly help believing the old man, and at length in a fit of desperation he seized the bottle — "Take the cow," said he, "and if you are telling a lie, the curse of the poor will be on you."

"I care neither for your curses nor your blessings, but I have spoken truth, Mick Purcell, and that you will find to-night, if you do what I tell you."

"And what's that?" says Mick.

"When you go home, never mind if your wife is angry, but be quiet yourself, and make her sweep the room clean, set the table out right, and spread a clean cloth over it; then put the bottle on the ground, saying these words: 'Bottle, do your duty,' and you will see the end of it."

"And is this all?" says Mick.

"No more," said the stranger. "Good bye, Mick Purcell — you are a rich man."

"God grant it!" said Mick, as the old man moved after the cow, and Mick retraced the road towards his cabin; but he could not help turning back his head, to look after the purchaser of his cow, who was nowhere to be seen.

"Lord between us and harm!" said Mick: "*He* can't belong to this earth; but where is the cow?" She too was gone, and Mick went homeward muttering prayers, and holding fast the bottle.

"And what would I do if it broke?" thought he. "Oh! but I'll take care of that;" so he put it into his bosom, and went on anxious to prove his bottle, and doubting of the reception he should meet from his wife; balancing his anxieties with his expectation, his fears with his hopes, he reached home in the evening, and surprised his wife, sitting over the turf fire in the big chimney.

"Oh! Mick, are you come back? Sure you weren't at Cork all the way! What has happened to you? Where is the cow? Did you sell her? How much money did you get for her? What news have you? Tell us every thing about it?"

"Why then, Molly, if you'll give me time, I'll tell you all about it. If you want to know where the cow is, 'tisn't Mick can tell you, for the never a know does he know where she is now."

"Oh! then, you sold her; and where's the money?"

"Arrah! stop awhile, Molly, and I'll tell you all about it."

"But what is that bottle under your waistcoat?" said Molly, spying its neck sticking out.

"Why, then, be easy now, can't you," says Mick, "till I tell it to you;" and putting the bottle on the table, "That's all I got for the cow."

His poor wife was thunderstruck. " All you got! and what good is that, Mick? Oh! I never thought you were such a fool; and what 'll we do for the rent, and what ——"

" Now, Molly," says Mick, " can't you hearken to reason? Didn't I tell you how the old man, or whatsomever he was, met me, — no, he did not meet me neither, but he was there with me — on the big hill, and how he made me sell him the cow, and told me the bottle was the only thing for me?"

" Yes, indeed, the only thing for you, you fool!" said Molly, seizing the bottle to hurl it at her poor husband's head; but Mick caught it, and quietly (for he minded the old man's advice) loosened his wife's grasp, and placed the bottle again in his bosom. Poor Molly sat down crying, while Mick told her his story, with many a crossing and blessing between him and harm. His wife could not help believing him, particularly as she had as much faith in fairies as she had in the priest, who indeed never discouraged her belief in the fairies; may be, he didn't know she believed in them, and may be, he believed in them himself. She got up, however, without saying one word, and began to sweep the earthen floor with a bunch of heath; then she tidied up every thing, and put out the long table, and spread the clean cloth, for she had only one, upon it, and Mick, placing the bottle on the ground, looked at it, and said, " Bottle, do your duty."

" Look there! look there, mammy!" said his chubby eldest son, a boy about five years old — " look there! look there!" and he sprang to his mother's side, as two tiny little fellows rose like light from the bottle, and in an instant covered the table with dishes and plates of gold and silver, full of the finest victuals that ever were seen, and when all was done went into the bottle again. Mick and his wife looked at every thing with astonishment; they had never seen such plates and dishes before, and didn't think they could ever admire them enough; the very sight almost took away their appetites; but at length Molly said, " Come and sit down, Mick, and try and eat a bit: sure you ought to be hungry after such a good day's work."

" Why, then, the man told no lie about the bottle."

Mick sat down, after putting the children to the table; and they made a hearty meal, though they couldn't taste half the dishes.

" Now," says Molly, " I wonder will those two good little gentlemen carry away these fine things again ?" They waited, but no one came; so Molly put up the dishes and plates very carefully, saying, " Why, then, Mick, that was no lie sure enough: but you'll be a rich man yet, Mick Purcell."

Mick and his wife and children went to their bed, not to sleep, but to settle about selling the fine things they did not want, and to take more land. Mick went to Cork and sold his plate, and bought a horse and cart, and began to show that he was making money; and they did all they could to keep the bottle a secret; but for all that, their landlord found it out, for he came to Mick one day, and asked him where he got all his money — sure it was not by the farm; and he bothered him so much, that at last Mick told him of the bottle.   His landlord offered him a deal of money for it, but Mick would not give it, till at last he offered to give him all his farm for ever: so Mick, who was very rich, thought he'd never want any more money, and gave him the bottle: but Mick was mistaken — he and his family spent money as if there was no end of it; and, to make the story short, they became poorer and poorer, till at last they had nothing left but one cow; and Mick once more drove his cow before him to sell her at Cork fair, hoping to meet the old man and get another bottle.   It was hardly daybreak when he left home, and he walked on at a good pace till he reached the big hill: the mists were sleeping in the valleys and curling like smoke-wreaths upon the brown heath around him.   The sun rose on his left, and just at his feet a lark sprang from its grassy couch and poured forth its joyous matin song, ascending into the clear blue sky,

> " Till its form like a speck in the airiness blending
>   And thrilling with music, was melting in light."

Mick crossed himself, listening as he advanced to the sweet song of the lark, but thinking, notwithstanding, all the time of the little old man; when, just as he reached the summit of the hill, and cast his eyes over the extensive prospect before and around him, he was startled and rejoiced by the same well-known voice: — " Well, Mick Purcell, I told you, you would be a rich man."

" Indeed, then, sure enough I was, that's no lie for you, sir. Good morning to you, but it is not rich I am now — but have you another bottle, for I want it now as much as I did long ago ; so if you have it, sir, here is the cow for it."

" And here is the bottle," said the old man, smiling ; " you know what to do with it."

" Oh ! then, sure I do, as good right I have."

" Well, farewell for ever, Mick Purcell : I told you, you would be a rich man."

" And good bye to you, sir," said Mick, as he turned back ; " and good luck to you, and good luck to the big hill — it wants a name — Bottle Hill. — Good bye, sir, good bye :" so Mick walked back as fast as he could, never looking after the white-faced little gentleman and the cow, so anxious was he to bring home the bottle. Well, he arrived with it safely enough, and called out, as soon as he saw Molly, " Oh! sure I've another bottle !"

" Arrah ! then, have you ? why, then, you're a lucky man, Mick Purcell, that's what you are."

In an instant she put every thing right ; and Mick, looking at his bottle, exultingly cried out, " Bottle, do your duty."   In a twinkling, two great stout men with big cudgels issued from the bottle (I do not know how they got room in it), and belaboured poor Mick and his wife and all his family, till they lay on the floor, when in they went again. Mick, as soon as he recovered, got up and looked about him ; he thought and thought, and at last he took up his wife and his children ; and, leaving them to recover as well as they could, he took the bottle under his coat, and went to his landlord, who had a great company : he got a servant to tell him he wanted to speak to him, and at last he came out to Mick.

" Well, what do you want now ?"

" Nothing, sir, only I have another bottle."

" Oh ! ho ! is it as good as the first ?"

" Yes, sir, and better ; if you like, I will show it to you before all the ladies and gentlemen."

" Come along, then."   So saying, Mick was brought into the great hall, where he saw his old bottle standing high up on a shelf : " Ah ! ha !" says he to himself, " may be I won't have you by and by."

" Now," says his landlord, " show us your bottle."   Mick set it on the floor, and uttered the words : in a moment the landlord was tumbled on the floor ; ladies and gentlemen, servants and all, were running and roaring, and sprawling, and kicking, and shrieking.   Wine cups and salvers were knocked about in every direction, until the landlord called out, " Stop those two devils, Mick Purcell, or I'll have you hanged !"

" They never shall stop," said Mick, " till I get my own bottle that I see up there at top of that shelf."

" Give it down to him, give it down to him, before we are all killed !" says the landlord.

Mick put his bottle in his bosom ; in jumped the two men into the new bottle, and he carried the bottles home. I need not lengthen my story by telling how he got richer than ever, how his son married his landlord's only daughter, how he and his wife died when they were very old, and how some of the servants, fighting at their wake, broke the bottles; but still the hill has the name upon it; ay, and so 't will be always Bottle Hill to the end of the world, and so it ought, for it is a strange story.

THE

CONFESSIONS OF TOM BOURKE.

VII.

Tom Bourke lives in a low long farm-house, resembling in outward appearance a large barn, placed at the bottom of the hill, just where the new road strikes off from the old one, leading from the town of Kilworth to that of Lismore. He is of a class of persons who are a sort of black swans in Ireland : he is a wealthy farmer. Tom's father had, in the good old times, when a hundred pounds were no inconsiderable treasure, either to lend or spend, accommodated his landlord with that sum, at interest ; and obtained, as a return for the civility, a long lease, about half a dozen times more valuable than the loan which procured it. The old man died worth several hundred pounds, the greater part of which, with his farm, he bequeathed to his son Tom. But, besides all this, Tom received from his father, upon his deathbed, another gift, far more valuable than worldly riches, greatly as he prized and is still known to prize them. He was invested with the privilege, enjoyed by few of the sons of men, of communicating with those mysterious beings called " the good people."

Tom Bourke is a little, stout, healthy, active

man, about fifty-five years of age. His hair is
perfectly white, short and bushy behind, but
rising in front erect and thick above his forehead,
like a new clothes-brush. His eyes are of that
kind which I have often observed with persons
of a quick but limited intellect—they are small,
grey, and lively. The large and projecting eyebrows under, or rather within, which they twinkle,
give them an expression of shrewdness and intelligence, if not of cunning. And this is very much
the character of the man. If you want to make
a bargain with Tom Bourke, you must act as if
you were a general besieging a town, and make
your advances a long time before you can hope to
obtain possession; if you march up boldly, and
tell him at once your object, you are for the most
part sure to have the gates closed in your teeth.
Tom does not wish to part with what you wish to
obtain, or another person has been speaking to
him for the whole of the last week. Or, it may
be, your proposal seems to meet the most favourable reception. " Very well, sir ; " " That's true,
sir ;" " I'm very thankful to your honour," and
other expressions of kindness and confidence,
greet you in reply to every sentence ; and you
part from him wondering how he can have obtained the character which he universally bears,
of being a man whom no one can make any thing
of in a bargain. But when you next meet him,
the flattering illusion is dissolved: you find you
are a great deal farther from your object than
you were when you thought you had almost suc_
ceeded: his eye and his tongue express a total
forgetfulness of what the mind within never lost

sight of for an instant; and you have to begin operations afresh, with the disadvantage of having put your adversary completely upon his guard.

Yet, although Tom Bourke is, whether from supernatural revealings, or (as many will think more probable) from the tell-truth, experience, so distrustful of mankind, and so close in his dealings with them, he is no misanthrope. No man loves better the pleasures of the genial board. The love of money, indeed, which is with him (and who will blame him?) a very ruling propensity, and the gratification which it has received from habits of industry, sustained throughout a pretty long and successful life, have taught him the value of sobriety, during those seasons, at least, when a man's business requires him to keep possession of his senses. He has therefore a general rule, never to get drunk but on Sundays. But, in order that it should be a general one to all intents and purposes, he takes a method which, according to better logicians than he is, always proves the rule. He has many exceptions: among these, of course, are the evenings of all the fair and market-days that happen in his neighbourhood; so also all the days on which funerals, marriages, and christenings take place among his friends within many miles of him. As to this last class of exceptions, it may appear at first very singular, that he is much more punctual in his attendance at the funerals than at the baptisms or weddings of his friends. This may be construed as an instance of disinterested affection for departed worth, very uncommon in this selfish woorld. But I am afraid that the motives which lead Tom Bourke to pay more court to the dead than the living are precisely those which lead to the opposite conduct in the generality of mankind — a hope of future benefit and a fear of future evil. For the good people, who are a race as powerful as they are capricious, have their favourites among those who inhabit this world; often show their affection, by easing the objects of it from the load of this burdensome life; and frequently reward or punish the living, according to the degree of reverence paid to the obsequies and the memory of the elected dead.

It is not easy to prevail on Tom to speak of those good people, with whom he is said to hold frequent and intimate communications. To the faithful, who believe in their power, and their occasional delegation of it to him, he seldom refuses, if properly asked, to exercise his high prerogative, when any unfortunate being is *struck*[1] in his neighbourhood. Still, he will not be won unsued: he is at first difficult of persuasion, and must be overcome by a little gentle violence. On these

1 The term " fairy struck " is applied to paralytic affections, which are supposed to proceed from a blow given by the invisible hand of an offended fairy; this belief, of course, creates fairy doctors, who by means of charms and mysterious journeys profess to cure the afflicted. It is only fair to add, that the term has also a convivial acceptation, the fairies being not unfrequently made to bear the blame of the effects arising from too copious a sacrifice to the jolly god.

The importance attached to the manner and place of burial by the peasantry is almost incredible; it is always a matter of consideration and often of dispute whether the deceased shall be buried with his or her " own people."

occasions he is unusually solemn and mysterious, and if one word of reward be mentioned, he at once abandons the unhappy patient, such a proposition being a direct insult to his supernatural superiors. It is true, that as the labourer is worthy of his hire, most persons, gifted as he is, do not scruple to receive a token of gratitude from the patients or their friends *after* their recovery.

To do Tom Bourke justice, he is on these occasions, as I have heard from many competent authorities, perfectly disinterested. Not many months since, he recovered a young woman (the sister of a tradesman living near him), who had been struck speechless after returning from a funeral, and had continued so for several days. He stedfastly refused receiving any compensation; saying, that even if he had not as much as would buy him his supper, he could take nothing in this case, because the girl had offended at the funeral one of the *good people* belonging to his own family, and though he would do her a kindness, he could take none from her.

About the time this last remarkable affair took place, my friend Mr. Martin, who is a neighbour of Tom's, had some business to transact with him, which it was exceedingly difficult to bring to a conclusion. At last Mr. Martin, having tried all quiet means, had recourse to a legal process, which brought Tom to reason, and the matter was arranged to their mutual satisfaction, and with perfect good humour between the parties. The accommodation took place after dinner at Mr. Martin's house, and he invited Tom to walk into the parlour and take a glass of punch, made of

some excellent *potteen*, which was on the table:
he had long wished to draw out his highly-
endowed neighbour on the subject of his supernatural powers, and as Mrs. Martin, who was in
the room, was rather a favourite of Tom's, this
seemed a good opportunity.

" Well, Tom," said Mr. Martin, " that was a
curious business of Molly Dwyer's, who recovered her speech so suddenly the other day."

" You may say that, sir," replied Tom Bourke;
" but I had to travel far for it: no matter for
that, now. Your health, ma'am," said he, turning
to Mrs. Martin.

" Thank you, Tom. But I am told you had
some trouble once in that way in your own family," said Mrs. Martin.

" So I had, ma'am; trouble enough; but you
were only a child at that time."

" Come, Tom," said the hospitable Mr. Martin,
interrupting him, " take another tumbler;" and
he then added, " I wish you would tell us something of the manner in which so many of your
children died. I am told they dropped off, one
after another, by the same disorder, and that your
eldest son was cured in a most extraordinary
way, when the physicians had given him over."

" 'Tis true for you, sir," returned Tom; " your
father, the doctor (God be good to him, I won't
belie him in his grave) told me, when my fourth
little boy was a week sick, that himself and Doctor Barry did all that man could do for him; but
they could not keep him from going after the
rest. No more they could, if the people that
took away the rest wished to take him too. But

they left him; and sorry to the heart I am I did
not know before why they were taking my boys
from me; if I did, I would not be left trusting to
two of 'em now."

"And how did you find it out, Tom?" enquired
Mr. Martin.

"Why, then, I'll tell you, sir," said Bourke.
"When your father said what I told you, I did
not know very well what to do. I walked down
the little *bohereen* you know, sir, that goes to the
river side near Dick Heafy's ground; for 't was
a lonesome place, and I wanted to think of myself.
I was heavy, sir, and my heart got weak in me,
when I thought I was to lose my little boy; and
I did not know well how to face his mother with
the news, for she doted down upon him. Beside,
she never got the better of all she cried at his
brother's berrin (burying) the week before. As I
was going down the bohereen, I met an old bo-
cough[1], that used to come about the place once or
twice a year, and used always sleep in our barn
while he staid in the neighbourhood. So he asked
me how I was. 'Bad enough, Shamous (James,)'
says I. 'I'm sorry for your trouble,' says he;
'but you're a foolish man, Mr. Bourke. Your son
would be well enough if you would only do what
you ought with him.' 'What more can I do with
him, Shamous?' says I: 'the doctors give him
over.' 'The doctors know no more what ails him
than they do what ails a cow when she stops her
milk,' says Shamous: 'but go to such a one,'

---

[1] A peculiar class of beggars resembling the Gaberlunzie
man of Scotland.

says he, telling me his name, 'and try what he'll
say to you.'"

"And who was that, Tom?" asked Mr. Martin.

"I could not tell you that, sir," said Bourke,
with a mysterious look: "howsoever, you often
saw him, and he does not live far from this. But
I had a trial of him before; and if I went to him
at first, may be I'd have now some of them that's
gone, and so Shamous often told me. Well, sir,
I went to this man, and he came with me to the
house. By course, I did every thing as he bid
me. According to his order, I took the little boy
out of the dwelling-house immediately, sick as he
was, and made a bed for him and myself in the
cow-house. Well, sir, I lay down by his side,
in the bed, between two of the cows, and he fell
asleep. He got into a perspiration, saving your
presence, as if he was drawn through the river,
and breathed hard, with a great *impression* (op-
pression) on his chest, and was very bad—very
bad entirely through the night. I thought about
twelve o'clock he was going at last, and I was just
getting up to go call the man I told you of; but
there was no occasion. My friends were getting
the better of them that wanted to take him away
from me. There was nobody in the cow-house but
the child and myself. There was only one halfpenny candle lighting, and that was stuck in the
wall at the far end of the house. I had just enough
of light where we were laying to see a person
walking or standing near us: and there was no
more noise than if it was a churchyard, except the
cows chewing the fodder in the stalls. Just as I
was thinking of getting up, as I told you—I

won't belie my father, sir — he was a good father
to me — I saw him standing at the bed-side, holding out his right hand to me, and leaning his
other hand on the stick he used to carry when he
was alive, and looking pleasant and smiling at me,
all as if he was telling me not to be afeard, for I
would not lose the child. ' Is that you, father?'
says I. He said nothing. ' If that's you,' says I
again, ' for the love of them that's gone, let me
catch your hand.' And so he did, sir; and his
hand was as soft as a child's. He stayed about as
long as you'd be going from this to the gate below
at the end of the avenue, and then went away. In
less than a week the child was as well as if nothing
ever ailed him ; and there isn't to-night a healthier
boy of nineteen, from this blessed house to the
town of Ballyporeen, across the Kilworth mountains."

"But I think, Tom," said Mr. Martin, " it
appears as if you are more indebted to your father
than to the man recommended to you by Shamous;
or do you suppose it was he who made favour
with your enemies among the good people, and
that then your father ——"

"I beg your pardon, sir," said Bourke, interrupting him; " but don't call them my enemies.
'Twould not be wishing to me for a good deal to
sit by when they are called so. No offence to
you, sir.—Here's wishing you a good health and
long life."

"I assure you," returned Mr. Martin, " I
meant no offence, Tom; but was it not as I
say?"

"I can't tell you that, sir," said Bourke; " I'm

bound down, sir. Howsoever, you may be sure the man I spoke of, and my father, and those they know, settled it between them."

There was a pause, of which Mrs. Martin took advantage to enquire of Tom, whether something remarkable had not happened about a goat and a pair of pigeons, at the time of his son's illness — circumstances often mysteriously hinted at by Tom.

" See that now," said he, turning to Mr. Martin, " how well she remembers it! True for you, ma'am. The goat I gave the mistress, your mother, when the doctors ordered her goats' whey."

Mrs. Martin nodded assent, and Tom Bourke continued — " Why, then, I'll tell you how that was. The goat was as well as e'er a goat ever was, for a month after she was sent to Killaan to your father's. The morning after the night I just told you of, before the child woke, his mother was standing at the gap, leading out of the barn-yard into the road, and she saw two pigeons flying from the town of Kilworth, off the church, down towards her. Well, they never stopped, you see, till they came to the house on the hill at the other side of the river, facing our farm. They pitched upon the chimney of that house, and after looking about them for a minute or two, they flew straight across the river, and stopped on the ridge of the cow-house where the child and I were lying. Do you think they came there for nothing, sir?"

" Certainly not, Tom," returned Mr. Martin.

" Well, the woman came in to me, frightened, and told me. She began to cry. — 'Whisht, you fool!' says I: ' 'tis all for the better.' 'Twas true for me.   What do you think, ma'am ; the goat that I gave your mother, that was seen feeding at sunrise that morning by Jack Cronin, as merry as a bee, dropped down dead, without any body knowing why, before Jack's face ; and at that very moment he saw two pigeons fly from the top of the house out of the town, towards the Lismore road. 'Twas at the same time my woman saw them, as I just told you."

" 'Twas very strange, indeed, Tom," said Mr. Martin ; " I wish you could give us some explanation of it."

" I wish I could, sir," was Tom Bourke's answer ; " but I'm bound down. I can't tell but what I'm allowed to tell, any more than a sentry is let walk more than his rounds."

" I think you said something of having had some former knowledge of the man that assisted in the cure of your son," said Mr. Martin.

" So I had, sir," returned Bourke. " I had a trial of that man. But that's neither here nor there. I can't tell you any thing about that, sir. But would you like to know how he got his skill ?"

" Oh ! very much, indeed," said Mr. Martin.

" But you can tell us his Christian name, that we may know him the better through the story," added Mrs. Martin. Tom Bourke paused for a minute to consider this proposition.

" Well, I believe I may tell you that, any how ; his name is Patrick. He was always a smart, active, 'cute boy, and would be a great clerk if he stuck to it. The first time I knew him, sir, was at my mother's wake. I was in great trouble, for I did not know where to bury her. Her people and my father's people — I mean their friends, sir, among the *good people*, had the greatest battle that was known for many a year, at Dunmanway-cross, to see to whose churchyard she'd be taken. They fought for three nights, one after another, without being able to settle it. The neighbours wondered how long I was before I buried my mother; but I had my reasons, though I could not tell them at that time. Well, sir, to make my story short, Patrick came on the fourth morning and told me he settled the business, and that day we buried her in Kilcrumper churchyard, with my father's people."

"He was a valuable friend, Tom," said Mrs. Martin, with difficulty suppressing a smile. "But you were about to tell how he became so skilful."

"So I will, and welcome," replied Bourke. "Your health, ma'am. I am drinking too much of this punch, sir; but to tell the truth, I never tasted the like of it: it goes down one's throat like sweet oil. But what was I going to say? — Yes — well — Patrick, many a long year ago, was coming home from a *berrin* late in the evening, and walking by the side of the river, opposite the big inch [1], near Ballyhefaan ford. [2] He had taken a drop, to be sure; but he was only a little merry, as you may say, and knew very well what he was doing. The moon was shining, for it was in the month of August, and the river was as smooth

---

[1] Inch — low meadow ground near a river.
[2] A ford of the river Funcheon (the Fanchin of Spenser), on the road leading from Fermoy to Araglin.

and as bright as a looking-glass. He heard nothing for a long time but the fall of the water at
the mill wier about a mile down the river, and now
and then the crying of the lambs on the other side
of the river.   All at once, there was a noise of a
great number of people, laughing as if they'd break
their hearts, and of a piper playing among them.
It came from the inch at the other side of the ford,
and he saw, through the mist that hung over the
river, a whole crowd of people dancing on the inch.
Patrick was as fond of a dance as he was of a glass,
and that's saying enough for him ; so he whipped [1]
off his shoes and stockings, and away with him
across the ford.   After putting on his shoes and
stockings at the other side of the river, he walked
over to the crowd, and mixed with them for some
time without being minded.   He thought, sir,
that he'd show them better dancing than any of
themselves, for he was proud of his feet, sir, and
good right he had, for there was not a boy in the
same parish could foot a double or treble with
him.   But pwah ! — his dancing was no more to
theirs than mine would be to the mistress there.
They did not seem as if they had a bone in their
bodies, and they kept it up as if nothing could
tire them.   Patrick was 'shamed within himself,
for he thought he had not his fellow in all the
country round ; and was going away, when a little
old man, that was looking at the company for
some time bitterly, as if he did not like what was
going on, came up to him.   'Patrick,' says he.

[1] *i. e.* " in the time of the crack of a whip," he took off his
shoes and stockings.

Patrick started, for he did not think any body there knew him. 'Patrick,' says he, 'you're discouraged, and no wonder for you. But you have a friend near you. I'm your friend, and your father's friend, and I think worse (more) of your little finger than I do of all that are here, though they think no one is as good as themselves. Go into the ring and call for a lilt. Don't be afeard. I tell you the best of them did not do as well as you shall, if you will do as I bid you.' Patrick felt something within him as if he ought not to gainsay the old man. He went into the ring, and called the piper to play up the best double he had. And, sure enough, all that the others were able for was nothing to him! He bounded like an eel, now here and now there, as light as a feather, although the people could hear the music answered by his steps, that beat time to every turn of it, like the left foot of the piper. He first danced a hornpipe on the ground. Then they got a table, and he danced a treble on it that drew down shouts from the whole company. At last he called for a trencher; and when they saw him, all as if he was spinning on it like a top, they did not know what to make of him. Some praised him for the best dancer that ever entered a ring; others hated him because he was better than themselves; although they had good right to think themselves better than him or any other man that never went the long journey."

"And what was the cause of his great success?" enquired Mr. Martin.

"He could not help it, sir," replied Tom Bourke. "They that could make him do more

than that made him do it.   Howsomever, when
he had done, they wanted him to dance again, but
he was tired, and they could not persuade him.
At last he got angry, and swore a big oath, saving
your presence, that he would not dance a step
more; and the word was hardly out of his mouth,
when he found himself all alone, with nothing but
a white cow grazing by his side."

" Did he ever discover why he was gifted with
these extraordinary powers in the dance, Tom ?"
said Mr. Martin.

" I'll tell you that too, sir," answered Bourke,
" when I come to it.   When he went home, sir,
he was taken with a shivering, and went to bed;
and the next day they found he got the fever, or
something like it, for he raved like as if he was
mad.   But they couldn't make out what it was
he was saying, though he talked constant.   The
doctors gave him over.   But it's little they
know what ailed him.   When he was, as you may
say, about ten days sick, and every body thought
he was going, one of the neighbours came in to
him with a man, a friend of his, from Ballinlacken,
that was keeping with him some time before.   I
can't tell you his name either, only it was Darby.
The minute Darby saw Patrick, he took a little
bottle, with the juice of herbs in it, out of his
pocket, and gave Patrick a drink of it.   He did
the same every day for three weeks, and then
Patrick was able to walk about, as stout and as
hearty as ever he was in his life.   But he was a
long time before he came to himself; and he used
to walk the whole day sometimes by the ditch
side, talking to himself, like as if there was some

one along with him.   And so there was, surely,
or he wouldn't be the man he is to-day.

"I suppose it was from some such companion
he learned his skill," said Mr. Martin.

"You have it all now, sir," replied Bourke.
"Darby told him his friends were satisfied with
what he did the night of the dance; and though
they couldn't hinder the fever, they'd bring him
over it, and teach him more than many knew beside him.   And so they did.   For you see all the
people he met on the inch that night were friends
of a different faction; only the old man that spoke
to him; he was a friend of Patrick's family, and
it went again' his heart, you see, that the others
were so light and active, and he was bitter in
himself to hear 'em boasting how they'd dance with
any set in the whole country round.   So he gave
Patrick the gift that night, and afterwards gave
him the skill that makes him the wonder of all
that know him.   And to be sure it was only
learning he was that time when he was wandering
in his mind after the fever."

"I have heard many strange stories about that
inch near Ballyhefaan ford," said Mr. Martin.
"'Tis a great place for the good people, isn't it,
Tom?"

"You may say that, sir," returned Bourke.
"I could tell you a great deal about it.   Many
a time I sat for as good as two hours by moonlight, at th' other side of the river, looking at 'em
playing goal as if they'd break their hearts over
it; with their coats and waistcoats off, and white
handkerchiefs on the heads of one party, and red
ones on th' other, just as you'd see on a Sunday

in Mr. Simming's big field. I saw 'em one night play till the moon set, without one party being able to take the ball from th' other. I'm sure they were going to fight, only 'twas near morning. I'm told your grandfather, ma'am, used to see 'em there, too," said Bourke, turning to Mrs. Martin.

"So I have been told, Tom," replied Mrs. Martin. "But don't they say that the church yard of Kilcrumper [1] is just as favourite a place with the good people, as Ballyhefaan inch."

"Why, then, may be, you never heard, ma'am, what happened to Davy Roche in that same churchyard," said Bourke; and turning to Mr. Martin, added, "'twas a long time before he went into your service, sir. He was walking home, of an evening, from the fair of Kilcummer, a little merry, to be sure, after the day, and he came up with a berrin. So he walked along with it, and thought it very queer, that he did not know a mother's soul in the crowd, but one man, and he was sure that man was dead many years afore. Howsomever, he went on with the berrin, till they came to Kilcrumper churchyard; and faith he went in and staid with the rest, to see the corpse buried. As soon as the grave was covered, what should they do but gather about a piper that *come* along with 'em and fall to dancing as if it was a wedding. Davy longed to be among 'em (for he hadn't a bad foot of his own, that time, whatever he may now); but he was loath to begin,

[1] About two hundred yards off the Dublin mail-coach road, nearly mid-way between Kilworth and Fermoy.

because they all seemed strange to him, only the
man I told you that he thought was dead.   Well,
at last this man saw what Davy wanted, and came
up to him.   'Davy,' says he, 'take out a partner,
and show what you can do, but take care and don't
offer to kiss her.'   'That I won't,' says Davy, ' although her lips were made of honey.'   And with
that he made his bow to the *purtiest* girl in the
ring, and he and she began to dance. 'Twas a jig
they danced, and they did it to th' admiration, do
you see, of all that were there.   'Twas all very
well till the jig was over ; but just as they had
done, Davy, for he had a drop in, and was warm
with the dancing, forgot himself, and kissed his
partner, according to custom.   The smack was
no sooner off of his lips, you see, than he was left
alone in the churchyard, without a creature near
him, and all he could see was the tall tombstones.
Davy said they seemed as if they were dancing
too, but I suppose that was only the wonder that
happened him, and he being a little in drink.
Howsomever, he found it was a great many hours
later than he thought it; 'twas near morning
when he came home ; but they couldn't get a
word out of him till the next day, when he 'woke
out of a dead sleep about twelve o'clock."

When Tom had finished the account of Davy
Roche and the berrin, it became quite evident
that spirits of some sort were working too strong
within him to admit of his telling many more tales
of the good people.   Tom seemed conscious of
this.— He muttered for a few minutes broken
sentences concerning churchyards, river-sides,
leprechans, and *dina magh*, which were quite un-

intelligible, perhaps to himself, certainly to Mr. Martin and his lady.   At length he made a slight motion of the head upwards, as if he would say, " I can talk no more;" stretched his arm on the table, upon which he placed the empty tumbler slowly, and with the most knowing and cautious air; and rising from his chair, walked, or rather rolled, to the parlour-door.   Here he turned round to face his host and hostess; but after various ineffectual attempts to bid them good night, the words, as they rose, being always choked by a violent hiccup, while the door, which he held by the handle, swung to and fro, carrying his unyielding body along with it, he was obliged to depart in silence.   The cow-boy, sent by Tom's wife, who knew well what sort of allurement detained him, when he remained out after a certain hour, was in attendance to conduct his master home.   I have no doubt that he returned without meeting any material injury, as I know that within the last month, he was, to use his own words, " As stout and hearty a man as any of his age in the county Cork."

FAIRIES OR NO FAIRIES.

VIII.

John Mulligan was as fine an old fellow as ever threw a Carlow spur into the sides of a horse. He was, besides, as jolly a boon companion over a jug of punch as you would meet from Carnsore Point to Bloody Farland. And a good horse he used to ride; and a stiffer jug of punch than his was not in nineteen baronies. May be he stuck more to it than he ought to have done—but that is nothing whatever to the story I am going to tell.

John believed devoutly in fairies; and an angry man was he if you doubted them. He had more fairy stories than would make, if properly printed in a rivulet of print running down a meadow of margin, two thick quartos for Mr. Murray, of Albemarle street; all of which he used to tell on all occasions that he could find listeners. Many believed his stories—many more did not believe them—but nobody, in process of time, used to contradict the old gentleman, for it was a pity to vex him. But he had a couple of young neighbours who were just come down from their first vacation in Trinity College to spend the summer months with an uncle of theirs, Mr. Whaley, an old Cromwellian, who lived at Ballybegmullinahone, and they were too full of logic to let the old man have his own way undisputed.

Every story he told they laughed at, and said that it was impossible — that it was merely old woman's gabble, and other such things. When he would insist that all his stories were derived from the most credible sources — nay, that some of them had been told him by his own grandmother, a very respectable old lady, but slightly affected in her faculties, as things that came under her own knowledge — they cut the matter short by declaring that she was in her dotage, and at the best of times had a strong propensity to pulling a long bow.

"But," said they, "Jack Mulligan, did you ever see a fairy yourself?"

"Never," was the reply. — Never, as I am a man of honour and credit."

"Well, then," they answered, "until you do, do not be bothering us with any more tales of my grandmother."

Jack was particularly nettled at this, and took up the cudgels for his grandmother; but the younkers were too sharp for him, and finally he got into a passion, as people generally do who have the worst of an argument. This evening — it was at their uncle's, an old crony of his with whom he had dined — he had taken a large portion of his usual beverage, and was quite riotous. He at last got up in a passion, ordered his horse, and, in spite of his host's entreaties, galloped off, although he had intended to have slept there, declaring that he would not have any thing more to do with a pair of jackanapes puppies, who, because they had learned how to read good-for-nothing books in cramp writing, and were taught by a parcel of wiggy, red-snouted, prating prigs, (" not," added he, " however, that I say a man may not be a good man and have a red nose,") they imagined they knew more than a man who had held buckle and tongue together facing the wind of the world for five dozen years.

He rode off in a fret, and galloped as hard as his horse Shaunbuie could powder away over the limestone. " Damn it !" hiccuped he, " Lord pardon me for swearing ! the brats had me in one thing — I never did see a fairy ; and I would give up five as good acres as ever grew apple-potatoes to get a glimpse of one — and, by the powers ! what is that ?"

He looked, and saw a gallant spectacle. His road lay by a noble demesne, gracefully sprinkled with trees, not thickly planted as in a dark forest, but disposed, now in clumps of five or six, now standing singly, towering over the plain of verdure around them, as a beautiful promontory arising out of the sea. He had come right opposite the glory of the wood. It was an oak, which in the oldest title-deeds of the county, and they were at least five hundred years old, was called the old oak of Ballinghassig. Age had hollowed its centre, but its massy boughs still waved with their dark serrated foliage. The moon was shining on it bright. If I were a poet, like Mr. Wordsworth, I should tell you how the beautiful light was broken into a thousand different fragments — and how it filled the entire tree with a glorious flood, bathing every particular leaf, and showing forth every particular bough ; but, as I am not a poet, I shall go on with my story. By this light Jack saw a brilliant company of lovely little forms dancing under the oak with an unsteady and rolling motion. The company was large. Some spread out far beyond the farthest boundary of the shadow of the oak's branches — some were seen glancing through the flashes of light shining through its leaves — some were barely visible, nestling under the trunk — some no doubt were entirely concealed from his eyes. Never did man see any thing more beautiful. They were not three inches in height, but they were white as the driven snow, and beyond number numberless. Jack threw the bridle over his horse's neck, and drew up to the low wall which bounded the demesne, and leaning over it, surveyed, with infinite delight, their diversified gambols. By looking long at them, he soon saw objects which had not struck him at first; in particular that in the middle was a chief of superior stature, round whom the group appeared to move. He gazed so long that he was quite overcome with joy, and could not help shouting out, " Bravo! little fellow," said he, " well kicked and strong." But the instant he uttered the words the night was darkened, and the fairies vanished with the speed of lightning.

" I wish," said Jack, " I had held my tongue; but no matter now. I shall just turn bridle about and go back to Ballybegmullinahone Castle, and beat the young Master Whaleys, fine reasoners as they think themselves, out of the field clean."

No sooner said than done; and Jack was back again as if upon the wings of the wind. He rapped fiercely at the door, and called aloud for the two collegians.

" Halloo!" said he, " young Flatcaps, come down now, if you dare. Come down, if you dare, and I shall give you *oc-oc*-ocular demonstration of the truth of what I was saying."

Old Whaley put his head out of the window, and said, " Jack Mulligan, what brings you back so soon?"

" The fairies," shouted Jack; " the fairies!"

" I am afraid," muttered the Lord of Ballybeg-mullinahone, " the last glass you took was too little watered: but, no matter—come in and cool yourself over a tumbler of punch."

He came in and sat down again at table. In great spirits he told his story;—how he had seen thousands and tens of thousands of fairies dancing about the old oak of Ballinghassig; he described their beautiful dresses of shining silver; their flat-crowned hats, glittering in the moonbeams; and the princely stature and demeanour of the central figure. He added, that he heard them singing, and playing the most enchanting music; but this was merely imagination. The young men laughed, but Jack held his ground. " Suppose," said one of the lads, " we join company with you on the road, and ride along to the place, where you saw that fine company of fairies?"

" Done!" cried Jack; " but I will not promise that you will find them there, for I saw them scudding up in the sky like a flight of bees, and heard their wings whizzing through the air." This, you know, was a bounce, for Jack had heard no such thing.

Off rode the three, and came to the demesne of Oakwood. They arrived at the wall flanking the field where stood the great oak; and the moon, by this time, having again emerged from the clouds, shone bright as when Jack had passed. " Look there," he cried, exultingly; for the same spectacle again caught his eyes, and he pointed to it with his horsewhip; " look, and deny if you can."

" Why," said one of the lads, pausing, " true it is that we do see a company of white creatures; but were they fairies ten times over, I shall go among them;" and he dismounted to climb over the wall.

" Ah, Tom! Tom;" cried Jack, " stop, man, stop! what are you doing? The fairies—the good people, I mean—hate to be meddled with. You will be pinched or blinded; or your horse will cast its shoe; or—look! a wilful man will have his way. Oh! oh! he is almost at the oak — God help him! for he is past the help of man."

By this time Tom was under the tree and burst out laughing. " Jack," said he, " keep your prayers to yourself. Your fairies are not bad at all. I believe they will make tolerably good catsup."

" Catsup," said Jack, who when he found that the two lads (for the second had followed his brother) were both laughing in the middle of the fairies, had dismounted and advanced slowly — " What do you mean by catsup?"

" Nothing," replied Tom, " but that they are mushrooms (as indeed they were); and your Oberon is merely this overgrown puff-ball."

Poor Mulligan gave a long whistle of amazement, staggered back to his horse without saying a word, and rode home in a hard gallop, never looking behind him. Many a long day was it before he ventured to face the laughers at Ballybegmullinahone ; and to the day of his death the people of the parish, aye, and five parishes round, called him nothing but Musharoon Jack, such being their pronunciation of mushroom.

I should be sorry if all my fairy stories ended with so little dignity ; but —

> " These our actors,
> As I foretold you, were all spirits, and
> Are melted into air — into thin air."

The name SHEFRO (variously written Siaḃnuġ, Siṫḃnoġ, Siġḃnoġ, Sioġḃnoġ, Sioġḃnuġ, &c.) by which the foregoing section is distinguished, literally signifies a fairy house or mansion, and is adopted as a general name for the Elves who are supposed to live in troops or communities, and were popularly supposed to have castles or mansions of their own. — See *Stewart's Popular Superstitions of the Highlands,* 1823. pp. 90, 91, &c.

Sia, sigh, sighe, sigheann, siabhra, siachaire, siogidh, are Irish words, evidently springing from a common Celtic root, used to express a fairy or goblin, and even a hag or witch. Thus we have the compounds *Leannan-sighe,* a familiar, from *Leannan,* a pet, and *Siogh-dhraoidheachd,* enchantment with or by spirits.

Sigh gàoithe or *siaheann-gàoithe,* a whirlwind, is so termed because it is said to be raised by the fairies. The close of day is called *Sia,* because twilight,

<blockquote>"That sweet hour, when day is almost closing,"</blockquote>

is the time when the fairies are most frequently seen. Again, *Sigh* is a hill or hillock, because the fairies are believed to dwell within. *Sidhe, sidheadh,* and *sigh,* are names for a blast or blight, because it is supposed to proceed from the fairies.

The term *Shoges,* i. e. *Sigh oges* (young or little Spirits), Fairies, is used in a curious poem printed under the name of "The Irish Hudibras," 1689. pp. 23. and 81.; a copy of which, entitled "The Fingallian Travesty," is among the Sloane MSS., No. 900. In the Third Part of O'Flaherty's Ogygia, it is related that St. Patrick and some of his followers, who were chanting matins beside a fountain, were taken for "*Sidhe,* or fairies," by some pagan ladies.

"The Irish," according to the Rev. James Hely's translation of O'Flaherty, " call these *Sidhe,* aërial spirits or phantoms, because they are seen to come out of pleasant hills, where the common people imagine they reside, which fictitious habitations are called by us *Sidhe* or *Siodha.*"

For a similar extended use of the German word *Alp, Elf,* &c. see Introductory Essay to the Grimms' *Irische Elfenmärchen,* pp. 55—62.

FAIRY LEGENDS.

THE CLURICAUNE.

" —————————— That sottish elf
Who quaffs with swollen lips the ruby wine,
Draining the cellar with as free a hand
As if it were his purse which ne'er lack'd coin ; —
And then, with feign'd contrition ruminates
Upon his wasteful pranks, and revelry,
In some secluded dell or lonely grove
Tinsel'd by Twilight." —

Δ.

LEGENDS OF THE CLURICAUNE.

THE HAUNTED CELLAR.

IX.

There are few people who have not heard of the Mac Carthies — one of the real old Irish families, with the true Milesian blood running in their veins, as thick as buttermilk. Many were the clans of this family in the south; as the Mac Carthy-more — and the Mac Carthy-reagh — and the Mac Carthy of Muskerry; and all of them were noted for their hospitality to strangers, gentle and simple.

But not one of that name, or of any other, exceeded Justin Mac Carthy, of Ballinacarthy, at putting plenty to eat and drink upon his table; and there was a right hearty welcome for every one who would share it with him. Many a wine-cellar would be ashamed of the name if that at Ballinacarthy was the proper pattern for one; large as that cellar was, it was crowded with bins of wine, and long rows of pipes, and hogsheads, and casks, that it would take more time to count than any sober man could spare in such a place, with plenty to drink about him, and a hearty welcome to do so.

There are many, no doubt, who will think that

the butler would have little to complain of in such a house; and the whole country round would have agreed with them, if a man could be found to remain as Mr. Mac Carthy's butler for any length of time worth speaking of; yet not one who had been in his service gave him a bad word.

" We have no fault," they would say, " to find with the master, and if he could but get any one to fetch his wine from the cellar, we might every one of us have grown gray in the house, and have lived quiet and contented enough in his service until the end of our days."

" 'Tis a queer thing that, surely," thought young Jack Leary, a lad who had been brought up from a mere child in the stables of Ballinacarthy to assist in taking care of the horses, and had occasionally lent a hand in the butler's pantry : — " 'tis a mighty queer thing, surely, that one man after another cannot content himself with the best place in the house of a good master, but that every one of them must quit, all through the means, as they say, of the wine-cellar.   If the master, long life to him ! would but make me his butler, I warrant never the word more would be heard of grumbling at his bidding to go to the wine-cellar."

Young Leary accordingly watched for what he conceived to be a favourable opportunity of presenting himself to the notice of his master.

A few mornings after, Mr. Mac Carthy went into his stable-yard rather earlier than usual, and called loudly for the groom to saddle his horse, as he intended going out with the hounds.   But there was no groom to answer, and young Jack Leary led Rainbow out of the stable.

" Where is William?" enquired Mr. Mac Carthy.

" Sir?" said Jack; and Mr. Mac Carthy repeated the question.

" Is it William, please your honour?" returned Jack; " why, then, to tell the truth, he had just *one* drop too much last night."

" Where did he get it?" said Mr. Mac Carthy; " for since Thomas went away, the key of the wine-cellar has been in my pocket, and I have been obliged to fetch what was drank myself."

" Sorrow a know I know," said Leary, " unless the cook might have given him the *least taste* in life of whiskey. But," continued he, performing a low bow by seizing with his right hand a lock of hair, and pulling down his head by it, whilst his left leg, which had been put forward, was scraped back against the ground, " may I make so bold as just to ask your honour one question?"

" Speak out, Jack," said Mr. Mac Carthy.

" Why, then, does your honour want a butler?"

" Can you recommend me one," returned his master, with the smile of good-humour upon his countenance, " and one who will not be afraid of going to my wine-cellar?"

" Is the wine-cellar all the matter?" said young Leary; " devil a doubt I have of myself then for that."

" So you mean to offer me your services in the capacity of butler?" said Mr. Mac Carthy, with some surprise.

" Exactly so," answered Leary, now for the first time looking up from the ground.

" Well, I believe you to be a good lad, and have no objection to give you a trial."

" Long may your honour reign over us, and the Lord spare you to us!" ejaculated Leary, with another national bow, as his master rode off; and he continued for some time to gaze after him with a vacant stare, which slowly and gradually assumed a look of importance.

" Jack Leary," said he at length, " Jack — is it Jack?" in a tone of wonder; " faith, 'tis not Jack now, but Mr. John, the butler;" and with an air of becoming consequence he strided out of the stable-yard towards the kitchen.

It is of little purport to my story, although it may afford an instructive lesson to the reader, to depict the sudden transition of nobody into somebody. Jack's former stable companion, a poor superannuated hound named Bran, who had been accustomed to receive many an affectionate pat on the head, was spurned from him with a kick and an " Out of the way, sirrah." Indeed, poor Jack's memory seemed sadly affected by this sudden change of situation. What established the point beyond all doubt was his almost forgetting the pretty face of Peggy, the kitchen wench, whose heart he had assailed but the preceding week by the offer of purchasing a gold ring for the fourth finger of her right hand, and a lusty imprint of good-will upon her lips.

When Mr. Mac Carthy returned from hunting, he sent for Jack Leary — so he still continued to call his new butler. " Jack," said he, " I believe you are a trustworthy lad, and here are the keys of my cellar. I have asked the gentlemen with whom I hunted to-day to dine with me, and I hope they may be satisfied at the way in which you will wait on them at table; but above all, let there be no want of wine after dinner."

Mr. John having a tolerably quick eye for such things, and being naturally a handy lad, spread his cloth accordingly, laid his plates and knives and forks in the same manner he had seen his predecessors in office perform these mysteries, and really, for the first time, got through attendance on dinner very well.

It must not be forgotten, however, that it was at the house of an Irish country squire, who was entertaining a company of booted and spurred fox-hunters, not very particular about what are considered matters of infinite importance under other circumstances and in other societies.

For instance, few of Mr. Mac Carthy's guests, (though all excellent and worthy men in their way,) cared much whether the punch produced after soup was made of Jamaica or Antigua rum; some even would not have been inclined to question the correctness of good old Irish whiskey; and, with the exception of their liberal host himself, every one in company preferred the port which Mr. Mac Carthy put on his table to the less ardent flavour of claret, — a choice rather at variance with modern sentiment.

It was waxing near midnight, when Mr. Mac Carthy rang the bell three times. This was a signal for more wine; and Jack proceeded to the cellar to procure a fresh supply, but it must be confessed not without some little hesitation.

The luxury of ice was then unknown in the

south of Ireland; but the superiority of cool wine had been acknowledged by all men of sound judgment and true taste.

The grandfather of Mr. Mac Carthy, who had built the mansion of Ballinacarthy upon the site of an old castle which had belonged to his ancestors, was fully aware of this important fact; and in the construction of his magnificent wine-cellar had availed himself of a deep vault, excavated out of the solid rock in former times as a place of retreat and security. The descent to this vault was by a flight of steep stone stairs, and here and there in the wall were narrow passages — I ought rather to call them crevices; and also certain projections, which cast deep shadows, and looked very frightful when any one went down the cellar stairs with a single light: indeed, two lights did not much improve the matter, for though the breadth of the shadows became less, the narrow crevices remained as dark and darker than ever.

Summoning up all his resolution, down went the new butler, bearing in his right hand a lantern and the key of the cellar, and in his left a basket, which he considered sufficiently capacious to contain an adequate stock for the remainder of the evening: he arrived at the door without any interruption whatever; but when he put the key, which was of an ancient and clumsy kind — for it was before the days of Bramah's patent, — and turned it in the lock, he thought he heard a strange kind of laughing within the cellar, to which some empty bottles that stood upon the floor outside vibrated so violently, that they struck against each other: in this he could not be mistaken, although he may have been deceived in the laugh, for the bottles were just at his feet, and he saw them in motion.

Leary paused for a moment, and looked about him with becoming caution. He then boldly seized the handle of the key, and turned it with all his strength in the lock, as if he doubted his own power of doing so; and the door flew open with a most tremendous crash, that, if the house had not been built upon the solid rock, would have shook it from the foundation.

To recount what the poor fellow saw would be impossible, for he seems not to know very clearly himself: but what he told the cook the next morning was, that he heard a roaring and bellowing like a mad bull, and that all the pipes and hogsheads and casks in the cellar went rocking backwards and forwards with so much force, that he thought every one would have been staved in, and that he should have been drowned or smothered in wine.

When Leary recovered, he made his way back as well as he could to the dining-room, where he found his master and the company very impatient for his return.

"What kept you?" said Mr. Mac Carthy in an angry voice; "and where is the wine? I rung for it half an hour since."

"The wine is in the cellar, I hope, sir," said Jack, trembling violently; "I hope 'tis not all lost."

"What do you mean, fool?" exclaimed Mr. Mac Carthy in a still more angry tone: "why did you not fetch some with you?"

Jack looked wildly about him, and only uttered a deep groan.

" Gentlemen," said Mr. Mac Carthy to his guests, " this is too much. When I next see you to dinner, I hope it will be in another house, for it is impossible I can remain longer in this, where a man has no command over his own wine-cellar, and cannot get a butler to do his duty. I have long thought of moving from Ballinacarthy; and I am now determined, with the blessing of God, to leave it to-morrow. But wine shall you have, were I to go myself to the cellar for it." So saying, he rose from table, took the key and lantern from his half stupified servant, who regarded him with a look of vacancy, and descended the narrow stairs, already described, which led to his cellar.

When he arrived at the door, which he found open, he thought he heard a noise, as if of rats or mice scrambling over the casks, and on advancing perceived a little figure, about six inches in height, seated astride upon the pipe of the oldest port in the place, and bearing a spigot upon his shoulder. Raising the lantern, Mr. Mac Carthy contemplated the little fellow with wonder: he wore a red nightcap on his head; before him was a short leather apron, which now, from his attitude, fell rather on one side; and he had stockings of a light blue colour, so long as nearly to cover the entire of his legs; with shoes, having huge silver buckles in them, and with high heels (perhaps out of vanity to make him appear taller). His face was like a withered winter apple; and his nose, which was of a bright crimson colour, about the tip wore a delicate purple bloom, like that of a plum: yet his eyes twinkled

> " like those mites
> Of candied dew in moony nights —

and his mouth twitched up at one side with an arch grin.

" Ha, scoundrel!" exclaimed Mr. Mac Carthy, " have I found you at last? disturber of my cellar — what are you doing there?"

" Sure, and master," returned the little fellow, looking up at him with one eye, and with the other throwing a sly glance towards the spigot on his shoulder, " a'n't we going to move to-morrow? and sure you would not leave your own little Cluricaune Naggeneen behind you?"

" Oh!" thought Mr. Mac Carthy, " if you are to follow me, master Naggeneen, I don't see much use in quitting Ballinacarthy." So filling with wine the basket which young Leary in his fright had left behind him, and locking the cellar door, he rejoined his guests.

For some years after Mr. Mac Carthy had always to fetch the wine for his table himself, as the little Cluricaune Naggeneen seemed to feel a personal respect towards him. Notwithstanding the labour of these journeys, the worthy lord of Ballinacarthy lived in his paternal mansion to a good round age, and was famous to the last for the excellence of his wine, and the conviviality of his company; but at the time of his death, that same conviviality had nearly emptied his wine-cellar; and as it was never so well filled again, nor so often visited, the revels of master Naggeneen became less celebrated, and are now only spoken of amongst the legendary lore of the country. It is even said that the poor little fellow took the declension of the cellar so to heart, that he became negligent and careless of himself, and that he has been sometimes seen going about with hardly a skreed to cover him.

Some, however, believe that he turned brogue maker, and assert that they have seen him at his work, and heard him whistling as merry as a blackbird on a May morning, under the shadow of a brown jug of foaming ale bigger — aye bigger than himself; decently dressed enough, they say; — only looking mighty old. But still 't is clear he has his wits about him, since no one ever had the luck to catch him, or to get hold of the purse he has with him, which they call *spré-na-skillinagh*, and 't said is never without a shilling in it.

MASTER AND MAN.

X.

BILLY MAC DANIEL was once as likely a young man as ever shook his brogue at a patron, emptied a quart, or handled a shillelagh: fearing for nothing but the want of drink; caring for nothing but who should pay for it; and thinking of nothing but how to make fun over it: drunk or sober, a word and a blow was ever the way with Billy Mac Daniel; and a mighty easy way it is of either getting into or ending a dispute. More is the pity that, through the means of his drinking, and fearing, and caring for nothing, this same Billy Mac Daniel fell into bad company; for surely the good people are the worst of all company any one could come across.

It so happened that Billy was going home one clear frosty night not long after Christmas; the moon was round and bright; but although it was as fine a night as heart could wish for, he felt pinched with the cold. "By my word," chattered Billy, "a drop of good liquor would be no bad thing to keep a man's soul from freezing in him; and I wish I had a full measure of the best."

"Never wish it twice, Billy," said a little man in a three-cornered hat, bound all about with gold lace, and with great silver buckles in his shoes, so big that it was a wonder how he could carry them, and he held out a glass as big as himself, filled with as good liquor as ever eye looked on or lip tasted.

" Success, my little fellow," said Billy Mac Daniel, nothing daunted, though well he knew the little man to belong to the *good people;* " here 's your health, any way, and thank you kindly ; no matter who pays for the drink;" and he took the glass and drained it to the very bottom, without ever taking a second breath to it.

" Success," said the little man ; " and you 're heartily welcome, Billy ; but don't think to cheat me as you have done others,—out with your purse and pay me like a gentleman."

" Is it I pay you?" said Billy : " could I not just take you up and put you in my pocket as easily as a blackberry? "

" Billy Mac Daniel," said the little man, getting very angry, " you shall be my servant for seven years and a day, and that is the way I will be paid ; so make ready to follow me."

When Billy heard this, he began to be very sorry for having used such bold words towards the little man ; and he felt himself, yet could not tell how, obliged to follow the little man the livelong night about the country, up and down, and over hedge and ditch, and through bog and brake, without any rest.

When morning began to dawn, the little man turned round to him and said, " You may now go home, Billy, but on your peril don't fail to meet me in the Fort-field to-night; or if you do, it may be the worse for you in the long run. If I find you a good servant, you will find me an indulgent master."

Home went Billy Mac Daniel; and though he was tired and weary enough, never a wink of sleep could he get for thinking of the little man; but he was afraid not to do his bidding, so up he got in the evening, and away he went to the Fort-field. He was not long there before the little man came towards him and said, " Billy, I want to go a long journey to-night; so saddle one of my horses, and you may saddle another for yourself, as you are to go along with me, and may be tired after your walk last night."

Billy thought this very considerate of his master, and thanked him accordingly: " But," said he, " if I may be so bold, sir, I would ask which is the way to your stable, for never a thing do I see but the fort here, and the old thorn-tree in the corner of the field, and the stream running at the bottom of the hill, with the bit of bog over against us."

" Ask no questions, Billy," said the little man, " but go over to that bit of bog, and bring me two of the strongest rushes you can find."

Billy did accordingly, wondering what the little man would be at; and he picked out two of the stoutest rushes he could find, with a little bunch of brown blossom stuck at the side of each, and brought them back to his master.

" Get up, Billy," said the little man, taking one of the rushes from him and striding across it.

" Where will I get up, please your honour?" said Billy.

" Why, upon horseback, like me, to be sure," said the little man.

" Is it after making a fool of me you'd be,"

said Billy, " bidding me get a horse-back upon that bit of a rush? May be you want to persuade me that the rush I pulled but while ago out of the bog over there is a horse?"

" Up! up! and no words," said the little man, looking very vexed; " the best horse you ever rode was but a fool to it." So Billy, thinking all this was in joke, and fearing to vex his master, straddled across the rush: " Borram! Borram! Borram!" cried the little man three times (which, in English, means to become great), and Billy did the same after him: presently the rushes swelled up into fine horses, and away they went full speed; but Billy, who had put the rush between his legs, without much minding how he did it, found himself sitting on horseback the wrong way, which was rather awkward, with his face to the horse's tail; and so quickly had his steed started off with him, that he had no power to turn round, and there was therefore nothing for it but to hold on by the tail.

At last they came to their journey's end, and stopped at the gate of a fine house: " Now, Billy," said the little man, " do as you see me do, and follow me close; but as you did not know your horse's head from his tail, mind that your own head does not spin round until you can't tell whether you are standing on it or on your heels: for remember that old liquor, though able to make a cat speak, can make a man dumb."

The little man then said some queer kind of words, out of which Billy could make no meaning; but he contrived to say them after him for all that; and in they both went through the key-hole of the door, and through one key-hole after another, until they got into the wine-cellar, which was well stored with all kinds of wine.

The little man fell to drinking as hard as he could, and Billy noway disliking the example, did the same. " The best of masters are you surely," said Billy to him; " no matter who is the next; and well pleased will I be with your service if you continue to give me plenty to drink."

" I have made no bargain with you," said the little man, " and will make none; but up and follow me." Away they went, through key-hole after key-hole; and each mounting upon the rush which he had left at the hall door, scampered off, kicking the clouds before them like snow-balls, as soon as the words, " Borram, Borram, Borram," had passed their lips.

When they came back to the Fort-field, the little man dismissed Billy, bidding him to be there the next night at the same hour. Thus did they go on, night after night, shaping their course one night here, and another night there—sometimes north, and sometimes east, and sometimes south, until there was not a gentleman's wine-cellar in all Ireland they had not visited, and could tell the flavour of every wine in it as well —aye, better than the butler himself.

One night when Billy Mac Daniel met the little man as usual in the Fort-field, and was going to the bog to fetch the horses for their journey, his master said to him, " Billy, I shall want another horse to-night, for may be we may bring back more company with us than we take."

So Billy, who now knew better than to question any order given to him by his master, brought a third rush, much wondering who it might be that would travel back in their company, and whether he was about to have a fellow-servant. "If I have," thought Billy, "he shall go and fetch the horses from the bog every night; for I don't see why I am not, every inch of me, as good a gentleman as my master."

Well, away they went, Billy leading the third horse, and never stopped until they came to a snug farmer's house in the county Limerick, close under the old castle of Carrigogunniel, that was built, they say, by the great Brian Boru. Within the house there was great carousing going forward, and the little man stopped outside for some time to listen; then turning round all of a sudden, said, "Billy, I will be a thousand years old to-morrow!"

"God bless us, sir," said Billy, "will you!"

"Don't say these words again, Billy," said the little man, "or you will be my ruin for ever. Now, Billy, as I will be a thousand years in the world to-morrow, I think it is full time for me to get married."

"I think so too, without any kind of doubt at all," said Billy, "if ever you mean to marry."

"And to that purpose," said the little man, "have I come all the way to Carrigogunniel; for in this house, this very night, is young Darby Riley going to be married to Bridget Rooney; and as she is a tall and comely girl, and has come of decent people, I think of marrying her myself, and taking her off with me."

" And what will Darby Riley say to that ?'
said Billy.

" Silence !" said the little man, putting on a
mighty severe look : " I did not bring you here
with me to ask questions ;" and without holding
further argument, he began saying the queer
words, which had the power of passing him
through the key-hole as free as air, and which
Billy thought himself mighty clever to be able to
say after him.

In they both went; and for the better viewing
the company, the little man perched himself up
as nimbly as a cock-sparrow upon one of the big
beams which went across the house over all their
heads, and Billy did the same upon another facing
him ; but not being much accustomed to roosting
in such a place, his legs hung down as untidy as
may be, and it was quite clear he had not taken
pattern after the way in which the little man had
bundled himself up together. If the little man
had been a tailor all his life, he could not have
sat more contentedly upon his haunches.

There they were, both master and man, looking
down upon the fun that was going forward — and
under them were the priest and piper — and the
father of Darby Riley, with Darby's two brothers
and his uncle's son — and there were both the
father and the mother of Bridget Rooney, and
proud enough the old couple were that night of
their daughter, as good right they had — and her
four sisters with bran new ribands in their caps,
and her three brothers all looking as clean and
as clever as any three boys in Munster — and
there were uncles and aunts, and gossips and

cousins enough besides to make a full house of it
— and plenty was there to eat and drink on the
table for every one of them, if they had been
double the number.

Now it happened, just as Mrs. Rooney had
helped his reverence to the first cut of the pig's
head which was placed before her, beautifully
bolstered up with white savoys, that the bride
gave a sneeze which made every one at table
start, but not a soul said " God bless us."   All
thinking that the priest would have done so, as
he ought if he had done his duty, no one wished
to take the word out of his mouth, which unfor-
tunately was pre-occupied with pig's head and
greens.   And after a moment's pause, the fun
and merriment of the bridal feast went on without
the pious benediction.

Of this circumstance both Billy and his master
were no inattentive spectators from their exalted
stations.   " Ha !" exclaimed the little man,
throwing one leg from under him with a joyous
flourish, and his eye twinkled with a strange
light, whilst his eyebrows became elevated into
the curvature of Gothic arches — " Ha !" said he,
leering down at the bride, and then up at Billy,
" I have half of her now, surely.   Let her sneeze
but twice more, and she is mine, in spite of priest,
mass-book and Darby Riley."

Again the fair Bridget sneezed ; but it was so
gently, and she blushed so much, that few except
the little man took, or seemed to take, any notice ; and no one thought of saying " God bless
us."

Billy all this time regarded the poor girl with

a most rueful expression of countenance; for he could not help thinking what a terrible thing it was for a nice young girl of nineteen, with large blue eyes, transparent skin, and dimpled cheeks, suffused with health and joy, to be obliged to marry an ugly little bit of a man who was a thousand years old, barring a day.

At this critical moment the bride gave a third sneeze, and Billy roared out with all his might, " God save us ! " Whether this exclamation resulted from his soliloquy, or from the mere force of habit, he never could tell exactly himself; but no sooner was it uttered, than the little man, his face glowing with rage and disappointment, sprung from the beam on which he had perched himself, and shrieking out in the shrill voice of a cracked bagpipe, " I discharge you my service, Billy Mac Daniel — take *that* for your wages," gave poor Billy a most furious kick in the back, which sent his unfortunate servant sprawling upon his face and hands right in the middle of the supper table.

If Billy was astonished, how much more so was every one of the company into which he was thrown with so little ceremony; but when they heard his story, Father Cooney laid down his knife and fork, and married the young couple out of hand with all speed; and Billy Mac Daniel danced the Rinka at their wedding, and plenty did he drink at it too, which was what he thought more of than dancing.

THE LITTLE SHOE.

XI.

" Now tell me, Molly," said Mr. Coote to Molly Cogan, as he met her on the road one day, close to one of the old gateways of Kilmallock, [1] " did you ever hear of the Cluricaune ? "

" Is it the Cluricaune ? why, then, sure I did, often and often ; many's the time I heard my father, rest his soul ! tell about 'em."

" But did you ever see one, Molly, yourself ? "

" Och ! no, I never *see* one in my life ; but my grandfather, that's my father's father, you know, he *see* one, one time, and caught him too."

" Caught him ! Oh ! Molly, tell me how ? "

" Why, then, I 'll tell you. My grandfather, you see, was out there above in the bog, drawing home turf, and the poor old mare was tired after her day's work, and the old man went out to the stable to look after her, and to see if she was eating her hay ; and when he came to the stable door there, my dear, he heard something hammering, hammering, hammering, just for all the world like a shoemaker making a shoe, and whistling all the time the prettiest tune he ever heard in his whole life before. Well, my grandfather, he thought it was the Cluricaune, and he said to himself, says he, ' I 'll catch you, if I can,

____

1 " Kilmallock seemed to me like the court of the Queen of Silence."—*O'Keeffe's Recollections.*

and then I 'll have money enough always.' So
he opened the door very quietly, and didn't make
a bit of noise in the world that ever was heard;
and looked all about, but the never a bit of the
little man he could see any where, but he heard
him hammering and whistling, and so he looked
and looked, till at last he *see* the little fellow;
and where was he, do you think, but in the girth
under the mare; and there he was with his little
bit of an apron on him, and hammer in his hand,
and a little red nightcap on his head, and he
making a shoe; and he was so busy with his
work, and he was hammering and whistling so
loud, that he never minded my grandfather till he
caught him fast in his hand. ' Faith, I have you
now,' says he, ' and I 'll never let you go till I get
your purse — that's what I won't; so give it here
to me at once, now.' — ' Stop, stop,' says the
Cluricaune, ' stop, stop,' says he, ' till I get it for
you.' So my grandfather, like a fool, you see,
opened his hand a little, and the little fellow
jumped away laughing, and he never saw him
any more, and the never the bit of the purse did
he get, only the Cluricaune left his little shoe that
he was making; and my grandfather was mad
enough angry with himself for letting him go; but
he had the shoe all his life, and my own mother
told me she often *see* it, and had it in her hand,
and 'twas the prettiest little shoe she ever saw."

"And did you see it yourself, Molly?"

"Oh! no, my dear, it was lost long afore I
was born: but my mother told me about it often
and often enough."

The main point of distinction between the Cluricaune and the Shefro, arises from the sottish and solitary habits of the former, who are rarely found in troops or communities.

The Cluricaune of the county of Cork, the Luricaune of Kerry, and the Lurigadaune of Tipperary, appear to be the same as the Leprechan or Leprochaune of Leinster, and the Loghery-man of Ulster ; and these words are probably all provincialisms of *luaċarmaṅ* the Irish for a pigmy.

It is possible, and is in some measure borne out by the text of one of the preceding stories [IX.], that the word *luacharman* is merely an Anglo-Irish induction, compounded of *luaċair* (a rush), and the English word, *man.* — A rushy man, — that may be, a man of the height of a rush, or a being who dwelt among rushes, *i. e.* unfrequented or boggy places.

The following dialogue is said to have taken place in an Irish court of justice, upon the witness having used the word Leprochaune : —

Court.—Pray what is a leprochaune ? the law knows no such character or designation.

Witness. — My Lord, it is a little counsellor man in the fairies, or an attorney that robs them all, and he always carries a purse that is full of money, and if you see him and keep your eyes on him, and that you never turn them aside, he cannot get away, and if you catch him he gives you the purse to let him go, and then you 're as rich as a Jew.

Court. — Did you ever know of any one that caught a Leprochaune ? I wish I could catch one.

Witness. — Yes, my Lord, there was one ——

Court. — That will do.

With respect to " money matters," there appears to be a strong resemblance between the ancient Roman Incubus and the Irish Cluricaune.—" Sed quomodo dicunt, ego nihil scio, sed audivi, quomodo incuboni pileum rapuisset et thesaurum invenit," are the words of Petronius.— See, for further arguments in support of the identity of the two spirits, the Brothers Grimm's Essay on the Nature of the Elves, prefixed to their translation of this work, under the head of " Ancient Testimonies."

" Old German and Northern poems contain numerous accounts of the skill of the dwarfs in curious smith's work." — " The Irish Cluricaune is heard hammering ; he is particularly fond of making shoes, but these were in ancient times made of metal (in the old northern language a shoe-maker is called a *shoe-smith*) ; and, singularly enough, the wights in a German tradition manifest the same propensity ; for, whatever work the shoe-maker has been able to cut out in the day, they finish with incredible quickness during the night."

THE BROTHERS GRIMM.

FAIRY LEGENDS.

THE BANSHEE.

" Who sits upon the heath forlorn,
With robe so free and tresses torn?
Anon she pours a harrowing strain,
And then — she sits all mute again !—
Now peals the wild funereal cry —
And now — it sinks into a sigh."

OURAWNS.

H

LEGENDS OF THE BANSHEE.

XII.

THE Reverend Charles Bunworth was rector of Buttevant, in the county of Cork, about the middle of the last century. He was a man of unaffected piety, and of sound learning; pure in heart, and benevolent in intention. By the rich he was respected, and by the poor beloved; nor did a difference of creed prevent their looking up to "*the minister*" (so was Mr. Bunworth called by them) in matters of difficulty and in seasons of distress, confident of receiving from him the advice and assistance that a father would afford to his children. He was the friend and the benefactor of the surrounding country — to him, from the neighbouring town of Newmarket, came both Curran and Yelverton for advice and instruction, previous to their entrance at Dublin College. Young, indigent and inexperienced, these afterwards eminent men received from him, in addition to the advice they sought, pecuniary aid; and the brilliant career which was theirs, justified the discrimination of the giver.

But what extended the fame of Mr. Bunworth far beyond the limits of the parishes adjacent to his own, was his performance on the Irish harp, and his hospitable reception and entertainment of the poor harpers who travelled from house to house about the country. Grateful to their patron, these itinerant minstrels sang his praises to the tingling accompaniment of their harps, invoking in return for his bounty abundant blessings on his white head, and celebrating in their rude verses the blooming charms of his daughters, Elizabeth and Mary. It was all these poor fellows could do; but who can doubt that their gratitude was sincere, when, at the time of Mr. Bunworth's death, no less than fifteen harps were deposited on the loft of his granary, bequeathed to him by the last members of a race which has now ceased to exist. Trifling, no doubt, in intrinsic value were these relics, yet there is something in gifts of the heart that merits preservation; and it is to be regretted that, when he died, these harps were broken up one after the other, and used as fire-wood by an ignorant follower of the family, who, on their removal to Cork for a temporary change of scene, was left in charge of the house.

The circumstances attending the death of Mr. Bunworth may be doubted by some; but there are still living credible witnesses who declare their authenticity, and who can be produced to attest most, if not all of the following particulars.

About a week previous to his dissolution, and early in the evening, a noise was heard at the hall-door resembling the shearing of sheep; but at the time no particular attention was paid to it. It was nearly eleven o'clock the same night, when Kavanagh, the herdsman, returned from Mallow, whither he had been sent in the afternoon for some medicine, and was observed by Miss Bunworth, to whom he delivered the parcel, to be much agitated. At this time, it must be observed, her father was by no means considered in danger.

"What is the matter, Kavanagh?" asked Miss Bunworth: but the poor fellow, with a bewildered look, only uttered, "The master, Miss — the master — he is going from us;" and, overcome with real grief, he burst into a flood of tears.

Miss Bunworth, who was a woman of strong nerve, enquired if any thing he had learned in Mallow induced him to suppose that her father was worse.

"No, Miss," said Kavanagh; "it was not in Mallow —— "

"Kavanagh," said Miss Bunworth, with that stateliness of manner for which she is said to have been remarkable, "I fear you have been drinking, which, I must say, I did not expect at such a time as the present, when it was your duty to have kept yourself sober;— I thought you might have been trusted: — what should we have done if you had broken the medicine bottle, or lost it? for the doctor said it was of the greatest consequence that your master should take the medicine to-night. But I will speak to you in the morning, when you are in a fitter state to understand what I say."

Kavanagh looked up with a stupidity of aspect which did not serve to remove the impression of his being drunk, as his eyes appeared heavy and dull after the flood of tears; — but his voice was not that of an intoxicated person.

"Miss," said he, "as I hope to receive mercy

hereafter, neither bit nor sup has passed my lips since I left this house: but the master ———"

"Speak softly," said Miss Bunworth; "he sleeps, and is going on as well as we could expect."

"Praise be to God for that, any way," replied Kavanagh; "but oh! Miss, he is going from us surely—we will lose him—the master—we will lose him, we will lose him!" and he wrung his hands together.

"What is it you mean, Kavanagh?" asked Miss Bunworth.

"Is it mean?" said Kavanagh: "the Banshee has come for him, Miss; and 'tis not I alone who have heard her."

"'Tis an idle superstition," said Miss Bunworth.

"May be so," replied Kavanagh, as if the words 'idle superstition' only sounded upon his ear without reaching his mind—"May be so," he continued; "but as I came through the glen of Ballybeg, she was along with me keening, and screeching, and clapping her hands, by my side, every step of the way, with her long white hair falling about her shoulders, and I could hear her repeat the master's name every now and then, as plain as ever I heard it. When I came to the old abbey, she parted from me there, and turned into the pigeon-field next the *berrin* ground, and folding her cloak about her, down she sat under the tree that was struck by the lightning, and began keening so bitterly, that it went through one's heart to hear it."

"Kavanagh," said Miss Bunworth, who had,

however, listened attentively to this remarkable relation, " my father is, I believe, better; and I hope will himself soon be up and able to convince you that all this is but your own fancy; nevertheless, I charge you not to mention what you have told me, for there is no occasion to frighten your fellow-servants with the story."

Mr. Bunworth gradually declined; but nothing particular occurred until the night previous to his death: that night both his daughters, exhausted with continued attendance and watching, were prevailed upon to seek some repose; and an elderly lady, a near relative and friend of the family, remained by the bedside of their father. The old gentleman then lay in the parlour, where he had been in the morning removed at his own request, fancying the change would afford him relief; and the head of his bed was placed close to the window. In a room adjoining sat some male friends, and, as usual on like occasions of illness, in the kitchen many of the followers of the family had assembled.

The night was serene and moonlight — the sick man slept — and nothing broke the stillness of their melancholy watch, when the little party in the room adjoining the parlour, the door of which stood open, was suddenly roused by a sound at the window near the bed: a rose-tree grew outside the window, so close as to touch the glass; this was forced aside with some noise, and a low moaning was heard, accompanied by clapping of hands, as if of a female in deep affliction. It seemed as if the sound proceeded from a person holding her mouth close to the window. The lady who sat by the bedside of Mr. Bunworth went into the adjoining room, and in the tone of alarm, enquired of the gentlemen there, if they had heard the Banshee? Sceptical of supernatural appearances, two of them rose hastily and went out to discover the cause of these sounds, which they also had distinctly heard. They walked all round the house, examining every spot of ground, particularly near the window from whence the voice had proceeded; the bed of earth beneath, in which the rose tree was planted, had been recently dug, and the print of a footstep — if the tree had been forced aside by mortal hand — would have inevitably remained; but they could perceive no such impression; and an unbroken stillness reigned without. Hoping to dispel the mystery, they continued their search anxiously along the road, from the straightness of which and the lightness of the night, they were enabled to see some distance around them; but all was silent and deserted, and they returned surprised and disappointed. How much more then were they astonished at learning that the whole time of their absence, those who remained within the house had heard the moaning and clapping of hands even louder and more distinct than before they had gone out; and no sooner was the door of the room closed on them, than they again heard the same mournful sounds! Every succeeding hour the sick man became worse, and as the first glimpse of the morning appeared, Mr. Bunworth expired.

LEGENDS OF THE BANSHEE.

XIII.

The family of Mac Carthy have for some generations possessed a small estate in the county of Tipperary. They are the descendants of a race, once numerous and powerful in the south of Ireland; and though it is probable that the property they at present hold is no part of the large possessions of their ancestors, yet the district in which they live is so connected with the name of Mac Carthy by those associations which are never forgotten in Ireland, that they have preserved with all ranks a sort of influence much greater than that which their fortune or connections could otherwise give them. They are, like most of this class, of the Roman Catholic persuasion, to which they adhere with somewhat of the pride of ancestry, blended with a something, call it what you will, whether bigotry, or a sense of wrong, arising out of repeated diminutions of their family possessions, during the more rigorous periods of the penal laws. Being an old family, and especially being an old Catholic family, they have of course their Banshee; and the circumstances under which the appearance, which I shall relate, of this mysterious harbinger of death took place, were told me by an old lady, a near connection of theirs, who knew many of the parties concerned, and who, though not deficient in understanding or education, cannot to this day be brought to give a decisive opinion as to the truth or authenticity of the story. The plain inference to be drawn from this is, that she believes it, though she does not own it; and as she was a contemporary of the persons concerned — as she heard the account from many persons about the same period, all concurring in the important particulars — as some of her authorities were themselves actors in the scene — and as none of the parties were interested in speaking what was false; I think we have about as good evidence that the whole is undeniably true as we have of many narratives of modern history, which I could name, and which many grave and sober-minded people would deem it very great pyrrhonism to question. This, however, is a point which it is not my province to determine. People who deal out stories of this sort must be content to act like certain young politicians, who tell very freely to their friends what they hear at a great man's table; not guilty of the impertinence of weighing the doctrines, and leaving it to their hearers to understand them in any sense, or in no sense, just as they may please.

Charles Mac Carthy was, in the year 1749, the only surviving son of a very numerous family. His father died when he was little more than twenty, leaving him the Mac Carthy estate, not much encumbered, considering that it was an Irish one. Charles was gay, handsome, unfettered either by poverty, a father, or guardians, and therefore was not, at the age of one-and-twenty, a pattern of regularity and virtue. In plain terms, he was an exceedingly dissipated — I fear I may say debauched young man. His companions were, as may be supposed, of the higher classes of the youth in his neighbourhood, and, in general, of those whose fortunes were larger than his own, whose dispositions to pleasure were therefore under still less restrictions, and in whose example he found at once an incentive and an apology for his irregularities. Besides, Ireland, a place to this day not very remarkable for the coolness and steadiness of its youth, was then one of the cheapest countries in the world in most of those articles which money supplies for the indulgence of the passions. The odious exciseman, with his portentous book in one hand, his unrelenting pen held in the other, or stuck beneath his hat-band, and the ink-bottle ('black emblem of the informer') dangling from his waistcoat-button — went not then from ale-house to ale-house, denouncing all those patriotic dealers in spirit, who preferred selling whiskey, which had nothing to do with English laws (but to elude them), to retailing that poisonous liquor, which derived its name from the British " Parliament," that compelled its circulation among a reluctant people. Or if the gauger — recording angel of the law — wrote down the peccadillo of a publican, he dropped a tear upon the word, and blotted it out for ever ! For, welcome to the tables of their hospitable neighbours, the guardians of the excise, where they existed at all, scrupled to abridge those luxuries which they freely shared ; and thus the competition in the market between the smuggler, who incurred little hazard, and the personage ycleped fair trader, who enjoyed little protection, made Ireland a land flowing, not merely with milk and honey, but with whiskey and wine.   In the enjoyments supplied by these, and in the many kindred pleasures to which frail youth is but too prone, Charles Mac Carthy indulged to such a degree, that just about the time when he had completed his four-and-twentieth year, after a week of great excesses, he was seized with a violent fever, which, from its malignity, and the weakness of his frame, left scarcely a hope of his recovery.   His mother, who had at first made many efforts to check his vices, and at last had been obliged to look on at his rapid progress to ruin in silent despair, watched day and night at his pillow.   The anguish of parental feeling was blended with that still deeper misery which those only know who have striven hard to rear in virtue and piety a beloved and favourite child ; have found him grow up all that their hearts could desire, until he reached manhood ; and then, when their pride was highest, and their hopes almost ended in the fulfilment of their fondest expectations, have seen this idol of their affections plunge headlong into a course of reckless profligacy, and, after a rapid career of vice, hang upon the verge of eternity, without the leisure for, or the power of, repentance.   Fervently she prayed that, if his life could not be spared, at least the delirium, which continued with increasing violence from the first few hours of his disorder, might vanish before death, and leave enough of light and of calm for making his peace with offended Heaven.   After several days, however, nature seemed quite exhausted, and he sunk into a state too like death to be mistaken for the repose of sleep. His face had that pale, glossy, marble look, which is in general so sure a symptom that life has left its tenement of clay. His eyes were closed and sunk; the lids having that compressed and stiffened appearance which seemed to indicate that some friendly hand had done its last office. The lips, half-closed and perfectly ashy, discovered just so much of the teeth as to give to the features of death their most ghastly, but most impressive look. He lay upon his back, with his hands stretched beside him, quite motionless; and his distracted mother, after repeated trials, could discover not the least symptom of animation. The medical man who attended, having tried the usual modes for ascertaining the presence of life, declared at last his opinion that it was flown, and prepared to depart from the house of mourning. His horse was seen to come to the door. A crowd of people who were collected before the windows, or scattered in groups on the lawn in front, gathered round when the door opened. These were tenants, fosterers, and poor relations of the family, with others attracted by affection, or by that interest which partakes of curiosity, but is something more, and which collects the lower ranks round a house where a human being is in his passage to another world. They saw the professional man come out from the hall door and approach his horse; and while slowly, and with a melancholy air, he prepared to mount, they clustered round him with enquiring and wishful looks. Not a word was spoken; but their meaning could not be misunderstood; and the physician, when he had got into his saddle, and while the servant was still holding the bridle, as if to delay him, and was looking anxiously at his face, as if expecting that he would relieve the general suspense, shook his head, and said in a low voice, "It's all over, James;" and moved slowly away. The moment he had spoken, the women present, who were very numerous, uttered a shrill cry, which, having been sustained for about half a minute, fell suddenly into a full, loud, continued and discordant but plaintive wailing, above which occasionally were heard the deep sounds of a man's voice, sometimes in broken sobs, sometimes in more distinct exclamations of sorrow. This was Charles's foster-brother, who moved about in the crowd, now clapping his hands, now rubbing them together in an agony of grief. The poor fellow had been Charles's playmate and companion when a boy, and afterwards his servant; had always been distinguished by his peculiar regard, and loved his young master, as much, at least, as he did his own life.

When Mrs. Mac Carthy became convinced that the blow was indeed struck, and that her beloved son was sent to his last account, even in the blossoms of his sin, she remained for some time gazing with fixedness upon his cold features; then, as if something had suddenly touched the string of her tenderest affections, tear after tear trickled down her cheeks, pale with anxiety and watching. Still she continued looking at her son, apparently unconscious that she was weeping, without once lifting her handkerchief to her eyes, until reminded of the sad duties which the custom of the country imposed upon her, by the crowd of females belonging to the better class of the peasantry, who now, crying audibly, nearly filled the apartment. She then withdrew, to give directions for the ceremony of waking, and for supplying the numerous visiters of all ranks with the refreshments usual on these melancholy occasions. Though her voice was scarcely heard, and though no one saw her but the servants and one or two old followers of the family, who assisted her in the necessary arrangements, every thing was conducted with the greatest regularity; and though she made no effort to check her sorrows, they never once suspended her attention, now more than ever required to preserve order in her household, which, in this season of calamity, but for her would have been all confusion.

The night was pretty far advanced; the boisterous lamentations which had prevailed during part of the day in and about the house had given place to a solemn and mournful stillness; and Mrs. Mac Carthy, whose heart, notwithstanding her long fatigue and watching, was yet too sore for sleep, was kneeling in fervent prayer in a chamber adjoining that of her son:—suddenly her devotions were disturbed by an unusual noise, proceeding from the persons who were watching round the body. First there was a low murmur—then all was silent, as if the movements of those in the chamber were checked by a sudden panic—and then a loud cry of terror burst from all within:—the door of the chamber was thrown open, and all who were not overturned in the press rushed wildly into the passage which led to the stairs, and into which Mrs. Mac Carthy's room opened.   Mrs. Mac Carthy made her way through the crowd into her son's chamber, where she found him sitting up in the bed, and looking vacantly around, like one risen from the grave. The glare thrown upon his sunk features and thin lathy frame gave an unearthly horror to his whole aspect.   Mrs. Mac Carthy was a woman of some firmness; but she was a woman, and not quite free from the superstitions of her country.   She dropped on her knees, and, clasping her hands, began to pray aloud.   The form before her moved only its lips, and barely uttered " Mother;"— but though the pale lips moved, as if there was a design to finish the sentence, the tongue refused its office.   Mrs. Mac Carthy sprung forward, and catching the arm of her son, exclaimed, " Speak! in the name of God and his saints, speak! are you alive?"

He turned to her slowly, and said, speaking still with apparent difficulty, " Yes, my mother, alive, and —— But sit down and collect yourself; I have that to tell, which will astonish you still more than what you have seen."   He leaned back upon his pillow, and while his mother remained kneeling by the bedside, holding one of his hands clasped in hers, and gazing on him with the look of one who distrusted all her senses, he proceeded :— " Do not interrupt me until I have done.   I wish to speak while the excitement of returning life is upon me, as I know I shall soon need much repose.   Of the commencement of my illness I have only a confused recollection;

but within the last twelve hours, I have been before the judgment-seat of God. Do not stare incredulously on me—'tis as true as have been my crimes, and, as I trust, shall be my repentance. I saw the awful Judge arrayed in all the terrors which invest him when mercy gives place to justice. The dreadful pomp of offended omnipotence, I saw,—I remember. It is fixed here; printed on my brain in characters indelible; but it passeth human language. What I *can* describe I *will*—I may speak it briefly. It is enough to say, I was weighed in the balance and found wanting. The irrevocable sentence was upon the point of being pronounced; the eye of my Almighty Judge, which had already glanced upon me, half spoke my doom; when I observed the guardian saint, to whom you so often directed my prayers when I was a child, looking at me with an expression of benevolence and compassion. I stretched forth my hands to him, and besought his intercession; I implored that one year, one month might be given to me on earth, to do penance and atonement for my transgressions. He threw himself at the feet of my Judge, and supplicated for mercy. Oh! never— not if I should pass through ten thousand successive states of being—never, for eternity, shall I forget the horrors of that moment, when my fate hung suspended—when an instant was to decide whether torments unutterable were to be my portion for endless ages! But Justice suspended its decree, and Mercy spoke in accents of firmness, but mildness, 'Return to that world in which thou hast lived but to outrage the laws of

Him who made that world and thee. Three years are given thee for repentance; when these are ended, thou shalt again stand here, to be saved or lost for ever.'—I heard no more; I saw no more, until I awoke to life, the moment before you entered."

Charles's strength continued just long enough to finish these last words, and on uttering them he closed his eyes, and lay quite exhausted. His mother, though, as was before said, somewhat disposed to give credit to supernatural visitations, yet hesitated whether or not she should believe that, although awakened from a swoon, which might have been the crisis of his disease, he was still under the influence of delirium. Repose, however, was at all events necessary, and she took immediate measures that he should enjoy it undisturbed. After some hours' sleep, he awoke refreshed, and thenceforward gradually but steadily recovered.

Still he persisted in his account of the vision, as he had at first related it; and his persuasion of its reality had an obvious and decided influence on his habits and conduct. He did not altogether abandon the society of his former associates, for his temper was not soured by his reformation; but he never joined in their excesses, and often endeavoured to reclaim them. How his pious exertions succeeded, I have never learnt; but of himself it is recorded, that he was religious without ostentation, and temperate without austerity; giving a practical proof that vice may be exchanged for virtue, without a loss of respectability, popularity, or happiness.

Time rolled on, and long before the three years were ended, the story of his vision was forgotten, or, when spoken of, was usually mentioned as an instance proving the folly of believing in such things. Charles's health, from the temperance and regularity of his habits, became more robust than ever. His friends, indeed, had often occasion to rally him upon a seriousness and abstractedness of demeanour, which grew upon him as he approached the completion of his seven-and-twentieth year, but for the most part his manner exhibited the same animation and cheerfulness for which he had always been remarkable. In company, he evaded every endeavour to draw from him a distinct opinion on the subject of the supposed prediction; but among his own family it was well known that he still firmly believed it. However, when the day had nearly arrived on which the prophecy was, if at all, to be fulfilled, his whole appearance gave such promise of a long and healthy life, that he was persuaded by his friends to ask a large party to an entertainment at Spring House, to celebrate his birth-day. But the occasion of this party, and the circumstances which attended it, will be best learned from a perusal of the following letters, which have been carefully preserved by some relations of his family. The first is from Mrs. Mac Carthy to a lady, a very near connection and valued friend of hers, who lived in the county of Cork, at about fifty miles' distance from Spring House.

" *To Mrs. Barry, Castle Barry.*

" Spring House, Tuesday morning,
October 15th, 1752.

" MY DEAREST MARY,

" I am afraid I am going to put your affection for your old friend and kinswoman to a severe trial. A two days' journey at this season, over bad roads and through a troubled country, it will indeed require friendship such as yours to persuade a sober woman to encounter. But the truth is, I have, or fancy I have, more than usual cause for wishing you near me. You know my son's story. I can't tell how it is, but as next Sunday approaches, when the prediction of his dream or his vision will be proved false or true, I feel a sickening of the heart, which I cannot suppress, but which your presence, my dear Mary, will soften, as it has done so many of my sorrows. My nephew, James Ryan, is to be married to Jane Osborne (who, you know, is my son's ward), and the bridal entertainment will take place here on Sunday next, though Charles pleaded hard to have it postponed a day or two longer. Would to God — but no more of this till we meet. Do prevail upon yourself to leave your good man for *one* week, if his farming concerns will not admit of his accompanying you ; and come to us, with the girls, as soon before Sunday as you can.

" Ever my dear Mary's attached cousin and friend,

" ANN MAC CARTHY."

Although this letter reached Castle Barry early on Wednesday, the messenger having travelled on foot, over bog and moor, by paths impassable to horse or carriage, Mrs. Barry, who at once determined on going, had so many arrangements to make for the regulation of her domestic affairs (which, in Ireland, among the middle orders of the gentry, fall soon into confusion when the mistress of the family is away), that she and her two younger daughters were unable to leave home until late on the morning of Friday. The eldest daughter remained, to keep her father company, and superintend the concerns of the household. As the travellers were to journey in an open one-horse vehicle, called a jaunting-car (still used in Ireland), and as the roads, bad at all times, were rendered still worse by the heavy rains, it was their design to make two easy stages; to stop about mid-way the first night, and reach Spring House early on Saturday evening. This arrangement was now altered, as they found that, from the lateness of their departure, they could proceed, at the utmost, no farther than twenty miles on the first day; and they therefore purposed sleeping at the house of a Mr. Bourke, a friend of theirs, who lived at somewhat less than that distance from Castle Barry. They reached Mr. Bourke's in safety, after rather a disagreeable drive. What befel them on their journey the next day to Spring House, and after their arrival there, is fully related in a letter from the second Miss Barry to her eldest sister.

" Spring House, Sunday evening,
20th October, 1752.

" DEAR ELLEN,

" As my mother's letter, which encloses this, will announce to you briefly the sad intelligence which I shall here relate more fully, I think it better to go regularly through the recital of the extraordinary events of the last two days.

" The Bourkes kept us up so late on Friday night, that yesterday was pretty far advanced before we could begin our journey, and the day closed when we were nearly fifteen miles distant from this place. The roads were excessively deep, from the heavy rains of the last week, and we proceeded so slowly, that at last my mother resolved on passing the night at the house of Mr. Bourke's brother (who lives about a quarter of a mile off the road), and coming here to breakfast in the morning. The day had been windy and showery, and the sky looked fitful, gloomy, and uncertain. The moon was full, and at times shone clear and bright; at others, it was wholly concealed behind the thick, black, and rugged masses of clouds, that rolled rapidly along, and were every moment becoming larger, and collecting together, as if gathering strength for a coming storm. The wind, which blew in our faces, whistled bleakly along the low hedges of the narrow road, on which we proceeded with difficulty from the number of deep sloughs, and which afforded not the least shelter, no plantation being within some miles of us. My mother, therefore, asked Leary, who drove the jaunting-car, how far

we were from Mr. Bourke's. ' 'T is about ten
spades from this to the cross, and we have then
only to turn to the left into the avenue, ma'am.'
' Very well, Leary : turn up to Mr. Bourke's as
soon as you reach the cross roads.'   My mother
had scarcely spoken these words, when a shriek,
that made us thrill as if our very hearts were
pierced by it, burst from the hedge to the right of
our way.   If it resembled any thing earthly, it
seemed the cry of a female, struck by a sudden
and mortal blow, and giving out her life in one
long deep pang of expiring agony. ' Heaven
defend us!' exclaimed my mother. ' Go you
over the hedge, Leary, and save that woman, if
she is not yet dead, while we run back to the hut
we just passed, and alarm the village near it.'
' Woman!' said Leary, beating the horse violently,
while his voice trembled—' that 's no woman : the
sooner we get on, ma'am, the better;' and he
continued his efforts to quicken the horse's pace.
We saw nothing.   The moon was hid.   It was
quite dark, and we had been for some time expecting a heavy fall of rain.   But just as Leary
had spoken, and had succeeded in making the
horse trot briskly forward, we distinctly heard a
loud clapping of hands, followed by a succession
of screams, that seemed to denote the last excess
of despair and anguish, and to issue from a person
running forward inside the hedge, to keep pace
with our progress.   Still we saw nothing; until,
when we were within about ten yards of the place
where an avenue branched off to Mr. Bourke's to
the left, and the road turned to Spring House on
the right, the moon started suddenly from behind

a cloud, and enabled us to see, as plainly as I now see this paper, the figure of a tall thin woman, with uncovered head, and long hair that floated round her shoulders, attired in something which seemed either a loose white cloak, or a sheet thrown hastily about her. She stood on the corner hedge, where the road on which we were met that which leads to Spring House, with her face towards us, her left hand pointing to this place, and her right arm waving rapidly and violently, as if to draw us on in that direction. The horse had stopped, apparently frightened at the sudden presence of the figure, which stood in the manner I have described, still uttering the same piercing cries, for about half a minute. It then leaped upon the road, disappeared from our view for one instant, and the next was seen standing upon a high wall a little way up the avenue, on which we purposed going, still pointing towards the road to Spring House, but in an attitude of defiance and command, as if prepared to oppose our passage up the avenue. The figure was now quite silent, and its garments, which had before flown loosely in the wind, were closely wrapped around it. ' Go on, Leary, to Spring House, in God's name,' said my mother ; ' whatever world it belongs to, we will provoke it no longer.' ' 'T is the Banshee, ma'am,' said Leary ; ' and I would not, for what my life is worth, go any where this blessed night but to Spring House. But I 'm afraid there 's something bad going forward, or *she* would not send us there.' So saying, he drove forward ; and as we turned on the road to the right, the moon suddenly withdrew its light, and we saw the apparition no more; but we heard plainly a prolonged clapping of hands, gradually dying away, as if it issued from a person rapidly retreating. We proceeded as quickly as the badness of the roads and the fatigue of the poor animal that drew us would allow, and arrived here about eleven o'clock last night. The scene which awaited us you have learned from my mother's letter. To explain it fully, I must recount to you some of the transactions which took place here during the last week.

" You are aware that Jane Osborne was to have been married this day to James Ryan, and that they and their friends have been here for the last week. On Tuesday last, the very day on the morning of which cousin Mac Carthy despatched the letter inviting us here, the whole of the company were walking about the grounds a little before dinner. It seems that an unfortunate creature, who had been seduced by James Ryan, was seen prowling in the neighbourhood in a moody melancholy state for some days previous. He had separated from her for several months, and, they say, had provided for her rather handsomely; but she had been seduced by the promise of his marrying her; and the shame of her unhappy condition, uniting with disappointment and jealousy, had disordered her intellects. During the whole forenoon of this Tuesday, she had been walking in the plantations near Spring House, with her cloak folded tight round her, the hood nearly covering her face; and she had avoided conversing with or even meeting any of the family.

" Charles Mac Carthy, at the time I mentioned, was walking between James Ryan and another, at a little distance from the rest, on a gravel path, skirting a shrubbery.   The whole party were thrown into the utmost consternation by the report of a pistol, fired from a thickly planted part of the shrubbery which Charles and his companions had just passed.   He fell instantly, and it was found that he had been wounded in the leg.   One of the party was a medical man ; his assistance was immediately given, and, on examining, he declared that the injury was very slight, that no bone was broken, that it was merely a flesh wound, and that it would certainly be well in a few days.   ' We shall know more by Sunday,' said Charles, as he was carried to his chamber.   His wound was immediately dressed, and so slight was the inconvenience which it gave, that several of his friends spent a portion of the evening in his apartment.

" On enquiry, it was found that the unlucky shot was fired by the poor girl I just mentioned. It was also manifest that she had aimed, not at Charles, but at the destroyer of her innocence and happiness, who was walking beside him.   After a fruitless search for her through the grounds, she walked into the house of her own accord, laughing, and dancing and singing wildly, and every moment exclaiming that she had at last killed Mr. Ryan.   When she heard that it was Charles, and not Mr. Ryan, who was shot, she fell into a violent fit, out of which, after working convulsively for some time, she sprung to the door, escaped from the crowd that pursued her, and could never

be taken until last night, when she was brought
here, perfectly frantic, a little before our arrival.

" Charles's wound was thought of such little
consequence, that the preparations went forward,
as usual, for the wedding entertainment on Sunday.   But on Friday night he grew restless and
feverish, and on Saturday (yesterday) morning
felt so ill, that it was deemed necessary to obtain
additional medical advice.   Two physicians and a
surgeon met in consultation about twelve o'clock
in the day, and the dreadful intelligence was an-
nounced, that unless a change, hardly hoped for,
took place before night, death must happen within
twenty-four hours after.   The wound, it seems,
had been too tightly bandaged, and otherwise in-
judiciously treated.   The physicians were right in
their anticipations.   No favourable symptom appeared, and long before we reached Spring House
every ray of hope had vanished.   The scene we
witnessed on our arrival would have wrung the
heart of a demon.   We heard briefly at the gate
that Mr. Charles was upon his death-bed.   When
we reached the house, the information was con-
firmed by the servant who opened the door.   But
just as we entered, we were horrified by the most
appalling screams issuing from the staircase.   My
mother thought she heard the voice of poor Mrs.
Mac Carthy, and sprung forward.   We followed,
and on ascending a few steps of the stairs, we
found a young woman, in a state of frantic passion,
struggling furiously with two men-servants, whose
united strength was hardly sufficient to prevent
her rushing up stairs over the body of Mrs. Mac
Carthy, who was lying in strong hysterics upon

the steps. This, I afterwards discovered, was the unhappy girl I before described, who was attempting to gain access to Charles's room, to 'get his forgiveness,' as she said, 'before he went away to accuse her for having killed him.' This wild idea was mingled with another, which seemed to dispute with the former possession of her mind. In one sentence she called on Charles to forgive her, in the next she would denounce James Ryan as the murderer both of Charles and her. At length she was torn away; and the last words I heard her scream were, ' James Ryan, 'twas you killed him, and not I —'t was you killed him, and not I.'

" Mrs. Mac Carthy, on recovering, fell into the arms of my mother, whose presence seemed a great relief to her. She wept — the first tears, I was told, that she had shed since the fatal accident. She conducted us to Charles's room, who, she said, had desired to see us the moment of our arrival, as he found his end approaching, and wished to devote the last hours of his existence to uninterrupted prayer and meditation. We found him perfectly calm, resigned, and even cheerful. He spoke of the awful event which was at hand with courage and confidence, and treated it as a doom for which he had been preparing ever since his former remarkable illness, and which he never once doubted was truly foretold to him. He bade us farewell with the air of one who was about to travel a short and easy journey ; and we left him with impressions which, notwithstanding all their anguish, will, I trust, never entirely forsake us.

" Poor Mrs. Mac Carthy —— but I am just called away. There seems a slight stir in the family; perhaps —— "

The above letter was never finished. The enclosure to which it more than once alludes told the sequel briefly, and it is all that I have farther learned of this branch of the Mac Carthy family. Before the sun had gone down upon Charles's seven-and-twentieth birthday, his soul had gone to render its last account to its Creator.

"Banshee, correctly written beanṡíðe, plural mná-ríðe, she fairies or women fairies, credulously supposed, by the common people, to be so affected to certain families, that they are heard to sing mournful lamentations about their houses at night, whenever any of the family labours under a sickness which is to end in death. But no families which are not of an ancient and noble stock are believed to be honoured with this fairy privilege."—O'Brien's *Irish Dictionary.*

For accounts of the appearance of the Irish Banshee, see "Personal Sketches, &c. by Sir Jonah Barrington;" Miss Lefanu's Memoirs of her Grandmother, Mrs. Frances Sheridan, (1824.) p. 32.; "The Memoirs of Lady Fanshaw," (quoted by Sir Walter Scott in a note on "the Lady of the Lake,") &c.

Sir Walter Scott terms the belief in the appearance of the Banshee "one of the most beautiful" of the leading superstitions of Europe. In his "Letters on Demonology," he says that "several families of the Highlands of Scotland anciently laid claim to the distinction of an attendant spirit, who performed the office of the Irish Banshee," and particularly refers to the supernatural cries and lamentations which foreboded the death of the gallant Mac Lean of Lochbuy.

"The Welsh Gwrâch y Rhibyn (or the hag of the Dribble) bears some resemblance to the Irish Banshee, being regarded as an omen of death. She is said to come after dusk and flap her leathern wings against the window where she warns of death, and in a broken, howling tone, to call on the one who is to quit mortality by his or her name several times, as thus, *A-a-a-n-ni-i-i-i! Anni.*"—*MS. Communication from* Dr. Owen Pughe. For some further particulars, see, in "A Relation of Apparitions, &c. by the Rev. Edmund Jones," his account of the *Kyhirraeth*, "a doleful foreboding noise before death;" and Howell's "Cambrian Superstitions," (Tipton, 1831.) p. 31.

The reader will probably remember the White Lady of the House of Brandenburgh, and the fairy Melusine, who usually prognosticated the recurrence of mortality in some noble family of Poitou. Prince, in his "Worthies of Devon," records the appearance of a white bird, performing the same office for the worshipful lineage of Oxenham.

"In the Tyrol, too, they believe in a spirit which looks in at the window of the house in which a person is to die (*Deutsche Sagen*, No. 266.); the white woman with a veil over her head (267.) answers to the Banshee; but the tradition of the *Klage-weib* (mourning woman), in the *Lüneburger Heath* (*Spiels Archiv.* ii. 297.), resembles it still more closely. On stormy nights, when the moon shines faintly through the fleeting clouds, she stalks, of gigantic stature, with death-like aspect, and black hollow eyes, wrapt in grave-clothes which float in the wind, and stretches her immense arm over the solitary hut, uttering lamentable cries in the tempestuous darkness. Beneath the roof over which the *Klage-weib* has leaned, one of the inmates must die in the course of the month."—The Brothers Grimm, *and MS. Communication from Dr.* William Grimm.

FAIRY LEGENDS.

THE PHOOKA.

" Ne let house-fires, nor lightnings helpless harms,
Ne let the *Pouke*, nor other evil spright,
Ne let mischievous witches with their charms,
Ne let hobgoblins, names whose sense we see not,
Fray us with things that be not.."

SPENSER.

LEGENDS OF THE PHOOKA.

THE SPIRIT HORSE.

XIV.

THE history of Morty Sullivan ought to be a warning to all young men to stay at home, and to live decently and soberly if they can, and not to go roving about the world. Morty, when he had just turned of fourteen, ran away from his father and mother, who were a mighty respectable old couple, and many and many a tear they shed on his account. It is said they both died heart-broken for his loss: all they ever learned about him was that he went on board of a ship bound to America.

Thirty years after the old couple had been laid peacefully in their graves, there came a stranger to Beerhaven enquiring after them—it was their son Morty; and, to speak the truth of him, his heart did seem full of sorrow when he heard that his parents were dead and gone;—but what else could he expect to hear? Repentance generally comes when it is too late.

Morty Sullivan, however, as an atonement for his sins, was recommended to perform a pilgrimage to the blessed chapel of Saint Gobnate, which is in a wild place called Ballyvourney.

This he readily undertook; and willing to lose no time, commenced his journey the same afternoon. He had not proceeded many miles before the evening came on: there was no moon, and the starlight was obscured by a thick fog, which ascended from the valleys. His way was through a mountainous country, with many cross-paths and by-ways, so that it was difficult for a stranger like Morty to travel without a guide. He was anxious to reach his destination, and exerted himself to do so; but the fog grew thicker and thicker, and at last he became doubtful if the track he was in led to the blessed chapel of Saint Gobnate. But seeing a light which he imagined not to be far off, he went towards it, and when he thought himself close to it the light suddenly seemed at a great distance, twinkling dimly through the fog. Though Morty felt some surprise at this, he was not disheartened, for he thought that it was a light sent by the holy Saint Gobnate to guide his feet through the mountains to her chapel.

And thus did he travel for many a mile, continually, as he believed, approaching the light, which would suddenly start off to a great distance. At length he came so close as to perceive that the light came from a fire; seated beside which he plainly saw an old woman;—then, indeed, his faith was a little shaken, and much did he wonder that both the fire and the old woman should travel before him, so many weary miles, and over such uneven roads.

" In the holy names of the pious Gobnate, and of her preceptor Saint Abban," said Morty, " how can that burning fire move on so fast before me, and who can that old woman be sitting beside the moving fire?"

These words had no sooner passed Morty's lips than he found himself, without taking another step, close to this wonderful fire, beside which the old woman was sitting munching her supper. With every wag of the old woman's jaw her eyes would roll fiercely upon Morty, as if she was angry at being disturbed; and he saw with more astonishment than ever that her eyes were neither black, nor blue, nor gray, nor hazel, like the human eye, but of a wild red colour, like the eye of a ferret. If before he wondered at the fire, much greater was his wonder at the old woman's appearance; and stout-hearted as he was, he could not but look upon her with fear—judging, and judging rightly, that it was for no good purpose her supping in so unfrequented a place, and at so late an hour, for it was near midnight. She said not one word, but munched and munched away, while Morty looked at her in silence.—" What's your name?" at last demanded the old hag, a sulphureous puff coming out of her mouth, her nostrils distending, and her eyes growing redder than ever, when she had finished her question.

Plucking up all his courage, " Morty Sullivan," replied he, " at your service;" meaning the latter words only in civility.

" *Ubbubbo!*" said the old woman, " we'll soon see that;" and the red fire of her eyes turned into a pale green colour. Bold and fearless as

Morty was, yet much did he tremble at hearing this dreadful exclamation: he would have fallen down on his knees and prayed to Saint Gobnate, or any other saint, for he was not particular; but he was so petrified with horror, that he could not move in the slightest way, much less go down on his knees.

" Take hold of my hand, Morty," said the old woman: " I'll give you a horse to ride that will soon carry you to your journey's end." So saying, she led the way, the fire going before them;—it is beyond mortal knowledge to say how, but on it went, shooting out bright tongues of flame, and flickering fiercely.

Presently they came to a natural cavern in the side of the mountain, and the old hag called aloud in a most discordant voice for her horse! In a moment a jet-black steed started from its gloomy stable, the rocky floor whereof rung with a sepulchral echo to the clanging hoofs.

" Mount, Morty, mount!" cried she, seizing him with supernatural strength, and forcing him upon the back of the horse. Morty finding human power of no avail, muttered, " O that I had spurs!" and tried to grasp the horse's mane; but he caught at a shadow; it nevertheless bore him up and bounded forward with him, now springing down a fearful precipice, now clearing the rugged bed of a torrent, and rushing like the dark midnight storm through the mountains.

The following morning Morty Sullivan was discovered by some pilgrims (who came that way after taking their rounds at Gougane Barra) lying on the flat of his back, under a steep cliff, down

which he had been flung by the Phooka. Morty
was severely bruised by the fall, and he is said to
have sworn on the spot, by the hand of O'Sullivan
(and that is no small oath),[1] never again to take
a full quart bottle of whisky with him on a pilgrimage.

[1] " Nulla manus,
Tam liberalis
Atque generalis
Atque universalis
Quam Sullivanis."

DANIEL O'ROURKE.

XV.

PEOPLE may have heard of the renowned adventures of Daniel O'Rourke, but how few are there who know that the cause of all his perils, above and below, was neither more nor less than his having slept under the walls of the Phooka's tower. I knew the man well: he lived at the bottom of Hungry Hill, just at the right hand side of the road as you go towards Bantry. An old man was he at the time that he told me the story, with gray hair, and a red nose; and it was on the 25th of June, 1813, that I heard it from his own lips, as he sat smoking his pipe under the old poplar tree, on as fine an evening as ever shone from the sky. I was going to visit the caves in Dursey Island, having spent the morning at Glengariff.

"I am often *axed* to tell it, sir," said he, "so that this is not the first time. The master's son, you see, had come from beyond foreign parts in France and Spain, as young gentlemen used to go, before Buonaparte or any such was heard of; and sure enough there was a dinner given to all the people on the ground, gentle and simple, high and low, rich and poor. The *ould* gentlemen were the gentlemen, after all, saving your honour's presence. They'd swear at a body a little, to be sure, and, may be, give one a cut of a whip now and then, but we were no losers by it in the end;

— and they were so easy and civil, and kept such rattling houses, and thousands of welcomes;— and there was no grinding for rent, and few agents; and there was hardly a tenant on the estate that did not taste of his landlord's bounty often and often in the year;—but now it's another thing : no matter for that, sir, for I'd better be telling you my story.

" Well, we had every thing of the best, and plenty of it ; and we ate, and we drank, and we danced, and the young master by the same token danced with Peggy Barry, from the Bohereen — a lovely young couple they were, though they are both low enough now. To make a long story short, I got, as a body may say, the same thing as tipsy almost, for I can't remember ever at all, no ways, how it was I left the place : only I did leave it, that's certain. Well, I thought, for all that, in myself, I'd just step to Molly Cronohan's, the fairy woman, to speak a word about the bracket heifer what was bewitched ; and so as I was crossing the stepping-stones of the ford of Ballyasheenough, and was looking up at the stars and blessing myself — for why ? it was Lady-day — I missed my foot, and souse I fell into the water. ' Death alive !' thought I, ' I'll be drowned now !' However, I began swimming, swimming, swimming away for the dear life, till at last I got ashore, somehow or other, but never the one of me can tell how, upon a *dissolute* island.

" I wandered and wandered about there, with-out knowing where I wandered, until at last I got into a big bog. The moon was shining as bright as day, or your fair lady's eyes, sir (with your pardon for mentioning her), and I looked east and west, and north and south, and every way, and nothing did I see but bog, bog, bog;— I could never find out how I got into it; and my heart grew cold with fear, for sure and certain I was that it would be my *berrin* place. So I sat down upon a stone which, as good luck would have it, was close by me, and I began to scratch my head and sing the *Ullagone* — when all of a sudden the moon grew black, and I looked up, and saw something for all the world as if it was moving down between me and it, and I could not tell what it was. Down it came with a pounce, and looked at me full in the face; and what was it but an eagle? as fine a one as ever flew from the kingdom of Kerry. So he looked at me in the face, and says he to me, 'Daniel O'Rourke,' says he, 'how do you do?' 'Very well, I thank you, sir,' says I: 'I hope you're well;' wondering out of my senses all the time how an eagle came to speak like a Christian. 'What brings you here, Dan?' says he. 'Nothing at all, sir,' says I: 'only I wish I was safe home again.' 'Is it out of the island you want to go, Dan?' says he. ''Tis, sir,' says I: so I up and told him how I had taken a drop too much, and fell into the water; how I swam to the island; and how I got into the bog and did not know my way out of it. 'Dan,' says he, after a minute's thought, 'though it is very improper for you to get drunk on Lady-day, yet as you are a decent sober man, who 'tends mass well, and never flings stones at me nor mine, nor cries out after us in the fields —

my life for yours,' says he; ' so get up on my back, and grip me well for fear you'd fall off, and I'll fly you out of the bog.'   ' I am afraid,' says I, ' your honour's making game of me; for who ever heard of riding a horseback on an eagle before?'   ' 'Pon the honour of a gentleman,' says he, putting his right foot on his breast, ' I am quite in earnest; and so now either take my offer or starve in the bog — besides, I see that your weight is sinking the stone.'

" It was true enough as he said, for I found the stone every minute going from under me. I had no choice; so thinks I to myself, faint heart never won fair lady, and this is fair per-suadance : — ' I thank your honour,' says I, ' for the loan of your civility; and I'll take your kind offer.'   I therefore mounted upon the back of the eagle, and held him tight enough by the throat, and up he flew in the air like a lark. Little I knew the trick he was going to serve me. Up — up — up — God knows how far up he flew. ' Why, then,' said I to him — thinking he did not know the right road home — very civilly, because why ? — I was in his power entirely ; — ' sir,' says I, ' please your honour's glory, and with humble submission to your better judgment, if you'd fly down a bit, you're now just over my cabin, and I could be put down there, and many thanks to your worship.'

" ' *Arrah*, Dan,' said he, ' do you think me a fool ?   Look down in the next field, and don't you see two men and a gun ?   By my word it would be no joke to be shot this way, to oblige a drunken blackguard that I picked up off of a *could*

stone in a bog.'   'Bother you,' said I to myself,
but I did not speak out, for where was the use?
Well, sir, up he kept, flying, flying, and I asking
him every minute to fly down, and all to no use.
'Where in the world are you going, sir?' says I
to him.   'Hold your tongue, Dan,' says he:
'mind your own business, and don't be inter-
fering with the business of other people.'   'Faith,
this is my business, I think,' says I.   'Be quiet,
Dan,' says he: so I said no more.

"At last where should we come to, but to the
moon itself.   Now you can't see it from this, but
there is, or there was in my time a reaping-hook
sticking out of the side of the moon, this way,
(drawing the figure thus 🌙 on the ground
with the end of his stick).

"'Dan,' said the eagle, 'I'm tired with this
long fly; I had no notion 't was so far.'   'And
my lord, sir,' said I, 'who in the world *axed* you
to fly so far — was it I? did not I beg, and pray,
and beseech you to stop half an hour ago?'
'There's no use talking, Dan,' said he; 'I'm
tired bad enough, so you must get off, and sit
down on the moon until I rest myself.'   'Is it
sit down on the moon?' said I; 'is it upon that
little round thing, then? why, then, sure I'd fall
off in a minute, and be *kilt* and split, and smashed
all to bits: you are a vile deceiver, — so you are.'
'Not at all, Dan,' said he: 'you can catch fast
hold of the reaping-hook that's sticking out of the
side of the moon, and 'twill keep you up.'   'I
won't, then,' said I.   'May be not,' said he, quite
quiet.   'If you don't, my man, I shall just give
you a shake, and one slap of my wing, and send

you down to the ground, where every bone in your body will be smashed as small as a drop of dew on a cabbage-leaf in the morning.' ' Why, then, I'm in a fine way,' said I to myself, ' ever to have come along with the likes of you;' and so giving him a hearty curse in Irish, for fear he'd know what I said, I got off his back with a heavy heart, took a hold of the reaping-hook, and sat down upon the moon; and a mighty cold seat it was, I can tell you that.

" When he had me there fairly landed, he turned about on me, and said, ' Good morning to you, Daniel O'Rourke,' said he : ' I think I've nicked you fairly now. You robbed my nest last year,' ('twas true enough for him, but how he found it out is hard to say,) ' and in return you are freely welcome to cool your heels dangling upon the moon like a cockthrow.'

" ' Is that all, and is this the way you leave me, you brute, you?' says I. ' You ugly unnatural *baste*, and is this the way you serve me at last ? Bad luck to yourself, with your hook'd nose, and to all your breed, you blackguard.' 'Twas all to no manner of use : he spread out his great big wings, burst out a laughing, and flew away like lightning. I bawled after him to stop; but I might have called and bawled for ever, without his minding me. Away he went, and I never saw him from that day to this — sorrow fly away with him! You may be sure I was in a disconsolate condition, and kept roaring out for the bare grief, when all at once a door opened right in the middle of the moon, creaking on its hinges as if it had not been opened for a month before. I suppose they never thought of greasing 'em, and out there walks — who do you think but the man in the moon himself? I knew him by his bush.

"'Good morrow to you, Daniel O'Rourke,' said he: 'How do you do?' 'Very well, thank your honour,' said I. 'I hope your honour's well.' 'What brought you here, Dan?' said he. So I told him how I was a little overtaken in liquor at the master's, and how I was cast on a *dissolute* island, and how I lost my way in the bog, and how the thief of an eagle promised to fly me out of it, and how instead of that he had fled me up to the moon.

"'Dan,' said the man in the moon, taking a pinch of snuff when I was done, 'you must not stay here.' 'Indeed, sir,' says I, ''tis much against my will I'm here at all; but how am I to go back?' 'That's your business,' said he, 'Dan: mine is to tell you that here you must not stay, so be off in less than no time.' 'I'm doing no harm,' says I, 'only holding on hard by the reaping-hook, lest I fall off.' 'That's what you must not do, Dan,' says he. 'Pray, sir,' says I, 'may I ask how many you are in family, that you would not give a poor traveller lodging: I'm sure 'tis not so often you're troubled with strangers coming to see you, for 'tis a long way.' 'I'm by myself, Dan,' says he; 'but you'd better let go the reaping-hook.' 'Faith, and with your leave,' says I, 'I'll not let go the grip, and the more you bids me, the more I won't let go;— so I will.' 'You had better, Dan,' says he again. 'Why, then, my little fellow,' says I, taking the whole weight of him with my eye from head to foot, ' there are two words to that bargain ; and I 'll not budge, but you may if you like.' ' We 'll see how that is to be,' says he ; and back he went, giving the door such a great bang after him (for it was plain he was huffed), that I thought the moon and all would fall down with it.

" Well, I was preparing myself to try strength with him, when back again he comes, with the kitchen cleaver in his hand, and without saying a word, he gives two bangs to the handle of the reaping-hook that was keeping me up, and *whap !* it came in two. ' Good morning to you, Dan,' says the spiteful little old blackguard, when he saw me cleanly falling down with a bit of the handle in my hand : ' I thank you for your visit, and fair weather after you, Daniel.' I had not time to make any answer to him, for I was tumbling over and over, and rolling and rolling at the rate of a fox-hunt. ' God help me,' says I, ' but this is a pretty pickle for a decent man to be seen in at this time of night : I am now sold fairly.' The word was not out of my mouth, when whiz ! what should fly by close to my ear but a flock of wild geese ; all the way from my own bog of Ballyasheenough, else how should they know *me ?* the *ould* gander, who was their general, turning about his head, cried out to me, ' Is that you, Dan ?' ' The same,' said I, not a bit daunted now at what he said, for I was by this time used to all kinds of *bedevilment*, and, besides, I knew him of *ould*. ' Good morrow to you,' says he, ' Daniel O'Rourke : how are you in health this morning?' 'Very well, sir,' says I, 'I thank you kindly,' drawing my breath, for I was mightily in want of some. 'I hope your honour's the same.' 'I think 'tis falling you are, Daniel,' says he. 'You may say that, sir,' says I. 'And where are you going all the way so fast?' said the gander. So I told him how I had taken the drop, and how I came on the island, and how I lost my way in the bog, and how the thief of an eagle flew me up to the moon, and how the man in the moon turned me out. 'Dan,' said he, 'I'll save you: put out your hand and catch me by the leg, and I'll fly you home.' 'Sweet is your hand in a pitcher of honey, my jewel,' says I, though all the time I thought in myself that I don't much trust you; but there was no help, so I caught the gander by the leg, and away I and the other geese flew after him as fast as hops.

"We flew, and we flew, and we flew, until we came right over the wide ocean. I knew it well, for I saw Cape Clear to my right hand, sticking up out of the water. 'Ah! my lord,' said I to the goose, for I thought it best to keep a civil tongue in my head any way, 'fly to land if you please.' 'It is impossible, you see, Dan,' said he, 'for a while, because you see we are going to Arabia.' 'To Arabia!' said I; 'that's surely some place in foreign parts, far away. Oh! Mr. Goose: why then, to be sure, I'm a man to be pitied among you.' 'Whist, whist, you fool,' said he, 'hold your tongue; I tell you Arabia is a very decent sort of place, as like West Carbery as one egg is like another, only there is a little more sand there.'

" Just as we were talking, a ship hove in sight, scudding so beautiful before the wind: ' Ah! then, sir,' said I, ' will you drop me on the ship, if you please?' ' We are not fair over it,' said he. ' We are,' said I. ' We are not,' said he : ' If I dropped you now, you would go splash into the sea.' ' I would not,' says I : ' I know better than that, for it is just clean under us, so let me drop now at once.'

" ' If you must, you must,' said he. ' There, take your own way ;' and he opened his claw, and faith he was right — sure enough I came down plump into the very bottom of the salt sea! Down to the very bottom I went, and I gave myself up then for ever, when a whale walked up to me, scratching himself after his night's sleep, and looked me full in the face, and never the word did he say, but lifting up his tail, he splashed me all over again with the cold salt water, till there wasn't a dry stitch upon my whole carcass ; and I heard somebody saying — 'twas a voice I knew too — ' Get up, you drunken brute, off of that ;' and with that I woke up, and there was Judy with a tub full of water, which she was splashing all over me ; — for, rest her soul ! though she was a good wife, she never could bear to see me in drink, and had a bitter hand of her own.

" ' Get up,' said she again : ' and of all places in the parish, would no place *sarve* your turn to lie down upon but under the *ould* walls of Carrig-aphooka ? an uneasy resting I am sure you had of it.' And sure enough I had ; for I was fairly bothered out of my senses with eagles, and men of the moon, and flying ganders, and whales, driving me through bogs, and up to the moon, and down to the bottom of the green ocean. If I was in drink ten times over, long would it be before I'd lie down in the same spot again, I know that."

THE CROOKENED BACK.

XVI.

PEGGY BARRETT was once tall, well-shaped, and comely. She was in her youth remarkable for two qualities, not often found together, of being the most thrifty housewife, and the best dancer in her native village of Ballyhooley. But she is now upwards of sixty years old; and during the last ten years of her life, she has never been able to stand upright. Her back is bent nearly to a level; yet she has the freest use of all her limbs that can be enjoyed in such a posture; her health is good, and her mind vigorous; and, in the family of her eldest son, with whom she has lived since the death of her husband, she performs all the domestic services which her age, and the infirmity just mentioned, allow. She washes the potatoes, makes the fire, sweeps the house (labours in which she good-humouredly says " she finds her crooked back mighty convenient"), plays with the children, and tells stories to the family and their neighbouring friends, who often collect round her son's fireside to hear them during the long winter evenings. Her powers of conversation are highly extolled, both for humour and in narration; and anecdotes of droll or awkward incidents, connected with the posture in which she has been so long fixed, as well as the history of the occurrence to which she owes that misfortune, are favourite topics of her discourse.

Among other matters she is fond of relating how, on a certain day, at the close of a bad harvest, when several tenants of the estate on which she lived concerted in a field a petition for an abatement of rent, they placed the paper on which they wrote upon her back, which was found no very inconvenient substitute for a table.

Peggy, like all experienced story-tellers, suited her tales, both in length and subject, to the audience and the occasion. She knew that, in broad daylight, when the sun shines brightly, and the trees are budding, and the birds singing around us, when men and women, like ourselves, are moving and speaking, employed variously in business or amusement; she knew, in short (though certainly without knowing or much caring wherefore), that when we are engaged about the realities of life and nature, we want that spirit of credulity, without which tales of the deepest interest will lose their power. At such times Peggy was brief, very particular as to facts, and never dealt in the marvellous. But round the blazing hearth of a Christmas evening, when infidelity is banished from all companies, at least in low and simple life, as a quality, to say the least of it, out of season; when the winds of " dark December" whistled bleakly round the walls, and almost through the doors of the little mansion, reminding its inmates, that as the world is vexed by elements superior to human power, so it may be visited by beings of a superior nature : — at such times would Peggy Barrett give full scope to her memory, or her imagination, or both; and upon one of these occasions, she gave the following circumstantial account of the " crookening of her back."

" It was of all days in the year, the day before May-day, that I went out to the garden to weed the potatoes. I would not have gone out that day, but I was dull in myself, and sorrowful, and wanted to be alone ; all the boys and girls were laughing and joking in the house, making goaling-balls and dressing out ribands for the mummers next day. I couldn't bear it 'Twas only at the Easter that was then past (and that's ten years last Easter—I won't forget the time), that I buried my poor man ; and I thought how gay and joyful I was, many a long year before that, at the May-eve before our wedding, when with Robin by my side, I sat cutting and sewing the ribands for the goaling-ball I was to give the boys on the next day, proud to be preferred above all the other girls of the banks of the Blackwater, by the hand-somest boy and the best hurler in the village ; so I left the house and went to the garden. I staid there all the day, and didn't come home to dinner. I don't know how it was, but some-how I continued on, weeding, and thinking sor-rowfully enough, and singing over some of the old songs that I sung many and many a time in the days that are gone, and for them that never will come back to me to hear them. The truth is, I hated to go and sit silent and mournful among the people in the house, that were merry and young, and had the best of their days before them. 'Twas late before I thought of returning home, and I did not leave the garden till some time after sunset. The moon was up; but though there wasn't a cloud to be seen, and though a star was winking here and there in the sky, the day wasn't long enough gone to have it clear moonlight; still it shone enough to make every thing on one side of the heavens look pale and silvery-like; and the thin white mist was just beginning to creep along the fields. On the other side, near where the sun was set, there was more of daylight, and the sky looked angry, red, and fiery through the trees, like as if it was lighted up by a great town burning below. Every thing was as silent as a churchyard, only now and then one could hear far off a dog barking, or a cow lowing after being milked. There wasn't a creature to be seen on the road or in the fields. I wondered at this first, but then I remembered it was May-eve, and that many a thing, both good and bad, would be wandering about that night, and that I ought to shun danger as well as others. So I walked on as quick as I could, and soon came to the end of the demesne wall, where the trees rise high and thick at each side of the road, and almost meet at the top. My heart misgave me when I got under the shade. There was so much light let down from the opening above, that I could see about a stone throw before me. All of a sudden I heard a rustling among the branches, on the right side of the road, and saw something like a small black goat, only with long wide horns turned out instead of being bent backwards, standing upon its hind legs upon the top of the wall, and looking down on me.

My breath was stopped, and I couldn't move for near a minute. I couldn't help, somehow, keeping my eyes fixed on it; and it never stirred, but kept looking in the same fixed way down at me. At last I made a rush, and went on; but I didn't go ten steps, when I saw the very same sight, on the wall to the left of me, standing in exactly the same manner, but three or four times as high, and almost as tall as the tallest man. The horns looked frightful: it gazed upon me as before; my legs shook, and my teeth chattered, and I thought I would drop down dead every moment. At last I felt as if I was obliged to go on—and on I went; but it was without feeling how I moved, or whether my legs carried me. Just as I passed the spot where this frightful thing was standing, I heard a noise as if something sprung from the wall, and felt like as if a heavy animal plumped down upon me, and held with the fore feet clinging to my shoulder, and the hind ones fixed in my gown, that was folded and pinned up behind me. 'Tis the wonder of my life ever since how I bore the shock; but so it was, I neither fell, nor even staggered with the weight, but walked on as if I had the strength of ten men, though I felt as if I couldn't help moving, and couldn't stand still if I wished it. Though I gasped with fear, I knew as well as I do now what I was doing. I tried to cry out, but couldn't; I tried to run, but wasn't able; I tried to look back, but my head and neck were as if they were screwed in a vice. I could barely roll my eyes on each side, and then I could see, as clearly and plainly as if it was in the broad light of the blessed sun, a black and cloven foot planted upon each of my shoulders. I heard a low breathing in my ear; I felt, at every step I took, my leg strike back against the feet of the creature that was on my back. Still I could do nothing but walk straight on. At last I came within sight of the house, and a welcome sight it was to me, for I thought I would be released when I reached it. I soon came close to the door, but it was shut; I looked at the little window, but it was shut too, for they were more cautious about May-eve than I was; I saw the light inside, through the chinks of the door; I heard 'em talking and laughing within; I felt myself at three yards distance from them that would die to save me;— and may the Lord save me from ever again feeling what I did that night, when I found myself held by what couldn't be good nor friendly, but without the power to help myself, or to call my friends, or to put out my hand to knock, or even to lift my leg to strike the door, and let them know that I was outside it! 'Twas as if my hands grew to my sides, and my feet were glued to the ground, or had the weight of a rock fixed to them. At last I thought of blessing myself; and my right hand, that would do nothing else, did that for me. Still the weight remained on my back, and all was as before. I blessed myself again: 'twas still all the same. I then gave myself up for lost: but I blessed myself a third time, and my hand no sooner finished the sign, than all at once I felt the burthen spring off of my back: the door flew open as if a clap of thunder burst it, and I was pitched forward on my forehead, in upon the middle of the floor. When I got up my back was crookened, and I never stood straight from that night to this blessed hour."

There was a pause when Peggy Barrett finished. Those who had heard the story before had listened with a look of half-satisfied interest, blended, however, with an expression of that serious and solemn feeling, which always attends a tale of supernatural wonders, how often soever told. They moved upon their seats out of the posture in which they had remained fixed during the narrative, and sat in an attitude which denoted that their curiosity as to the cause of this strange occurrence had been long since allayed. Those to whom it was before unknown still retained their look and posture of strained attention, and anxious but solemn expectation. A grandson of Peggy's, about nine years old (not the child of the son with whom she lived), had never before heard the story. As it grew in interest, he was observed to cling closer and closer to the old woman's side; and at the close he was gazing steadfastly at her, with his body bent back across her knees, and his face turned up to hers, with a look, through which a disposition to weep seemed contending with curiosity. After a moment's pause, he could no longer restrain his impatience, and catching her gray locks in one hand, while the tear of dread and wonder was just dropping from his eye-lash, he cried, " Granny, what was it ? "

The old woman smiled first at the elder part of her audience, and then at her grandson, and patting him on the forehead, she said, " It was the Phooka."

The *Pouke* or *Phooka,* as the word is pronounced, means, in plain terms, the Evil One. " Playing the puck," a common Anglo-Irish phrase, is equivalent to " playing the devil." Much learning has been displayed in tracing this word through various languages, vide Quarterly Review [vol. xxii.] &c. The commentators on Shakspeare derive the beautiful and frolicksome Puck of the Midsummer Night's Dream from the mischievous Pouke.—Vide Drayton's Nymphidia.

> " This Puck seems but a dreaming dolt,
>   Still walking like a ragged colt," &c.

In Golding's translation of Ovid's Metamorphoses (1587) we find,

> " —— and the countrie where Chymæra, that same *Pooke*,
>   Hath goatish bodie," &c.

The Irish Phooka, in its nature, perfectly resembles the *Mahr*; and we have only to observe, that there is a particular German tradition of a spirit, which sits among reeds and alder bushes ; and which, like the Phooka, leaps upon the back of those who pass by in the night, and does not leave them till they faint and fall to the earth.

THE BROTHERS GRIMM.

FAIRY LEGENDS.

THIERNA NA OGE.

" On Lough-Neagh's bank, as the fisherman strays
When the clear cold eve 's declining,
He sees the round towers of other days
In the wave beneath him shining."

MOORE.

FIOR USGA.

XVII.

A LITTLE way beyond the Gallows Green of Cork, and just outside the town, there is a great lough of water, where people in the winter go and skate for the sake of diversion; but the sport above the water is nothing to what is under it, for at the very bottom of this lough there are buildings and gardens, far more beautiful than any now to be seen, and how they came there was in this manner.

Long before Saxon foot pressed Irish ground, there was a great king called Corc, whose palace stood where the lough now is, in a round green valley, that was just a mile about. In the middle of the court-yard was a spring of fair water, so pure, and so clear, that it was the wonder of all the world. Much did the king rejoice at having so great a curiosity within his palace; but as people came in crowds from far and near to draw the precious water of this spring, he was sorely afraid that in time it might become dry; so he caused a high wall to be built up round it, and would allow nobody to have the water, which was a very great loss to the poor people living about the palace. Whenever he wanted any for himself, he would send his daughter to get it, not liking to trust his servants with the key of the well-door, fearing that they might give some away.

One night the king gave a grand entertainment, and there were many great princes present, and lords and nobles without end; and there were wonderful doings throughout the palace: there were bonfires, whose blaze reached up to the very sky; and dancing was there, to such sweet music, that it ought to have waked up the dead out of their graves; and feasting was there in the greatest of plenty for all who came; nor was any one turned away from the palace gates — but "you're welcome — you're welcome, heartily," was the porter's salute for all.

Now it happened at this grand entertainment there was one young prince above all the rest mighty comely to behold, and as tall and as straight as ever eye would wish to look on. Right merrily did he dance that night with the old king's daughter, wheeling here, and wheeling there, as light as a feather, and footing it away to the admiration of every one. The musicians played the better for seeing their dancing; and they danced as if their lives depended upon it. After all this dancing came the supper; and the young prince was seated at table by the side of his beautiful partner, who smiled upon him as often as he spoke to her; and that was by no means so often as he wished, for he had constantly to turn to the company and thank them for the many compliments passed upon his fair partner and himself.

In the midst of this banquet, one of the great lords said to King Corc, " May it please your majesty, here is every thing in abundance that heart can wish for, both to eat and drink, except water."

"Water!" said the king, mightily pleased at some one calling for that of which purposely there was a want: "water shall you have, my lord, speedily, and that of such a delicious kind, that I challenge all the world to equal it. Daughter," said he, "go fetch some in the golden vessel which I caused to be made for the purpose."

The king's daughter, who was called Fior Usga, (which signifies, in English, Spring Water,) did not much like to be told to perform so menial a service before so many people, and though she did not venture to refuse the commands of her father, yet hesitated to obey him, and looked down upon the ground. The king, who loved his daughter very much, seeing this, was sorry for what he had desired her to do, but having said the word, he was never known to recall it; he therefore thought of a way to make his daughter go speedily and fetch the water, and it was by proposing that the young prince her partner should go along with her. Accordingly, with a loud voice, he said, "Daughter, I wonder not at your fearing to go alone so late at night; but I doubt not the young prince at your side will go with you." The prince was not displeased at hearing this; and taking the golden vessel in one hand, with the other led the king's daughter out of the hall so gracefully that all present gazed after them with delight.

When they came to the spring of water, in the court-yard of the palace, the fair Usga unlocked the door with the greatest care, and stooping down with the golden vessel to take some of the water out of the well, found the vessel so heavy that she lost her balance and fell in. The young prince tried in vain to save her, for the water rose and rose so fast, that the entire court-yard was speedily covered with it, and he hastened back almost in a state of distraction to the king.

The door of the well being left open, the water, which had been so long confined, rejoiced at obtaining its liberty, rushed forth incessantly, every moment rising higher and higher, and was in the hall of the entertainment sooner than the young prince himself, so that when he attempted to speak to the king he was up to his neck in water. At length the water rose to such a height, that it filled the entire of the green valley in which the king's palace stood, and so the present lough of Cork was formed.

Yet the king and his guests were not drowned, as would now happen, if such an awful inundation were to take place; neither was his daughter, the fair Usga, who returned to the banquet hall the very next night after this dreadful event; and every night since the same entertainment and dancing goes on in the palace at the bottom of the lough, and will last until some one has the luck to bring up out of it the golden vessel which was the cause of all this mischief.

Nobody can doubt that it was a judgment upon the king for his shutting up the well in the court-yard from the poor people: and if there are any who do not credit my story, they may go and see the lough of Cork, for there it is to be seen to this day; the road to Kinsale passes at one side of it; and when its waters are low and clear, the tops of towers and stately buildings may be plainly viewed in the bottom by those who have good eyesight, without the help of spectacles.

CORMAC AND MARY.

XVIII.

" She is not dead — she has no grave —
    She lives beneath Lough Corrib's water[1];
And in the murmur of each wave
    Methinks I catch the songs I taught her."

Thus many an evening on the shore
    Sat Cormac raving wild and lowly;
Still idly muttering o'er and o'er,
    " She lives, detain'd by spells unholy.

" Death claims her not, too fair for earth,
    Her spirit lives — alien of heaven;
Nor will it know a second birth
    When sinful mortals are forgiven !

" Cold is this rock — the wind comes chill,
    And mists the gloomy waters cover;
But oh ! her soul is colder still —
    To lose her God — to leave her lover !"

The lake was in profound repose,
    Yet one white wave came gently curling,
And as it reach'd the shore, arose
    Dim figures — banners gay unfurling.

[1] In the county of Galway.

Onward they move, an airy crowd:
  Through each thin form a moonlight ray shone;
While spear and helm, in pageant proud,
  Appear in liquid undulation.

Bright barbed steeds curvetting tread
  Their trackless way with antic capers;
And curtain clouds hang overhead,
  Festoon'd by rainbow-colour'd vapours.

And when a breath of air would stir
  That drapery of Heaven's own wreathing,
Light wings of prismy gossamer
  Just moved and sparkled to the breathing.

Nor wanting was the choral song,
  Swelling in silv'ry chimes of sweetness;
To sound of which this subtile throng
  Advanced in playful grace and fleetness.

With music's strain, all came and went
  Upon poor Cormac's doubting vision;
Now rising in wild merriment,
  Now softly fading in derision.

" Christ, save her soul," he boldly cried;
  And when that blessed name was spoken,
Fierce yells and fiendish shrieks replied,
  And vanished all, — the spell was broken.

M

And now on Corrib's lonely shore,
 Freed by his word from power of faëry,
To life, to love, restored once more,
 Young Cormac welcomes back his Mary.

THE LEGEND OF LOUGH GUR.

XIX.

LARRY COTTER had a farm on one side of Lough Gur [1], and was thriving in it, for he was an industrious proper sort of man, who would have lived quietly and soberly to the end of his days, but for the misfortune that came upon him, and you shall hear how that was. He had as nice a bit of meadow-land, down by the water-side, as ever a man would wish for; but its growth was spoiled entirely on him, and no one could tell how.

One year after the other it was all ruined just in the same way: the bounds were well made up, and not a stone of them was disturbed; neither could his neighbours' cattle have been guilty of the trespass, for they were spancelled [2]; but however it was done, the grass of the meadow was destroyed, which was a great loss to Larry.

"What in the wide world will I do?" said Larry Cotter to his neighbour, Tom Welsh, who was a very decent sort of man himself: "that bit of meadow-land, which I am paying the great rent for, is doing nothing at all to make it for me; and the times are bitter bad, without the help of that to make them worse."

"'Tis true for you, Larry," replied Welsh: "the times are bitter bad — no doubt of that;

---

[1] In the county of Limerick.
[2] Spancelled — fettered.

but may be if you were to watch by night, you might make out all about it: sure there 's Mick and Terry, my two boys, will watch with you; for 't is a thousand pities any honest man like you should be ruined in such a scheming way."

Accordingly, the following night, Larry Cotter, with Welch's two sons, took their station in a corner of the meadow. It was just at the full of the moon, which was shining beautifully down upon the lake, that was as calm all over as the sky itself; not a cloud was there to be seen any where, nor a sound to be heard, but the cry of the corncreaks answering one another across the water.

"Boys! boys!" said Larry, "look there! look there! but for your lives don't make a bit of noise, nor stir a step till I say the word."

They looked, and saw a great fat cow, followed by seven milk-white heifers, moving on the smooth surface of the lake towards the meadow.

"'T is not Tim Dwyer the piper's cow, any way, that danced all the flesh off her bones," whispered Mick to his brother.

"Now, boys!" said Larry Cotter, when he saw the fine cow and her seven white heifers fairly in the meadow, "get between them and the lake if you can, and, no matter who they belong to, we 'll just put them into the pound."

But the cow must have overheard Larry speaking, for down she went in a great hurry to the shore of the lake, and into it with her, before all their eyes: away made the seven heifers after her, but the boys got down to the bank before them, and work enough they had to drive them up from the lake to Larry Cotter.

Larry drove the seven heifers, and beautiful beasts they were, to the pound; but after he had them there for three days, and could hear of no owner, he took them out, and put them up in a field of his own. There he kept them, and they were thriving mighty well with him, until one night the gate of the field was left open, and in the morning the seven heifers were gone. Larry could not get any account of them after; and, beyond all doubt, it was back into the lake they went. Wherever they came from, or to whatever world they belonged, Larry Cotter never had a crop of grass off the meadow through their means. So he took to drink, fairly out of the grief; and it was the drink that killed him, they say.

THE ENCHANTED LAKE.

XX.

In the west of Ireland there was a lake, and no doubt it is there still, in which many young men had been at various times drowned. What made the circumstance remarkable was, that the bodies of the drowned persons were never found. People naturally wondered at this: and at length the lake came to have a bad repute. Many dreadful stories were told about that lake; some would affirm, that on a dark night its waters appeared like fire — others would speak of horrid forms which were seen to glide over it; and every one agreed that a strange sulphureous smell issued from out of it.

There lived, not far distant from this lake, a young farmer, named Roderick Keating, who was about to be married to one of the prettiest girls in that part of the country. On his return from Limerick, where he had been to purchase the wedding-ring, he came up with two or three of his acquaintance, who were standing on the shore, and they began to joke with him about Peggy Honan. One said that young Delaney, his rival, had in his absence contrived to win the affection of his mistress; — but Roderick's confidence in his intended bride was too great to be disturbed at this tale, and putting his hand in his pocket, he produced and held up with a significant look the wedding-ring. As he was turning it between his fore-finger and thumb, in token of triumph, somehow or other the ring fell from his hand, and rolled into the lake: Roderick looked after it with the greatest sorrow; it was not so much for its value, though it had cost him half-a-guinea, as for the ill-luck of the thing; and the water was so deep, that there was little chance of re-covering it. His companions laughed at him, and he in vain endeavoured to tempt any of them by the offer of a handsome reward to dive after the ring: they were all as little inclined to venture as Roderick Keating himself; for the tales which they had heard when children were strongly im-pressed on their memories, and a superstitious dread filled the mind of each.

"Must I then go back to Limerick to buy an-other ring?" exclaimed the young farmer. "Will not ten times what the ring cost tempt any one of you to venture after it?"

There was within hearing a man who was con-sidered to be a poor, crazy, half-witted fellow, but he was as harmless as a child, and used to go wandering up and down through the country from one place to another. When he heard of so great a reward, Paddeen, for that was his name, spoke out, and said, that if Roderick Keating would give him encouragement equal to what he had offered to others, he was ready to venture after the ring into the lake; and Paddeen, all the while he spoke, looked as covetous after the sport as the money.

"I'll take you at your word," said Keating. So Paddeen pulled off his coat, and without a single syllable more, down he plunged, head foremost, into the lake : what depth he went to, no one can tell exactly ; but he was going, going, going down through the water, until the water parted from him, and he came upon the dry land ; the sky, and the light, and every thing, was there just as it is here ; and he saw fine pleasure-grounds, with an elegant avenue through them, and a grand house, with a power of steps going up to the door. When he had recovered from his wonder at finding the land so dry and comfortable under the water, he looked about him, and what should he see but all the young men that were drowned working away in the pleasure-grounds as if nothing had ever happened to them. Some of them were mowing down the grass, and more were· settling out the gravel walks, and doing all manner of nice work, as neat and as clever as if they had never been drowned ; and they were singing away with high glee : —

> " She is fair as Cappoquin :
> Have you courage her to win ?
> And her wealth it far outshines
> Cullen's bog and Silvermines.
> She exceeds all heart can wish ;
> Not brawling like the Foherish,
> But as the brightly-flowing Lee,
> Graceful, mild, and pure is she ! "

Well, Paddeen could not but look at the young men, for he knew some of them before they were lost in the lake ; but he said nothing, though he thought a great deal more for all that, like an oyster : — no, not the wind of a word passed his lips ; so on he went towards the big house, bold enough, as if he had seen nothing to speak of ;

yet all the time mightily wishing to know who the young woman could be that the young men were singing the song about.

When he had nearly reached the door of the great house, out walks from the kitchen a powerful fat woman, moving along like a beer-barrel on two legs, with teeth as big as horses' teeth, and up she made towards him.

" Good morrow, Paddeen," said she.

" Good morrow, Ma'am," said he.

" What brought you here ?" said she.

" 'Tis after Rory Keating's gold ring," said he, " I'm come."

" Here it is for you," said Paddeen's fat friend, with a smile on her face that moved like boiling stirabout [gruel].

" Thank you, Ma'am," replied Paddeen, taking it from her :—" I need not say the Lord increase you, for you're fat enough already.   Will you tell me, if you please, am I to go back the same way I came ?"

" Then you did not come to marry me ?" cried the corpulent woman, in a desperate fury.

" Just wait till I come back again, my darling," said Paddeen : " I'm to be paid for my message, and I must return with the answer, or else they'll wonder what has become of me."

" Never mind the money," said the fat woman : " if you marry me, you shall live for ever and a day in that house, and want for nothing."

Paddeen saw clearly that, having got possession of the ring, the fat woman had no power to detain him ; so without minding any thing she said, he kept moving and moving down the avenue, quite quietly, and looking about him ; for, to tell the truth, he had no particular inclination to marry a fat fairy. When he came to the gate, without ever saying good b'ye, out he bolted, and he found the water coming all about him again. Up he plunged through it, and wonder enough there was, when Paddeen was seen swimming away at the opposite side of the lake ; but he soon made the shore, and told Roderick Keating, and the other boys that were standing there looking out for him, all that had happened. Roderick paid him the five guineas for the ring on the spot ; and Paddeen thought himself so rich with such a sum of money in his pocket, that he did not go back to marry the fat lady with the fine house at the bottom of the lake, knowing she had plenty of young men to choose a husband from, if she pleased to be married.

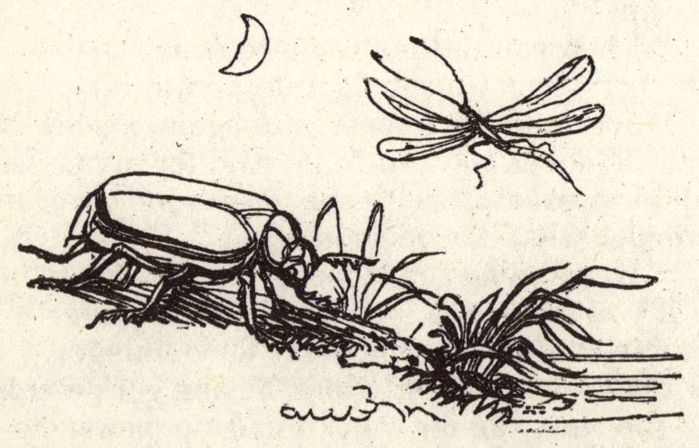

THE LEGEND OF O'DONOGHUE.

XXI.

In an age so distant that the precise period is unknown, a chieftain named O'Donoghue ruled over the country which surrounds the romantic Lough Lean, now called the lake of Killarney. Wisdom, beneficence, and justice distinguished his reign, and the prosperity and happiness of his subjects were their natural results. He is said to have been as renowned for his warlike exploits as for his pacific virtues ; and as a proof that his domestic administration was not the less rigorous because it was mild, a rocky island is pointed out to strangers, called "O'Donoghue's Prison," in which this prince once confined his own son for some act of disorder and disobedience.

His end — for it cannot correctly be called his death — was singular and mysterious. At one of those splendid feasts for which his court was celebrated, surrounded by the most distinguished of his subjects, he was engaged in a prophetic relation of the events which were to happen in ages yet to come. His auditors listened, now wrapt in wonder, now fired with indignation, burning with shame, or melted into sorrow, as he faithfully detailed the heroism, the injuries, the crimes, and the miseries of their descendants. In the midst of his predictions he rose slowly from his seat, advanced with a solemn, measured, and majestic tread to the shore of the lake, and walked forward composedly upon its unyielding surface. When he had nearly reached the centre, he paused for a moment, then turning slowly round, looked towards his friends, and waving his arms to them with the cheerful air of one taking a short farewell, disappeared from their view.

The memory of the good O'Donoghue has been cherished by successive generations with affectionate reverence: and it is believed that at sunrise, on every May-day morning, the anniversary of his departure, he revisits his ancient domains: a favoured few only are in general permitted to see him, and this distinction is always an omen of good fortune to the beholders: when it is granted to many, it is a sure token of an abundant harvest,—a blessing, the want of which during this prince's reign was never felt by his people.

Some years have elapsed since the last appearance of O'Donoghue. The April of that year had been remarkably wild and stormy; but on May-morning the fury of the elements had altogether subsided. The air was hushed and still; and the sky, which was reflected in the serene lake, resembled a beautiful but deceitful countenance, whose smiles, after the most tempestuous emotions, tempt the stranger to believe that it belongs to a soul which no passion has ever ruffled.

The first beams of the rising sun were just gilding the lofty summit of Glenaa, when the waters near the eastern shores of the lake became suddenly and violently agitated, though all the rest of its surface lay smooth and still as a tomb of polished marble; the next moment a foaming wave darted forward, and, like a proud high-crested war-horse, exulting in his strength, rushed across the lake towards Toomies mountain. Behind this wave appeared a stately warrior fully armed, mounted upon a milk-white steed; his snowy plume waved gracefully from a helmet of polished steel, and at his back fluttered a light blue scarf. The horse, apparently exulting in his noble burden, sprang after the wave along the water, which bore him up like firm earth, while showers of spray that glittered brightly in the morning sun were dashed up at every bound.

The warrior was O'Donoghue; he was followed by numberless youths and maidens, who moved lightly and unconstrained over the watery plain, as the moonlight fairies glide through the fields of air; they were linked together by garlands of delicious spring flowers, and they timed their movements to strains of enchanting melody. When O'Donoghue had nearly reached the western side of the lake, he suddenly turned his steed, and directed his course along the wood-fringed shore of Glenaa, preceded by the huge wave that curled and foamed up as high as the horse's neck, whose fiery nostrils snorted above it. The long train of attendants followed with playful deviations the track of their leader, and moved on with unabated fleetness to their celestial music, till gradually, as they entered the narrow strait between Glenaa and Dinis, they became involved in the mists which still partially floated over the lakes, and faded from the view of the wondering beholders : but the sound of their music still fell upon the ear, and echo, catching up the harmonious strains, fondly repeated and prolonged them in soft and softer tones, till the last faint repetition died away, and the hearers awoke as from a dream of bliss.

---

[1] *Thierna na Oge,* or the Country of Youth, is the name given to the foregoing section, from the belief that those who dwell in regions of enchantment beneath the water are not affected by the movements of time.

FAIRY LEGENDS.

THE MERROW.

______

——" The mysterious depths
And wild and wondrous forms of ocean old."
Mattima's Conchologist.

LEGENDS OF THE MERROW.

THE LADY OF GOLLERUS.

XXII.

On the shore of Smerwick harbour, one fine summer's morning, just at day-break, stood Dick Fitzgerald "shoghing the dudeen," which may be translated, smoking his pipe. The sun was gradually rising behind the lofty Brandon, the dark sea was getting green in the light, and the mists clearing away out of the valleys went rolling and curling like the smoke from the corner of Dick's mouth.

"'Tis just the pattern of a pretty morning," said Dick, taking the pipe from between his lips, and looking towards the distant ocean, which lay as still and tranquil as a tomb of polished marble. "Well, to be sure," continued he, after a pause, "'tis mighty lonesome to be talking to one's self by way of company, and not to have another soul to answer one — nothing but the child of one's own voice, the echo! I know this, that if I had the luck, or may be the misfortune," said Dick with a melancholy smile, "to have the woman, it would not be this way with me!—and what in the wide world is a man without a wife? He's no more surely than a bottle without a drop of drink in it, or dancing without music, or the left leg of a scissars, or a fishing line without a hook, or any other matter that is no ways complete.—Is it not so?" said Dick Fitzgerald, casting his eyes towards a rock upon the strand, which, though it could not speak, stood up as firm and looked as bold as ever Kerry witness did.

But what was his astonishment at beholding, just at the foot of that rock, a beautiful young creature combing her hair, which was of a sea-green colour; and now the salt water shining on it, appeared, in the morning light, like melted butter upon cabbage.

Dick guessed at once that she was a Merrow, although he had never seen one before, for he spied the *cohuleen driuth*, or little enchanted cap, which the sea people use for diving down into the ocean, lying upon the strand, near her; and he had heard, that if once he could possess himself of the cap, she would lose the power of going away into the water: so he seized it with all speed, and she, hearing the noise, turned her head about as natural as any Christian.

When the Merrow saw that her little diving-cap was gone, the salt tears — doubly salt, no doubt, from her — came trickling down her cheeks, and she began a low mournful cry with just the tender voice of a new-born infant. Dick, although he knew well enough what she was crying for, determined to keep the *cohuleen driuth*, let her cry never so much, to see what luck would come

out of it.   Yet he could not help pitying her
and when the dumb thing looked up in his face,
and her cheeks all moist with tears, 'twas enough
to make any one feel, let alone Dick, who had
ever and always, like most of his countrymen,
a mighty tender heart of his own.

"Don't cry, my darling," said Dick Fitzgerald;
but the Merrow, like any bold child, only cried
the more for that.

Dick sat himself down by her side, and took
hold of her hand, by way of comforting her.
'Twas in no particular an ugly hand, only there
was a small web between the fingers, as there is
in a duck's foot; but 'twas as thin and as white
as the skin between egg and shell.

"What's your name, my darling?" says Dick,
thinking to make her conversant with him; but
he got no answer; and he was certain sure now,
either that she could not speak, or did not understand him: he therefore squeezed her hand in
his, as the only way he had of talking to her.
It's the universal language; and there's not a
woman in the world, be she fish or lady, that does
not understand it.

The Merrow did not seem much displeased at
this mode of conversation; and, making an end
of her whining all at once — "Man," says she,
looking up in Dick Fitzgerald's face, "Man, will
you eat me?"

"By all the red petticoats and check aprons
between Dingle and Tralee," cried Dick, jumping
up in amazement, "I'd as soon eat myself, my
jewel! Is it I eat you, my pet?— Now, 'twas
some ugly ill-looking thief of a fish put that notion

into your own pretty head, with the nice green
hair down upon it, that is so cleanly combed out
this morning!"

" Man," said the Merrow, " what will you do
with me, if you won't eat me?"

Dick's thoughts were running on a wife: he
saw, at the first glimpse, that she was handsome;
but since she spoke, and spoke too like any real
woman, he was fairly in love with her. 'Twas
the neat way she called him man, that settled
the matter entirely.

" Fish," says Dick, trying to speak to her after
her own short fashion; " fish," says he, " here's
my word, fresh and fasting, for you this blessed
morning, that I'll make you mistress Fitzgerald
before all the world, and that's what I'll do."

" Never say the word twice," says she; " I'm
ready and willing to be yours, mister Fitzgerald;
but stop, if you please, 'till I twist up my hair."

It was some time before she had settled it entirely to her liking; for she guessed, I suppose,
that she was going among strangers, where she
would be looked at. When that was done, the
Merrow put the comb in her pocket, and then
bent down her head and whispered some words
to the water that was close to the foot of the
rock.

Dick saw the murmur of the words upon the
top of the sea, going out towards the wide ocean,
just like a breath of wind rippling along, and,
says he, in the greatest wonder, " Is it speaking
you are, my darling, to the salt water?"

" It's nothing else," says she, quite carelessly,
" I'm just sending word home to my father, not

to be waiting breakfast for me; just to keep him from being uneasy in his mind."

"And who's your father, my duck?" says Dick.

"What!" said the Merrow, "did you never hear of my father? he's the king of the waves, to be sure!"

"And yourself, then, is a real king's daughter?" said Dick, opening his two eyes to take a full and true survey of his wife that was to be.

"Oh, I'm nothing else but a made man with you, and a king your father;—to be sure he has all the money that's down in the bottom of the sea!"

"Money," repeated the Merrow, "what's money?"

"'Tis no bad thing to have when one wants it," replied Dick; "and may be now the fishes have the understanding to bring up whatever you bid them?"

"Oh! yes," said the Merrow, "they bring me what I want."

"To speak the truth, then," said Dick, "'tis a straw bed I have at home before you, and that, I'm thinking, is no ways fitting for a king's daughter: so if 't would not be displeasing to you, just to mention, a nice feather bed, with a pair of new blankets—but what am I talking about? may be you have not such things as beds down under the water?"

"By all means," said she, "Mr. Fitzgerald—plenty of beds at your service. I've fourteen oyster beds of my own, not to mention one just planting for the rearing of young ones."

"You have," says Dick, scratching his head and looking a little puzzled. "'Tis a feather bed I was speaking of — but clearly, yours is the very cut of a decent plan, to have bed and supper so handy to each other, that a person when they'd have the one, need never ask for the other."

However, bed or no bed, money or no money, Dick Fitzgerald determined to marry the Merrow, and the Merrow had given her consent. Away they went, therefore, across the strand, from Gollerus to Ballinrunnig, where Father Fitzgibbon happened to be that morning.

"There are two words to this bargain, Dick Fitzgerald," said his Reverence, looking mighty glum. "And is it a fishy woman you'd marry? — the Lord preserve us! — Send the scaly creature home to her own people, that's my advice to you, wherever she came from."

Dick had the *cohuleen driuth* in his hand, and was about to give it back to the Merrow, who looked covetously at it, but he thought for a moment, and then, says he —

"Please your Reverence, she's a king's daughter."

"If she was the daughter of fifty kings," said Father Fitzgibbon, "I tell you, you can't marry her, she being a fish."

"Please your Reverence," said Dick again, in an under tone, "she is as mild and as beautiful as the moon."

"If she was as mild and as beautiful as the sun, moon, and stars, all put together, I tell you, Dick Fitzgerald," said the Priest, stamping his right foot, " you can't marry her, she being a fish ! "

" But she has all the gold that's down in the sea only for the asking, and I'm a made man if I marry her ; and," said Dick, looking up slily, " I can make it worth any one's while to do the job."

" Oh ! that alters the case entirely," replied the Priest ; " why there's some reason now in what you say : why didn't you tell me this before ? — marry her by all means if she was ten times a fish.   Money, you know, is not to be refused in these bad times, and I may as well have the hansel of it as another, that may be would not take half the pains in counselling you as I have done."

So Father Fitzgibbon married Dick Fitzgerald to the Merrow, and like any loving couple, they returned to Gollerus well pleased with each other. Every thing prospered with Dick — he was at the sunny side of the world ; the Merrow made the best of wives, and they lived together in the greatest contentment.

It was wonderful to see, considering where she had been brought up, how she would busy herself about the house, and how well she nursed the children ; for, at the end of three years, there were as many young Fitzgeralds — two boys and a girl.

In short, Dick was a happy man, and so he might have continued to the end of his days, if he had only the sense to take proper care of what he had got ; many another man, however, beside Dick, has not had wit enough to do that.

One day when Dick was obliged to go to Tralee, he left his wife, minding the children at home after him, and thinking she had plenty to do without disturbing his fishing tackle.

Dick was no sooner gone than Mrs. Fitzgerald set about cleaning up the house, and chancing to pull down a fishing net, what should she find behind it in a hole in the wall but her own *cohuleen driuth*.

She took it out and looked at it, and then she thought of her father the king, and her mother the queen, and her brothers and sisters, and she felt a longing to go back to them.

She sat down on a little stool and thought over the happy days she had spent under the sea; then she looked at her children, and thought on the love and affection of poor Dick, and how it would break his heart to lose her. "But," says she, "he won't lose me entirely, for I'll come back to him again, and who can blame me for going to see my father and my mother after being so long away from them."

She got up and went towards the door, but came back again to look once more at the child that was sleeping in the cradle. She kissed it gently, and as she kissed it, a tear trembled for an instant in her eye and then fell on its rosy cheek. She wiped away the tear, and turning to the eldest little girl, told her to take good care of her brothers, and to be a good child herself, until she came back. The Merrow then went down to the strand. — The sea was lying calm and smooth, just heaving and glittering in the sun, and she thought she heard a faint sweet singing, inviting her to come down. All her old ideas and feelings came flooding over her mind, Dick and her children were at the instant forgotten, and placing the *cohuleen driuth* on her head, she plunged in.

Dick came home in the evening, and missing his wife, he asked Kathelin, his little girl, what had become of her mother, but she could not tell him. He then enquired of the neighbours, and he learned that she was seen going towards the strand with a strange looking thing like a cocked hat in her hand. He returned to his cabin to search for the *cohuleen driuth*. It was gone, and the truth now flashed upon him.

Year after year did Dick Fitzgerald wait, expecting the return of his wife, but he never saw her more. Dick never married again, always thinking that the Merrow would sooner or later return to him, and nothing could ever persuade him but that her father the king kept her below by main force; " For," said Dick, " she surely would not of herself give up her husband and her children."

While she was with him, she was so good a wife in every respect, that to this day she is spoken of in the tradition of the country as the pattern for one, under the name of THE LADY OF GOLLERUS.

FLORY CANTILLON'S FUNERAL.

XXIII.

THE ancient burial-place of the Cantillon family was on an island in Ballyheigh Bay. This island was situated at no great distance from the shore, and at a remote period was overflowed in one of the incroachments which the Atlantic has made on that part of the coast of Kerry. The fishermen declare they have often seen the ruined walls of an old chapel beneath them in the water, as they sailed over the clear green sea, of a sunny afternoon.[1] However this may be, it is well known that the Cantillons were, like most other Irish families, strongly attached to their ancient burial-place; and this attachment led to the custom, when any of the family died, of carrying the corpse to the sea-side, where the coffin was left on the shore within reach of the tide. In the morning it had disappeared, being, as was traditionally believed, conveyed away by the ancestors of the deceased to their family tomb.

[1] " The neighbouring inhabitants," says Dr. Smith, in his History of Kerry, speaking of Ballyheigh, " show some rocks visible in this bay only at low tides, which, they say, are the remains of an island, that was formerly the burial-place of the family of Cantillon, the ancient proprietors of Ballyheigh." p. 210.

Connor Crowe, a county Clare man, was related to the Cantillons by marriage. " Connor Mac in Cruagh, of the seven quarters of Breintragh," as he was commonly called, and a proud man he was of the name. Connor, be it known, would drink a quart of salt water, for its medicinal virtues, before breakfast; and for the same reason, I suppose, double that quantity of raw whiskey between breakfast and night, which last he did with as little inconvenience to himself as any man in the barony of Moyferta; and were I to add Clanderalaw and Ibrickan, I don't think I should say wrong.

On the death of Florence Cantillon, Connor Crowe was determined to satisfy himself about the truth of this story of the old church under the sea: so when he heard the news of the old fellow's death, away with him to Ardfert, where Flory was laid out in high style, and a beautiful corpse he made.

Flory had been as jolly and as rollocking a boy in his day as ever was stretched, and his wake was in every respect worthy of him. There was all kind of entertainment and all sort of diversion at it, and no less than three girls got husbands there — more luck to them. Every thing was as it should be: all that side of the country, from Dingle to Tarbert, was at the funeral. The Keen was sung long and bitterly; and, according to the family custom, the coffin was carried to Ballyheigh strand, where it was laid upon the shore with a prayer for the repose of the dead.

The mourners departed, one group after another, and at last Connor Crowe was left alone:

he then pulled out his whiskey bottle, his drop of comfort as he called it, which he required, being in grief; and down he sat upon a big stone that was sheltered by a projecting rock, and partly concealed from view, to await with patience the appearance of the ghostly undertakers.

The evening came on mild and beautiful; he whistled an old air which he had heard in his childhood, hoping to keep idle fears out of his head; but the wild strain of that melody brought a thousand recollections with it, which only made the twilight appear more pensive.

" If 'twas near the gloomy tower of Dunmore, in my own sweet county, I was," said Connor Crowe, with a sigh, " one might well believe that the prisoners, who were murdered long ago, there in the vaults under the castle, would be the hands to carry off the coffin out of envy, for never a one of them was buried decently, nor had as much as a coffin amongst them all. 'Tis often, sure enough, I have heard lamentations and great mourning coming from the vaults of Dunmore Castle; but," continued he, after fondly pressing his lips to the mouth of his companion and silent comforter, the whiskey bottle, " didn't I know all the time well enough, 'twas the dismal sounding waves working through the cliffs and hollows of the rocks, and fretting themselves to foam. Oh then, Dunmore Castle, it is you that are the gloomy looking tower on a gloomy day, with the gloomy hills behind you; when one has gloomy thoughts on their heart, and sees you like a ghost rising out of the smoke made by the kelp burners on the strand, there is, the Lord save us! as fearful a look about you as about the Blue Man's Lake at midnight.   Well then, any how," said Connor, after a pause, " is it not a blessed night, though surely the moon looks mighty pale in the face? St. Senan himself between us and all kinds of harm."

It was, in truth, a lovely moonlight night; nothing was to be seen around but the dark rocks, and the white pebbly beach, upon which the sea broke with a hoarse and melancholy murmur. Connor, notwithstanding his frequent draughts, felt rather queerish, and almost began to repent his curiosity.   It was certainly a solemn sight to behold the black coffin resting upon the white strand.   His imagination gradually converted the deep moaning of old ocean into a mournful wail for the dead, and from the shadowy recesses of the rocks he imaged forth strange and visionary forms.

As the night advanced, Connor became weary with watching; he caught himself more than once in the fact of nodding, when suddenly giving his head a shake, he would look towards the black coffin.   But the narrow house of death remained unmoved before him.

It was long past midnight, and the moon was sinking into the sea, when he heard the sound of many voices, which gradually became stronger, above the heavy and monotonous roll of the sea: he listened, and presently could distinguish a Keen, of exquisite sweetness, the notes of which rose and fell with the heaving of the waves, whose deep murmur mingled with and supported the strain!

The Keen grew louder and louder, and seemed to approach the beach, and then fell into a low plaintive wail.   As it ended, Connor beheld a number of strange, and in the dim light, mysterious-looking figures, emerge from the sea, and surround the coffin, which they prepared to launch into the water.

"This comes of marrying with the creatures of earth," said one of the figures, in a clear, yet hollow tone.

"True," replied another, with a voice still more fearful, " our king would never have commanded his gnawing white-toothed waves to de vour the rocky roots of the island cemetery, had not his daughter, Durfulla, been buried there by her mortal husband!"

"But the time will come," said a third, bending over the coffin.

"When mortal eye — our work shall spy,
    And mortal ear — our dirge shall hear."

"Then," said a fourth, " our burial of the Cantillons is at an end for ever!"

As this was spoken, the coffin was borne from the beach by a retiring wave, and the company of sea people prepared to follow it : but at the moment, one chanced to discover Connor Crowe, as fixed with wonder and as motionless with fear as the stone on which he sat.

"The time is come," cried the unearthly being, " the time is come; a human eye looks on the forms of ocean, a human ear has heard their voices; farewell to the Cantillons ; the sons of the sea are no longer doomed to bury the dust of the earth!"

One after the other turned slowly round, and regarded Connor Crowe, who still remained as if bound by a spell. Again arose their funeral song; and on the next wave they followed the coffin. The sound of the lamentation died away, and at length nothing was heard but the rush of waters. The coffin and the train of sea people sank over the old church-yard, and never, since the funeral of old Flory Cantillon, have any of the family been carried to the strand of Ballyheigh, for conveyance to their rightful burial-place, beneath the waves of the Atlantic.

THE LORD OF DUNKERRON.

XXIV.

THE lord of Dunkerron [1] — O'Sullivan More,
Why seeks he at midnight the sea-beaten shore?
His bark lies in haven, his hounds are asleep;
No foes are abroad on the land or the deep.

Yet nightly the lord of Dunkerron is known
On the wild shore to watch and to wander alone;
For a beautiful spirit of ocean, 't is said,
The lord of Dunkerron would win to his bed.

When, by moonlight, the waters were hush'd to repose,
That beautiful spirit of ocean arose;
Her hair, full of lustre, just floated and fell
O'er her bosom, that heav'd with a billowy swell.

Long, long had he lov'd her — long vainly essay'd
To lure from her dwelling the coy ocean maid;
And long had he wander'd and watch'd by the tide,
To claim the fair spirit O'Sullivan's bride!

[1] The remains of Dunkerron Castle are distant about a mile from the village of Kenmare, in the county of Kerry. It is recorded to have been built in 1596, by Owen O'Sullivan More. — [*More*, is merely an epithet signifying *the Great.*]

The maiden she gazed on the creature of earth,
Whose voice in her breast to a feeling gave birth;
Then smiled; and, abashed as a maiden might be,
Looking down, gently sank to her home in the sea.

Though gentle that smile, as the moonlight above,
O'Sullivan felt 't was the dawning of love,
And hope came on hope, spreading over his mind,
Like the eddy of circles her wake left behind.

The lord of Dunkerron he plunged in the waves,
And sought through the fierce rush of waters,
    their caves;
The gloom of whose depth studded over with
    spars,
Had the glitter of midnight when lit up by stars.

Who can tell or can fancy the treasures that sleep
Intombed in the wonderful womb of the deep?
The pearls and the gems, as if valueless, thrown
To lie 'mid the sea-wrack concealed and unknown.

Down, down went the maid, — still the chieftain
    pursued;
Who flies must be followed ere she can be wooed.
Untempted by treasures, unawed by alarms,
The maiden at length he has clasped in his arms!

They rose from the deep by a smooth-spreading
    strand,
Whence beauty and verdure stretch'd over the
    land.

'T was an isle of enchantment ! and lightly the
    breeze,
With a musical murmur, just crept through the
    trees.

The haze-woven shroud of that newly born isle,
Softly faded away, from a magical pile,
A palace of crystal, whose bright-beaming sheen
Had the tints of the rainbow — red, yellow, and
    green.

And grottoes, fantastic in hue and in form,
Were there, as flung up — the wild sport of the
    storm ;
Yet all was so cloudless, so lovely, and calm,
It seemed but a region of sunshine and balm.

" Here, here shall we dwell in a dream of delight,
Where the glories of earth and of ocean unite !
Yet, loved son of earth ! I must from thee away ;
There are laws which e'en spirits are bound to
    obey !

" Once more must I visit the chief of my race,
His sanction to gain ere I meet thy embrace.
In a moment I dive to the chambers beneath :
One cause can detain me — one only — 't is
    death !"

They parted in sorrow, with vows true and fond ;
The language of promise had nothing beyond.
His soul all on fire, with anxiety burns :
The moment is gone — but no maiden returns.

What sounds from the deep meet his terrified ear—
What accents of rage and of grief does he hear?
What sees he? what change has come over the
    flood—
What tinges its green with a jetty of blood?

Can he doubt what the gush of warm blood would
    explain?
That she sought the consent of her monarch in
    vain!
For see all around him, in white foam and froth,
The waves of the ocean boil up in their wroth!

The palace of crystal has melted in air,
And the dies of the rainbow no longer are there;
The grottoes with vapour and clouds are o'ercast,
The sunshine is darkness — the vision has past!

Loud, loud was the call of his serfs for their chief;
They sought him with accents of wailing and grief:
He heard, and he struggled — a wave to the shore,
Exhausted and faint, bears O'Sullivan More!

THE WONDERFUL TUNE.

XXV.

MAURICE CONNOR was the king, and that's no small word, of all the pipers in Munster. He could play jig and planxty without end, and Ollistrum's March, and the Eagle's Whistle, and the Hen's Concert, and odd tunes of every sort and kind. But he knew one, far more surprising than the rest, which had in it the power to set every thing dead or alive dancing.

In what way he learned it is beyond my knowledge, for he was mighty cautious about telling how he came by so wonderful a tune. At the very first note of that tune, the brogues began shaking upon the feet of all who heard it — old or young it mattered not — just as if their brogues had the ague; then the feet began going — going — going from under them, and at last up and away with them, dancing like mad! — whisking here, there, and everywhere, like a straw in a storm — there was no halting while the music lasted!

Not a fair, nor a wedding, nor a patron in the seven parishes round, was counted worth the speaking of without " blind Maurice and his pipes." His mother, poor woman, used to lead him about from one place to another, just like a dog.

Down through Iveragh — a place that ought to be proud of itself, for 't is Daniel O'Connell's coun-

try — Maurice Connor and his mother were taking
their rounds. Beyond all other places Iveragh is
the place for stormy coast and steep mountains:
as proper a spot it is as any in Ireland to get yourself drowned, or your neck broken on the land,
should you prefer that. But, notwithstanding,
in Ballinskellig bay there is a neat bit of ground,
well fitted for diversion, and down from it, towards the water, is a clean smooth piece of strand
— the dead image of a calm summer's sea on a
moonlight night, with just the curl of the small
waves upon it.

Here it was that Maurice's music had brought
from all parts a great gathering of the young men
and the young women — *O the darlints!* — for
'twas not every day the strand of Trafraska was
stirred up by the voice of a bagpipe. The dance
began; and as pretty a rinkafadda it was as ever
was danced. " Brave music," said every body,
" and well done," when Maurice stopped.

" More power to your elbow, Maurice, and a
fair wind in the bellows," cried Paddy Dorman,
a hump-backed dancing-master, who was there to
keep order. " 'Tis a pity," said he, " if we'd let
the piper run dry after such music; 'twould be a
disgrace to Iveragh, that didn't come on it since
the week of the three Sundays." So, as well became him, for he was always a decent man, says
he: " Did you drink, piper?"

" I will, sir," says Maurice, answering the question on the safe side, for you never yet knew piper
or schoolmaster who refused his drink.

" What will you drink, Maurice?" says Paddy.

" I'm no ways particular," says Maurice; " I

drink any thing, and give God thanks, barring *raw* water : but if 'tis all the same to you, mister Dorman, may be you wouldn't lend me the loan of a glass of whiskey."

" I've no glass, Maurice," said Paddy ; " I've only the bottle."

" Let that be no hindrance," answered Maurice ; " my mouth just holds a glass to the drop ; often I've tried it, sure."

So Paddy Dorman trusted him with the bottle — more fool was he ; and, to his cost, he found that though Maurice's mouth might not hold more than the glass at one time, yet, owing to the hole in his throat, it took many a filling.

" That was no bad whiskey neither," says Maurice, handing back the empty bottle.

" By the holy frost, then !" says Paddy, " 'tis but *could* comfort there's in that bottle now ; and 'tis your word we must take for the strength of the whiskey, for you've left us no sample to judge by :" and to be sure Maurice had not.

Now I need not tell any gentleman or lady with common understanding, that if he or she was to drink an honest bottle of whiskey at one pull, it is not at all the same thing as drinking a bottle of water ; and in the whole course of my life, I never knew more than five men who could do so without being overtaken by the liquor. Of these Maurice Connor was not one, though he had a stiff head enough of his own — he was fairly tipsy. Don't think I blame him for it ; 'tis often a good man's case ; but true is the word that says, " when liquor 's in sense is out ;" and puff, at a breath, before you could say " Lord, save us !" out he blasted his wonderful tune.

'Twas really then beyond all belief or telling the dancing. Maurice himself could not keep quiet; staggering now on one leg, now on the other, and rolling about like a ship in a cross sea, trying to humour the tune. There was his mother too, moving her old bones as light as the youngest girl of them all: but her dancing, no, nor the dancing of all the rest, is not worthy the speaking about to the work that was going on down upon the strand. Every inch of it covered with all manner of fish jumping and plunging about to the music, and every moment more and more would tumble in out of the water, charmed by the wonderful tune. Crabs of monstrous size spun round and round on one claw with the nimbleness of a dancing-master, and twirled and tossed their other claws about like limbs that did not belong to them. It was a sight surprising to behold. But perhaps you may have heard of father Florence Conry, a Franciscan friar, and a great Irish poet; *bolg an dàna*, as they used to call him — a wallet of poems. If you have not, he was as pleasant a man as one would wish to drink with of a hot summer's day; and he has rhymed out all about the dancing fishes so neatly, that it would be a thousand pities not to give you his verses; so here's my hand at an upset of them into English:

> The big seals in motion,
> Like waves of the ocean
>   Or gouty feet prancing,
> Came heading the gay fish,
> Crabs, lobsters, and cray fish,
>   Determined on dancing.

The sweet sounds they follow'd,
The gasping cod swallow'd;
  'T was wonderful, really!
And turbot and flounder,
'Mid fish that were rounder,
  Just caper'd as gaily.

John-dories came tripping;
Dull hake by their skipping
  To frisk it seem'd given;
Bright mackrel went springing,
Like small rainbows winging
  Their flight up to heaven.

The whiting and haddock
Left salt water paddock
  This dance to be put in:
Where skate with flat faces
Edged out some odd plaices;
  But soles kept their footing.

Sprats and herrings in powers
Of silvery showers
  All number out-number'd.
And great ling so lengthy
Were there in such plenty
  The shore was encumber'd.

The scollop and oyster
Their two shells did roister,
  Like castanets fitting;
While limpets moved clearly,
And rocks very nearly
  With laughter were splitting.

Never was such an ullabulloo in this world, before or since; 'twas as if heaven and earth were coming together; and all out of Maurice Connor's wonderful tune!

In the height of all these doings, what should there be dancing among the outlandish set of fishes but a beautiful young woman — as beautiful as the dawn of day!   She had a cocked hat upon her head; from under it her long green hair — just the colour of the sea — fell down behind, without hinderance to her dancing.   Her teeth were like rows of pearl; her lips for all the world looked like red coral; and she had an elegant gown, as white as the foam of the wave, with little rows of purple and red sea weeds settled out upon it: for you never yet saw a lady, under the water or over the water, who had not a good notion of dressing herself out.

Up she danced at last to Maurice, who was flinging his feet from under him as fast as hops — for nothing in this world could keep still while that tune of his was going on — and says she to him, chaunting it out with a voice as sweet as honey —

> " I'm a lady of honour
>   Who live in the sea;
>   Come down, Maurice Connor,
>   And be married to me.

> " Silver plates and gold dishes
>   You shall have, and shall be
>   The king of the fishes,
>   When you 're married to me."

Drink was strong in Maurice's head, and out he chaunted in return for her great civility.   It is not every lady, may be, that would be after making such an offer to a blind piper; therefore 'twas only right in him to give her as good as she gave herself — so says Maurice,

> " I'm obliged to you, madam :
>   Off a gold dish or plate,
> If a king, and I had 'em,
>   I could dine in great state.

> " With your own father's daughter
>   I 'd be sure to agree ;
> But to drink the salt water
>   Wouldn't do so with me ! "

The lady looked at him quite amazed, and swinging her head from side to side like a great scholar, " Well," says she, " Maurice, if you 're not a poet, where is poetry to be found ? "

In this way they kept on at it, framing high compliments ; one answering the other, and their feet going with the music as fast as their tongues. All the fish kept dancing too : Maurice heard the clatter, and was afraid to stop playing lest it might be displeasing to the fish, and not knowing what so many of them may take it into their heads to do to him if they got vexed.

Well, the lady with the green hair kept on coaxing of Maurice with soft speeches, till at last she overpersuaded him to promise to marry her, and be king over the fishes, great and small. Maurice was well fitted to be their king, if they wanted one that could make them dance ; and he surely would drink, barring the salt water, with any fish of them all.

When Maurice's mother saw him, with that unnatural thing in the form of a green-haired lady as his guide, and he and she dancing down together so lovingly to the water's edge, through the thick of the fishes, she called out after him to stop and come back. " Oh then," says she, " as if I was not widow enough before, there he is going away from me to be married to that scaly woman. And who knows but 'tis grandmother I may be to a hake or a cod — Lord help and pity me, but 'tis a mighty unnatural thing!—and may be 'tis boiling and eating my own grandchild I'll be, with a bit of salt butter, and I not knowing it !— Oh Maurice, Maurice, if there's any love or nature left in you, come back to your own *ould* mother, who reared you like a decent Christian !"

Then the poor woman began to cry and ullagoane so finely that it would do any one good to hear her.

Maurice was not long getting to the rim of the water ; there he kept playing and dancing on as if nothing was the matter, and a great thundering wave coming in towards him ready to swallow him up alive ; but as he could not see it, he did not fear it. His mother it was who saw it plainly through the big tears that were rolling down her cheeks ; and though she saw it, and her heart was aching as much as ever mother's heart ached for a son, she kept dancing, dancing, all the time for the bare life of her. Certain it was she could not help it, for Maurice never stopped playing that wonderful tune of his.

He only turned the bothered ear to the sound of his mother's voice, fearing it might put him

out in his steps, and all the answer he made back
was —

"Whisht with you, mother — sure I'm going
to be king over the fishes down in the sea, and
for a token of luck, and a sign that I'm alive and
well, I'll send you in, every twelvemonth on this
day, a piece of burned wood to Trafraska." Maurice had not the power to say a word more, for
the strange lady with the green hair seeing the
wave just upon them, covered him up with herself in a thing like a cloak with a big hood to it,
and the wave curling over twice as high as their
heads, burst upon the strand, with a rush and a
roar that might be heard as far as Cape Clear.

That day twelvemonth the piece of burned
wood came ashore in Trafraska. It was a queer
thing for Maurice to think of sending all the way
from the bottom of the sea. A gown or a pair of
shoes would have been something like a present
for his poor mother; but he had said it, and he
kept his word. The bit of burned wood regularly
came ashore on the appointed day for as good,
ay, and better than a hundred years. The day
is now forgotten, and may be that is the reason
why people say how Maurice Connor has stopped
sending the luck-token to his mother. Poor woman, she did not live to get as much as one of
them; for what through the loss of Maurice, and
the fear of eating her own grandchildren, she died
in three weeks after the dance — some say it was
the fatigue that killed her, but whichever it
was, Mrs. Connor was decently buried with her
own people.

Seafaring men have often heard, off the coast

of Kerry, on a still night, the sound of music coming up from the water; and some, who have had good ears, could plainly distinguish Maurice Connor's voice singing these words to his pipes:—

Beautiful shore, with thy spreading strand,
Thy crystal water, and diamond sand;
Never would I have parted from thee
But for the sake of my fair ladie.[1]

[1] This is almost a literal translation of a Rann in the well-known song of Deardra.

The Irish *Merrow*, correctly written ᾶοηύαὄ or ᾶοηύαċ, answer
exactly to the English Mermaid, being compounded of ᾶuηη, the Sea
and Οιᴣ, a maid.   It is also used to express a sea-monster, like the Ar-
moric and Cornish *Morhuch*, to which it evidently bears analogy.

In Irish, ᾶuηὄuċαη, ᾶuηη-ᴣειlτ, Sαηᴣuбα, and Suιηe are
various names for sea-nymphs or mermaids.   The romantic historians of
Ireland describe the *Suire* as playing round the ships of the Milesians when
on their passage to that Island.

FAIRY LEGENDS.

THE DULLAHAN.

"Then wonder not at *headless folk*,
  Since every day you greet 'em;
Nor treat old stories as a joke,
  When fools you daily meet 'em."—*The Legendary.*

"Says the friar, 't is strange headless horses should trot."
                                          OLD SONG.

THE DULLAHAN.

THE GOOD WOMAN.

XXVI.

In a pleasant and not unpicturesque valley of the White Knight's Country, at the foot of the Galtee mountains, lived Larry Dodd and his wife Nancy. They rented a cabin and a few acres of land, which they cultivated with great care, and its crops rewarded their industry. They were independent and respected by their neighbours; they loved each other in a marriageable sort of way, and few couples had altogether more the appearance of comfort about them.

Larry was a hard working, and, occasionally, a hard drinking, Dutch-built, little man, with a fiddle head and a round stern; a steady-going straight-forward fellow, barring when he carried too much whiskey, which, it must be confessed, might occasionally prevent his walking the chalked line with perfect philomathical accuracy. He had a moist ruddy countenance, rather inclined to an expression of gravity, and particularly so in the morning; but, taken all together, he was gene-rally looked upon as a marvellously proper person, notwithstanding he had, every day in the year, a sort of unholy dew upon his face, even in the coldest weather, which gave rise to a supposition (amongst censorious persons, of course), that Larry was apt to indulge in strong and frequent potations. However, all men of talents have their faults, — indeed, who is without them ; — and as Larry, setting aside his domestic virtues and skill in farming, was decidedly the most distinguished breaker of horses for forty miles round, he must be in some degree excused, considering the inducements of " the stirrup cup," and the fox-hunting society in which he mixed, if he had also been the greatest drunkard in the county : but, in truth, this was not the case.

Larry was a man of mixed habits, as well in his mode of life and his drink, as in his costume. His dress accorded well with his character — a sort of half-and-half between farmer and horse-jockey. He wore a blue coat of coarse cloth, with short skirts, and a stand-up collar ; his waistcoat was red, and his lower habiliments were made of leather, which in course of time had shrunk so much, that they fitted like a second skin ; and long use had absorbed their moisture to such a degree, that they made a strange sort of crackling noise as he walked along. A hat covered with oil skin ; a cutting-whip, all worn and jagged at the end ; a pair of second-hand, or, to speak more correctly, second-footed, greasy top-boots, that seemed never to have imbibed a refreshing draught of Warren's blacking of matchless lustre ! — and one spur without a rowel, completed the every-day dress of Larry Dodd.

Thus equipped was Larry returning from Ca-
shel, mounted on a rough-coated and wall-eyed
nag, though, notwithstanding these and a few other
trifling blemishes, a well-built animal; having
just purchased the said nag, with a fancy that he
could make his own money again of his bargain,
and, may be, turn an odd penny more by it at the
ensuing Kildorrery fair. Well pleased with himself, he trotted fair and easy along the road in the
delicious and lingering twilight of a lovely June
evening, thinking of nothing at all, only whistling,
and wondering would horses always be so low.
" If they go at this rate," said he to himself, "for
half nothing, and that paid in butter buyer's notes,
who would be the fool to walk?" This very
thought, indeed, was passing in his mind, when
his attention was roused by a woman pacing
quickly by the side of his horse, and hurrying on,
as if endeavouring to reach her destination before
the night closed in. Her figure, considering the
long strides she took, appeared to be under the
common size — rather of the dumpy order; but
further, as to whether the damsel was young or
old, fair or brown, pretty or ugly, Larry could
form no precise notion, from her wearing a large
cloak (the usual garb of the female Irish peasant),
the hood of which was turned up, and completely
concealed every feature.

Enveloped in this mass of dark and concealing
drapery, the strange woman, without much exer-
tion, contrived to keep up with Larry Dodd's steed
for some time, when his master very civilly offered
her a lift behind him, as far as he was going her
way. " Civility begets civility," they say; how-

ever he received no answer; and thinking that the lady's silence proceeded only from bashfulness, like a man of true gallantry, not a word more said Larry until he pulled up by the side of a gap, and then says he, " *Ma colleen beg* [1], just jump up behind me, without a word more, though never a one have you spoke, and I'll take you save and sound through the lonesome bit of road that is before us."

She jumped at the offer, sure enough, and up with her on the back of the horse as light as a feather. In an instant there she was seated up behind Larry, with her hand and arm buckled round his waist holding on.

" I hope you're comfortable there, my dear," said Larry, in his own good-humoured way; but there was no answer; and on they went — trot, trot, trot — along the road; and all was so still and so quiet, that you might have heard the sound of the hoofs on the limestone a mile off: for that matter there was nothing else to hear except the moaning of a distant stream, that kept up a continued *cronane* [2], like a nurse *hushoing*. Larry, who had a keen ear, did not, however, require so profound a silence to detect the click of one of the shoes. " 'T is only loose the shoe is," said he to his companion, as they were just entering on the lonesome bit of road of which he had before spoken. Some old trees, with huge trunks, all covered, and irregular branches festooned with ivy, grew over a dark pool of water, which had been formed as a drinking-place for cattle; and in the distance

[1] My little girl.
[2] A monotonous song; a drowsy humming noise.

was seen the majestic head of Gaultee-more. Here the horse, as if in grateful recognition, made a dead halt ; and Larry, not knowing what vicious tricks his new purchase might have, and unwilling that through any odd chance the young woman should get *spilt* in the water, dismounted, thinking to lead the horse quietly by the pool.

" By the piper's luck, that always found what he wanted," said Larry, recollecting himself, " I've a nail in my pocket : 'tis not the first time I've put on a shoe, and may be it won't be the last ; for here is no want of paving-stones to make hammers in plenty."

No sooner was Larry off than off with a spring came the young woman just at his side. Her feet touched the ground without making the least noise in life, and away she bounded like an ill-mannered wench, as she was, without saying " by your leave," or no matter what else. She seemed to glide rather than run, not along the road, but across a field, up towards the old ivy-covered walls of Kilnaslattery church — and a pretty church it was.

" Not so fast, if you please, young woman — not so fast," cried Larry, calling after her : but away she ran, and Larry followed, his leathern garment, already described, crack, crick, crackling at every step he took. " Where's my wages ?" said Larry : " *Thorum pog, ma colleen oge* [1], — sure I've earned a kiss from your pair of pretty lips — and I'll have it too !" But she went on faster and faster, regardless of these and other

---

[1] Give me a kiss, my young girl.

flattering speeches from her pursuer: at last she came to the churchyard wall, and then over with her in an instant.

"Well, she's a mighty smart creature anyhow. To be sure, how neat she steps upon her pasterns! Did any one ever see the like of that before;— but I'll not be baulked by any woman that ever wore a head, or any ditch either," exclaimed Larry, as with a desperate bound he vaulted, scrambled, and tumbled over the wall into the churchyard. Up he got from the elastic sod of a newly made grave in which Tade Leary that morning was buried—rest his soul!—and on went Larry, stumbling over head-stones and foot-stones, over old graves and new graves, pieces of coffins, and the skulls and bones of dead men—the Lord save us!—that were scattered about there as plenty as paving-stones; floundering amidst great overgrown dock-leaves and brambles that, with their long prickly arms, tangled round his limbs, and held him back with a fearful grasp. Mean time the merry wench in the cloak moved through all these obstructions as evenly and as gaily as if the churchyard, crowded up as it was with graves and gravestones (for people came to be buried there from far and near), had been the floor of a dancing-room. Round and round the walls of the old church she went. "I'll just wait," said Larry, seeing this, and thinking it all nothing but a trick to frighten him; "when she comes round again, if I don't take the kiss, I won't, that's all, —and here she is!" Larry Dodd sprang forward with open arms, and clasped in them—a woman, it is true — but a woman without any lips to kiss, by reason of her having no head!

"Murder!" cried he. "Well, that accounts for her not speaking." Having uttered these words, Larry himself became dumb with fear and astonishment; his blood seemed turned to ice, and a dizziness came over him; and, staggering like a drunken man, he rolled against the broken window of the ruin, horrified at the conviction that he had actually held a Dullahan in his embrace!

When he recovered to something like a feeling of consciousness, he slowly opened his eyes, and then, indeed, a scene of wonder burst upon him. In the midst of the ruin stood an old wheel of torture, ornamented with heads, like Cork gaol, when the heads of Murty Sullivan and other gentlemen were stuck upon it. This was plainly visible in the strange light which spread itself around. It was fearful to behold, but Larry could not choose but look, for his limbs were powerless through the wonder and the fear. Useless as it was, he would have called for help, but his tongue cleaved to the roof of his mouth, and not one word could he say. In short, there was Larry, gazing through a shattered window of the old church, with eyes bleared and almost starting from their sockets; his breast rested on the thickness of the wall, over which, on one side, his head and outstretched neck projected, and on the other, although one toe touched the ground, it derived no support from thence: terror, as it were, kept him balanced. Strange noises assailed his ears, until at last they tingled painfully to the sharp clatter of little bells, which kept up a continued ding — ding — ding — ding : marrowless bones rattled and clanked, and the deep and solemn sound of a great bell came booming on the night wind.

> 'T was a spectre rung
> That bell when it swung —
>   Swing-swang !
> And the chain it squeaked,
> And the pulley creaked,
>   Swing-swang !
>
> And with every roll
> Of the deep death toll
>   Ding-dong !
> The hollow vault rang
> As the clapper went bang,
>   Ding-dong !

It was strange music to dance by; nevertheless, moving to it, round and round the wheel set with skulls, were well dressed ladies and gentlemen, and soldiers and sailors, and priests and publicans, and jockeys and jennys, but all without their heads. Some poor skeletons, whose bleached bones were ill covered by moth-eaten palls, and who were not admitted into the ring, amused themselves by bowling their brainless noddles at one another, which seemed to enjoy the sport beyond measure.

Larry did not know what to think; his brains were all in a mist; and losing the balance which he had so long maintained, he fell head foremost into the midst of the company of Dullahans.

" I'm done for and lost for ever," roared Larry, with his heels turned towards the stars, and souse down he came.

" Welcome, Larry Dodd, welcome," cried every head, bobbing up and down in the air. " A drink for Larry Dodd," shouted they, as with one voice, that quavered like a shake on the bagpipes. No sooner said than done, for a player at heads, catching his own as it was bowled at him, for fear of its going astray, jumped up, put the head, without a word, under his left arm, and, with the right stretched out, presented a brimming cup to Larry, who, to show his manners, drank it off like a man.

" 'Tis capital stuff," he would have said, which surely it was, but he got no further than cap, when decapitated was he, and his head began dancing over his shoulders like those of the rest of the party. Larry, however, was not the first man who lost his head through the temptation of looking at the bottom of a brimming cup. Nothing more did he remember clearly,—for it seems body and head being parted is not very favourable to thought, — but a great hurry scurry with the noise of carriages and the cracking of whips.

When his senses returned, his first act was to put up his hand to where his head formerly grew, and to his great joy there he found it still. He then shook it gently, but his head remained firm enough, and somewhat assured at this, he proceeded to open his eyes and look around him. It was broad daylight, and in the old church of Kilnaslattery he found himself lying, with that head, the loss of which he had anticipated, quietly resting, poor youth, " upon the lap of earth." Could it have been an ugly dream? " Oh no," said Larry, " a dream could never have brought me here, stretched on the flat of my back, with that death's head and cross marrow bones forenenting me on the fine old tombstone there that was *faced* by Pat Kearney [1] of Kilcrea — but where is the horse?"   He got up slowly, every joint aching with pain from the bruises he had received, and went to the pool of water, but no horse was there. " 'Tis home I must go," said Larry, with a rueful countenance ; " but how will I face Nancy ? — what will I tell her about the horse, and the seven I. O. U.'s that he cost me ?—'Tis them Dullahans that have made their own of him from me — the horsestealing robbers of the world, that have no fear of the gallows ! — but what's gone is gone, that's a clear case !" — so saying, he turned his steps homewards, and arrived at his cabin about noon without encountering any further adventures.   There he found Nancy, who, as he expected, looked as black as a thundercloud at him for being out all night.   She listened to the marvellous relation which he gave with exclamations of astonishment, and, when he had concluded, of grief, at the loss of the horse that he had paid for like an honest man with seven I. O. U.'s, three of which she knew to be as good as gold.

" But what took you up to the old church at all, out of the road, and at that time of the night, Larry ?" enquired his wife.

Larry looked like a criminal for whom there was no reprieve ; he scratched his head for an excuse, but not one could he muster up, so he knew not what to say.

---

[1] *Faced,* so written by the Chantrey of Kilcrea, for "*fecit.*"

" Oh ! Larry, Larry," muttered Nancy, after waiting some time for his answer, her jealous fears during the pause rising like barm ; " 'tis the very same way with you as with any other man — you are all alike for that matter — I've no pity for you — but, confess the truth !"

Larry shuddered at the tempest which he perceived was about to break upon his devoted head. " Nancy," said he, " I do confess : — it was a young woman without any head that ——"

His wife heard no more. " A woman I knew it was," cried she ; " but a woman without a head, Larry ! — well, it is long before Nancy Gollagher ever thought it would come to that with her ! — that she would be left dissolute and alone here by her *baste* of a husband, for a woman without a head ! — O father, father ! and O mother, mother ! it is well you are low to-day ! — that you don't see this affliction and disgrace to your daughter that you reared decent and tender.

" O Larry, you villain, you'll be the death of your lawful wife going after such O — O — O —"

" Well," says Larry, putting his hands in his coat-pockets, " least said is soonest mended. Of the young woman I know no more than I do of Moll Flanders : but this I know, that a woman without a head may well be called a Good Woman, because she has no tongue !"

How this remark operated on the matrimonial dispute history does not inform us. It is, however, reported that the lady had the last word.

HANLON'S MILL.

XXVII.

ONE fine summer's evening Michael Noonan went over to Jack Brien's the shoemaker, at Ballyduff, for the pair of brogues which Jack was mending for him. It was a pretty walk the way he took, but very lonesome; all along by the riverside, down under the oak-wood, till he came to Hanlon's mill, that used to be, but that had gone to ruin many a long year ago.

Melancholy enough the walls of that same mill looked; the great old wheel, black with age, all covered over with moss and ferns, and the bushes all hanging down about it. There it stood, silent and motionless; and a sad contrast it was to its former busy clack, with the stream which once gave it use rippling idly along.

Old Hanlon was a man that had great knowledge of all sorts; there was not an herb that grew in the field but he could tell the name of it and its use, out of a big book he had written, every word of it in the real Irish *karacter*. He kept a school once, and could teach the Latin; that surely is a blessed tongue all over the wide world; and I hear tell as how " the great Burke " went to school to him. Master Edmund lived up at the old house there, which was then in the family, and it was the Nagles that got it afterwards, but they sold it.

But it was Michael Noonan's walk I was about speaking of. It was fairly between lights, the day was clean gone, and the moon was not yet up, when Mick was walking smartly across the Inch. Well, he heard, coming down out of the wood, such blowing of horns and hallooing, and the cry of all the hounds in the world, and he thought they were coming after him; and the golloping of the horses, and the voice of the whipper-in, and he shouting out, just like the fine old song,

"Hallo Piper, Lilly, agus Finder;"

and the echo over from the grey rock across the river giving back every word as plainly as it was spoken. But nothing could Mick see, and the shouting and hallooing following him every step of the way till he got up to Jack Brien's door; and he was certain, too, he heard the clack of old Hanlon's mill going, through all the clatter. To be sure, he ran as fast as fear and his legs could carry him, and never once looked behind him, well knowing that the Duhallow hounds were out in quite another quarter that day, and that nothing good could come out of the noise of Hanlon's mill.

Well, Michael Noonan got his brogues, and well heeled they were, and well pleased was he with them; when who should be seated at Jack Brien's before him, but a gossip of his, one Darby Haynes, a mighty decent man, that had a horse and car of his own, and that used to be travelling with it, taking loads like the royal mail coach between Cork and Limerick; and when he was at home, Darby was a near neighbour of Michael Noonan's.

"Is it home you're going with the brogues this blessed night?" said Darby to him.

"Where else would it be?" replied Mick: "but, by my word, 't is not across the Inch back again I'm going, after all I heard coming here; 't is to no good that old Hanlon's mill is busy again."

"True, for you," said Darby; "and may be you'd take the horse and car home for me, Mick, by way of company, as 't is along the road you go. I'm waiting here to see a sister's son of mine that I expect from Kilcoleman." "That same I'll do," answered Mick, "with a thousand welcomes." So Mick drove the car fair and easy, knowing that the poor beast had come off a long journey; and Mick — God reward him for it — was always tender-hearted and good to the dumb creatures.

The night was a beautiful one; the moon was better than a quarter old; and Mick, looking up at her, could not help bestowing a blessing on her beautiful face, shining down so sweetly upon the gentle Awbeg. He had now got out of the open road, and had come to where the trees grew on each side of it: he proceeded for some space in the chequered light which the moon gave through them. At one time, when a big old tree got between him and the moon, it was so dark, that he could hardly see the horse's head; then, as he passed on, the moonbeams would stream through the open boughs and variegate the road with light and shade. Mick was lying down in the car at his ease, having got clear of the plantation, and was watching the bright piece of a moon in a little pool at the road side, when he saw it disappear all of a sudden as if a great cloud came over the sky. He turned round on his elbow to see if it was so; but how was Mick astonished at finding, close along-side of the car, a great high black coach drawn by six black horses, with long black tails reaching almost down to the ground, and a coachman dressed all in black sitting up on the box. But what surprised Mick the most was, that he could see no sign of a head either upon coachman or horses. It swept rapidly by him, and he could perceive the horses raising their feet as if they were in a fine slinging trot, the coachman touching them up with his long whip, and the wheels spinning round like hoddy-doddies; still he could hear no noise, only the regular step of his gossip Darby's horse, and the squeaking of the gudgeons of the car, that were as good as lost entirely for want of a little grease.

Poor Mick's heart almost died within him, but he said nothing, only looked on; and the black coach swept away, and was soon lost among some distant trees. Mick saw nothing more of it, or, indeed, of any thing else. He got home just as the moon was going down behind Mount Hillery — took the tackling off the horse, turned the beast out in the field for the night, and got to his bed.

Next morning, early, he was standing at the road-side, thinking of all that had happened the night before, when he saw Dan Madden, that was Mr. Wrixon's huntsman, coming on the master's best horse down the hill, as hard as ever he went at the tail of the hounds. Mick's mind instantly misgave him that all was not right, so he stood out in the very middle of the road, and caught hold of Dan's bridle when he came up.

"Mick, dear — for the love of God! don't stop me," cried Dan.

"Why, what's the hurry?" said Mick.

"Oh, the master!—he's off,—he's off—he'll never cross a horse again till the day of judgment!"

"Why, what would ail his honour?" said Mick; "sure it is no later than yesterday morning that I was talking to him, and he stout and hearty; and says he to me, Mick, says he — "

"Stout and hearty was he?" answered Madden; "and was he not out with me in the kennel last night, when I was feeding the dogs; and didn't he come out to the stable, and give a ball to Peg Pullaway with his own hand, and tell me he'd ride the old General to-day; and sure," said Dan, wiping his eyes with the sleeve of his coat, "who'd have thought that the first thing I'd see this morning was the mistress standing at my bed-side, and bidding me get up and ride off like fire for Doctor Galway; for the master had got a fit, and" — poor Dan's grief choked his voice — "oh, Mick! if you have a heart in you, run over yourself, or send the gossoon for Kate Finnigan, the midwife; she's a cruel skilful woman, and may be she might save the master, till I get the doctor."

Dan struck his spurs into the hunter, and Michael Noonan flung off his newly-mended brogues,

and cut across the fields to Kate Finnigan's; but
neither the doctor nor Katty was of any avail,
and the next night's moon saw Ballygibblin —
and more's the pity — a house of mourning.

THE DEATH COACH.

XXVIII.

'T is midnight! — how gloomy and dark!
  By Jupiter there 's not a star! —
'T is fearful! — 't is awful! — and hark!
  What sound is that comes from afar?

Still rolling and rumbling, that sound
  Makes nearer and nearer approach;
Do I tremble, or is it the ground? —
  Lord save us! — what is it? — a coach! —

A coach! — but that coach has no head;
  And the horses are headless as it:
Of the driver the same may be said,
  And the passengers inside who sit.

See the wheels! how they fly o'er the stones!
  And whirl, as the whip it goes crack:
Their spokes are of dead men's thigh bones,
  And the pole is the spine of the back!

The hammer-cloth, shabby display,
  Is a pall rather mildew'd by damps;
And to light this strange coach on its way,
  Two hollow sculls hang up for lamps!

From the gloom of Rathcooney church-yard,
    They dash down the hill of Glanmire;
Pass Lota in gallop as hard
    As if horses were never to tire!

With people thus headless 't is fun
    To drive in such furious career;
Since *headlong* their horses can't run,
    Nor coachman be *headdy* from beer.

Very steep is the Tivoli lane,
    But up-hill to them is as down;
Nor the charms of Woodhill can detain
    These Dullahans rushing to town.

Could they feel as I 've felt — in a song —
    A spell that forbade them depart;
They 'd a lingering visit prolong,
    And after their head lose their heart!

No matter! — 't is past twelve o'clock;
    Through the streets they sweep on like the
        wind,
And, taking the road to Blackrock,
    Cork city is soon left behind.

Should they hurry thus reckless along,
    To supper instead of to bed,
The landlord will surely be wrong,
    If he charge it at so much a head!

Yet mine host may suppose them too poor
    To bring to his wealth an increase;
As till now, all who drove to his door,
    Possess'd at least *one crown* a-piece.

Up the Deadwoman's hill they are roll'd;
    Boreenmannah is quite out of sight;
Ballintemple they reach, and behold!
    At its church-yard they stop and alight.

" Who's there?" said a voice from the ground
    " We 've no room, for the place is quite full."
" O! room must be speedily found,
    For we come from the parish of Skull.

" Though Murphys and Crowleys appear
    On headstones of deep-letter'd pride;
Though Scannels and Murleys lie here,
    Fitzgeralds and Toomies beside;

" Yet here for the night we lie down,
    To-morrow we speed on the gale;
For having no heads of our own,
    We seek the Old Head of Kinsale."

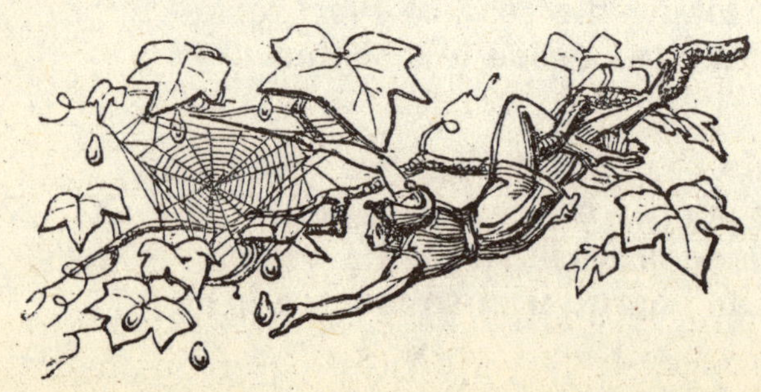

THE HEADLESS HORSEMAN.

XXIX.

"God speed you, and a safe journey this night to you, Charley," ejaculated the master of the little sheebeen house at Ballyhooley after his old friend and good customer, Charley Culnane, who at length had turned his face homewards, with the prospect of as dreary a ride and as dark a night as ever fell upon the Blackwater, along the banks of which he was about to journey.

Charley Culnane knew the country well, and moreover, was as bold a rider as any Mallow-boy that ever *rattled* a four-year-old upon Drumrue race-course. He had gone to Fermoy in the morning, as well for the purpose of purchasing some ingredients required for the Christmas dinner by his wife, as to gratify his own vanity by having new reins fitted to his snaffle, in which he intended showing off the old mare at the approaching St. Stephen's day hunt.

Charley did not get out of Fermoy until late; for although he was not one of your "nasty particular sort of fellows" in any thing that related to the common occurrences of life, yet in all the appointments connected with hunting, riding, leaping, in short, in whatever was connected with the old mare, "Charley," the saddlers said, "was the devil to *plāse*." An illustration of this fastidiousness was afforded by his going such a distance for a snaffle bridle. Mallow was full twelve miles nearer " Charley's farm " (which lay just three quarters of a mile below Carrick) than Fermoy ; but Charley had quarrelled with all the Mallow saddlers, from hard-working and hard-drinking Tim Clancey, up to Mr. Ryan, who wrote himself " Saddler to the Duhallow Hunt;" and no one could content him in all particulars but honest Michael Twomey of Fermoy, who used to assert — and who will doubt it — that he could stitch a saddle better than the lord-lieutenant, although they made him all as one as king over Ireland.

This delay in the arrangement of the snaffle bridle did not allow Charley Culnane to pay so long a visit as he had at first intended to his old friend and gossip, Con Buckley, of the " Harp of Erin."   Con, however, knew the value of time, and insisted upon Charley making good use of what he had to spare. " I won't bother you waiting for water, Charley, because I think you 'll have enough of that same before you get home ; so drink off your liquor, man. It 's as good *parliament* as ever a gentleman tasted, ay, and holy church too, for it will bear ' x *waters*,' and carry the bead after that, may be."

Charley, it must be confessed, nothing loth, drank success to Con, and success to the jolly " Harp of Erin," with its head of beauty and its strings of the hair of gold, and to their better acquaintance, and so on, from the bottom of his soul, until the bottom of the bottle reminded him that Carrick was at the bottom of the hill on the other side of Castletown Roche, and that he had got no

further on his journey than his gossip's at Ballyhooley, close to the big gate of Convamore. Catching hold of his oil-skin hat, therefore, whilst Con
Buckley went to the cupboard for another bottle
of the " real stuff," he regularly, as it is termed,
bolted from his friend's hospitality, darted to the
stable, tightened his girths, and put the old mare
into a canter towards home.

The road from Ballyhooley to Carrick follows
pretty nearly the course of the Blackwater, occasionally diverging from the river and passing
through rather wild scenery, when contrasted with
the beautiful seats that adorn its banks. Charley
cantered gaily, regardless of the rain, which, as his
friend Con had anticipated, fell in torrents: the
good woman's currants and raisins were carefully
packed between the folds of his yeomanry cloak,
which Charley, who was proud of showing that
he belonged to the " Royal Mallow Light Horse
Volunteers," always strapped to the saddle before
him, and took care never to destroy the military
effect of by putting it on.—Away he went singing
like a thrush —

> " Sporting, belleing, dancing, drinking,
> Breaking windows — (*hiccup!*) — sinking,
> Ever raking — never thinking,
>   Live the rakes of Mallow.
>
> Spending faster than it comes,
> Beating — (*hiccup, hic*), and duns,
> Duhallow's true-begotten sons,
>   Live the rakes of Mallow."

Notwithstanding that the visit to the jolly " Harp
of Erin " had a little increased the natural com-

placency of his mind, the drenching of the new snaffle reins began to disturb him; and then followed a train of more anxious thoughts than even were occasioned by the dreaded defeat of the pride of his long-anticipated *turn out* on St. Stephen's day. In an hour of good fellowship, when his heart was warm, and his head not over cool, Charley had backed the old mare against Mr. Jephson's bay filly Desdemona for a neat hundred, and he now felt sore misgivings as to the prudence of the match. In a less gay tone he continued

> " Living short, but merry lives,
> Going where the devil drives,
> Keeping——"

" Keeping " he muttered, as the old mare had reduced her canter to a trot at the bottom of Kilcummer Hill. Charley's eye fell on the old walls that belonged, in former times, to the Templars: but the silent gloom of the ruin was broken only by the heavy rain which splashed and pattered on the gravestones. He then looked up at the sky, to see if there was, among the clouds, any hopes for mercy on his new snaffle reins ; and no sooner were his eyes lowered, than his attention was arrested by an object so extraordinary as almost led him to doubt the evidence of his senses. The head, apparently, of a white horse, with short cropped ears, large open nostrils and immense eyes, seemed rapidly to follow him. No connection with body, legs, or rider, could possibly be traced — the head advanced — Charley's old mare, too, was moved at this unnatural sight, and snorting violently, increased her trot up the hill. The head moved forward, and passed on: Charley pursuing it with astonished gaze, and wondering by what means, and for what purpose, this detached head thus proceeded through the air, did not perceive the corresponding body until he was suddenly started by finding it close at his side. Charley turned to examine what was thus so sociably jogging on with him, when a most unexampled apparition presented itself to his view. A figure, whose height (judging as well as the obscurity of the night would permit him) he computed to be at least eight feet, was seated on the body and legs of a white horse full eighteen hands and a half high. In this measurement Charley could not be mistaken, for his own mare was exactly fifteen hands, and the body that thus jogged alongside he could at once determine, from his practice in horseflesh, was at least three hands and a half higher.

After the first feeling of astonishment, which found vent in the exclamation " I'm sold now for ever !" was over ; the attention of Charley, being a keen sportsman, was naturally directed to this extraordinary body, and having examined it with the eye of a connoisseur, he proceeded to reconnoitre the figure so unusually mounted, who had hitherto remained perfectly mute. Wishing to see whether his companion's silence proceeded from bad temper, want of conversational powers, or from a distaste to water, and the fear that the opening of his mouth might subject him to have it filled by the rain, which was then drifting in violent gusts against them, Charley endeavoured to catch a sight of his companion's face, in order to form an opinion on that point.   But his vision failed in carrying him further than the top of the collar of the figure's coat, which was a scarlet single-breasted hunting frock, having a waist of a very old fashioned cut reaching to the saddle, with two huge shining buttons at about a yard distance behind.   " I ought to see further than this, too," thought Charley, " although he is mounted on his high horse, like my cousin Darby, who was made barony constable last week, unless 'tis Con's whiskey that has blinded me entirely." However, see further he could not, and after straining his eyes for a considerable time to no purpose, he exclaimed, with pure vexation, " By the big bridge of Mallow, it is no head at all he has !"

" Look again, Charley Culnane," said a hoarse voice, that seemed to proceed from under the right arm of the figure.

Charley did look again, and now in the proper place, for he clearly saw, under the aforesaid right arm, that head from which the voice had proceeded, and such a head no mortal ever saw before. It looked like a large cream cheese hung round with black puddings: no speck of colour enlivened the ashy paleness of the depressed features ; the skin lay stretched over the unearthly surface, almost like the parchment head of a drum.   Two fiery eyes of prodigious circumference, with a strange and irregular motion, flashed like meteors upon Charley, and to complete all, a mouth reached from either extremity of two ears, which peeped forth from under a profusion of matted locks of lustreless blackness. This head, which the figure had evidently hitherto concealed from Charley's eyes, now burst upon his view in all its hideousness. Charley, although a lad of proverbial courage in the county of Cork, yet could not but feel his nerves a little shaken by this unexpected visit from the headless horseman, whom he considered his fellow traveller must be. The cropped-eared head of the gigantic horse moved steadily forward, always keeping from six to eight yards in advance. The horseman, unaided by whip or spur, and disdaining the use of stirrups, which dangled uselessly from the saddle, followed at a trot by Charley's side, his hideous head now lost behind the lappet of his coat, now starting forth in all its horror as the motion of the horse caused his arm to move to and fro. The ground shook under the weight of its supernatural burthen, and the water in the pools became agitated into waves as he trotted by them.

On they went — heads without bodies, and bodies without heads. — The deadly silence of night was broken only by the fearful clattering of hoofs, and the distant sound of thunder, which rumbled above the mystic hill of Cecaune a Mona Finnea. Charley, who was naturally a merry-hearted, and rather a talkative fellow, had hitherto felt tongue-tied by apprehension, but finding his companion showed no evil disposition towards him, and having become somewhat more reconciled to the Patago-nian dimensions of the horseman and his headless steed, plucked up all his courage, and thus ad-dressed the stranger : —

" Why, then, your honour rides mighty well without the stirrups !"

" Humph," growled the head from under the horseman's right arm.

" 'Tis not an over civil answer," thought Charley ; " but no matter, he was taught in one of them riding-houses, may be, and thinks nothing at all about bumping his leather breeches at the rate of ten miles an hour. I'll try him on the other tack. Ahem !" said Charley, clearing his throat, and feeling at the same time rather daunted at this second attempt to establish a conversation. " Ahem ! that's a mighty neat coat of your honour's, although 'tis a little too long in the waist for the present cut."

" Humph," growled again the head.

This second humph was a terrible thump in the face to poor Charley, who was fairly bothered to know what subject he could start that would prove more agreeable. " 'Tis a sensible head," thought Charley, " although an ugly one, for 'tis plain enough the man does not like flattery." A third attempt, however, Charley was determined to make, and having failed in his observations as to the riding and coat of his fellow-traveller, thought he would just drop a trifling allusion to the wonderful headless horse, that was jogging on so sociably beside his old mare ; and as Charley was considered about Carrick to be very knowing in horses, besides being a full private in the Royal Mallow Light Horse Volunteers, which were every one of them mounted like real Hessians, he felt rather sanguine as to the result of his third attempt.

" To be sure, that's a brave horse your honour rides," recommenced the persevering Charley.

" You may say that, with your own ugly mouth," growled the head.

Charley, though not much flattered by the compliment, nevertheless chuckled at his success in obtaining an answer, and thus continued :—

" May be your honour wouldn't be after riding him across the country ?"

" Will you try me, Charley ?" said the head, with an inexpressible look of ghastly delight.

" Faith, and that's what I'd do," responded Charley, " only I'm afraid, the night being so dark, of laming the old mare, and I've every halfpenny of a hundred pounds on her heels."

This was true enough ; Charley's courage was nothing dashed at the headless horseman's proposal ; and there never was a steeple-chase, nor a fox-chase, riding or leaping in the country, that Charley Culnane was not at it, and foremost in it.

" Will you take my word," said the man who carried his head so snugly under his right arm, " for the safety of your mare ?"

" Done," said Charley ; and away they started, helter, skelter, over every thing, ditch and wall, pop, pop, the old mare never went in such style, even in broad daylight : and Charley had just the start of his companion, when the hoarse voice called out " Charley Culnane, Charley, man, stop for your life, stop !"

Charley pulled up hard. " Ay," said he, " you may beat me by the head, because it always goes so much before you ; but if the bet was neck-and-neck, and that's the go between the old mare and Desdemona, I'd win it hollow!"

It appeared as if the stranger was well aware of what was passing in Charley's mind, for he suddenly broke out quite loquacious.

"Charley Culnane," says he, "you have a stout soul in you, and are every inch of you a good rider. I've tried you, and I ought to know; and that's the sort of man for my money. A hundred years it is since my horse and I broke our necks at the bottom of Kilcummer hill, and ever since I have been trying to get a man that dared to ride with me and never found one before. Keep, as you have always done, at the tail of the hounds, never baulk a ditch, nor turn away from a stone wall, and the headless horseman will never desert you nor the old mare."

Charley, in amazement, looked towards the stranger's right arm, for the purpose of seeing in his face whether or not he was in earnest, but behold! the head was snugly lodged in the huge pocket of the horseman's scarlet hunting-coat. The horse's head had ascended perpendicularly above them, and his extraordinary companion, rising quickly after his avant courier, vanished from the astonished gaze of Charley Culnane.

Charley, as may be supposed, was lost in wonder, delight, and perplexity; the pelting rain, the wife's pudding, the new snaffle — even the match against squire Jephson — all were forgotten; nothing could he think of, nothing could he talk of, but the headless horseman. He told it, directly that he got home, to Judy; he told it the following morning to all the neighbours; and he told it to the hunt on St. Stephen's day: but what provoked him after all the pains he took in describing the head, the horse, and the man, was that one and all attributed the creation of the headless horseman to his friend Con Buckley's " X water parliament." This, however, should be told, that Charley's old mare beat Mr. Jephson's bay filly, Desdemona, by Diamond, and Charley pocketed his cool hundred; and if he didn't win by means of the headless horseman, I am sure I don't know any other reason for his doing so.

Dullahan or Dulachan (oublacaí) signifies a dark sullen person. The word *Durrachan* or *Dullahan,* by which in some places the goblin is known, has the same signification. It comes from *Dorr* or *Durr,* anger, or *Durrach,* malicious, fierce, &c. — *M.S. communication from the late* Mr. Edward O'Reilly.

The correctness of this last etymology may be questioned, as oub black, is evidently a component part of the word.

The Death Coach, or Headless Coach and Horses, is called in Ireland " *Coach a bower* ; " and its appearance is generally regarded as a sign of death, or an omen of some misfortune.

The belief in the appearance of headless people and horses appears to be, like most popular superstitions, widely extended.

In England, see the Spectator (No. 110.) for mention of a spirit that had appeared in the shape of a black horse without a head.

In Wales, the apparition of " *Fenyw heb un pen,*" the headless woman, and " *Ceffyl heb un pen* " the headless horse, are generally accredited." — *M.S. communication from* Miss Williams.

" The Irish Dullahan puts me in mind of a spectre at Drumlarick Castle, of no less a person than the Duchess of Queensberry, — ' Fair Killy, blooming, young, and gay ' — who, instead of setting fire to the world in mamma's chariot, amuses herself with wheeling her own head in a wheel barrow through the great gallery." — *M.S. communication from* Sir Walter Scott.

In Scotland, so recently as January, 1826, that veritable paper, the Glasgow Chronicle, records, upon the occasion of some silk-weavers being out of employment at Paisley, that " Visions have been seen of carts, caravans, and coaches, going up Gleniffer braes without horses, with horses without heads," &c.

Cervantes mentions tales of the " *Caballo sin cabeça* among the *cuentos de viejas con que se entretienen al fuego las dilatadas noches del invierno,*" &c.

" The people of Basse Bretagne believe, that when the death of any person is at hand, a hearse drawn by skeletons (which they call *carriquet au nankon*), and covered with a white sheet, passes by the house where the sick person lies, and the creaking of the wheels may be plainly heard." — *Journal des Sciences,* 1826, *communicated by* Dr. William Grimm.

See also *Thiele's Danske Folkesagn,* vol. iv. p. 66, &c.

FAIRY LEGENDS.

THE FIR DARRIG.

Whene'er such wanderers I meete,
  As from their night-sports they trudge home,
With counterfeiting voice I greete,
  And call them on, with me to roame
    Through woods, through lakes,
    Through bogs, through brakes;
  Or else, unseene, with them I go,
    All in the nicke,
    To play some tricke,
  And frolicke it, with ho, ho, ho!   *Old Song.*

DIARMID BAWN, THE PIPER.

XXX.

ONE stormy night Patrick Burke was seated in the chimney corner, smoking his pipe quite contentedly after his hard day's work; his two little boys were roasting potatoes in the ashes, while his rosy daughter held a splinter [1] to her mother, who, seated on a siesteen [2], was mending a rent in Patrick's old coat; and Judy, the maid, was singing merrily to the sound of her wheel, that kept up a beautiful humming noise, just like the sweet drone of a bagpipe. Indeed they all seemed quite contented and happy; for the storm howled without, and they were warm and snug within, by the side of a blazing turf fire. "I was just thinking," said Patrick, taking the dudeen from his mouth and giving it a rap on his thumb-nail to shake out the ashes — "I was just thinking how thankful we ought to be to have a snug bit of a cabin this pelting night over our heads, for in all my born days I never heard the like of it."

"And that's no lie for you, Pat," said his wife; "but, whisht; what noise is that I *hard?*" and she dropped her work upon her knees, and looked

---

[1] A splinter, or slip of bog-deal, which, being dipped in tallow, is used as a candle.

[2] Siesteen is a low block-like seat, made of straw bands firmly sewed or bound together.

fearfully towards the door. "The *Vargin* herself
defend us all!" cried Judy, at the same time rapidly making a pious sign on her forehead, "if
'tis not the banshee!"

"Hold your tongue, you fool," said Patrick,
"it's only the old gate swinging in the wind;"
and he had scarcely spoken, when the door was
assailed by a violent knocking. Molly began to
mumble her prayers, and Judy proceeded to mut-
ter over the muster-roll of saints; the youngsters
scampered off to hide themselves behind the settle-
bed; the storm howled louder and more fiercely
than ever, and the rapping was renewed with re-
doubled violence.

"Whisht, whisht!" said Patrick — "what a
noise ye're all making about nothing at all. Judy
a-roon, can't you go and see who's at the door?"
for, notwithstanding his assumed bravery, Pat
Burke preferred that the maid should open the
door.

"Why, then, is it me you're speaking to?"
said Judy, in the tone of astonishment; "and is
it cracked mad you are, Mister Burke; or is it,
may be, that you want me to be *rund* away with,
and made a horse of, like my grandfather was? —
the sorrow a step will I stir to open the door, if
you were as great a man again as you are, Pat
Burke."

"Bother you, then! and hold your tongue, and
I'll go myself." So saying, up got Patrick, and
made the best of his way to the door. "Who's
there?" said he, and his voice trembled mightily
all the while. In the name of Saint Patrick,
who's there?" " 'Tis I, Pat," answered a voice

which he immediately knew to be the young
squire's.   In a moment the door was opened, and
in walked a young man, with a gun in his hand,
and a brace of dogs at his heels.   " Your honour's
honour is quite welcome, entirely," said Patrick ;
who was a very civil sort of a fellow, especially
to his betters.   " Your honour's honour is quite
welcome ; and if ye'll be so condescending as to
demean yourself by taking off your wet jacket,
Molly can give ye a bran new blanket, and ye can
sit forenent the fire while the clothes are drying."
" Thank you, Pat," said the squire, as he wrapt
himself, like Mr. Weld, in the proffered blanket. [1]

" But what made you keep me so long at the
door ?"

" Why, then, your honour 'twas all along of
Judy, there, being so much afraid of the good
people ; and a good right she has, after what happened to her grandfather — the Lord rest his
soul !"

" And what was that, Pat ?" said the squire.

" Why, then, your honour must know that
Judy had a grandfather ; and he was *ould* Diarmid Bawn, the piper, as personable a looking
man as any in the five parishes he was ; and he
could play the pipes so sweetly, and make them
spake to such perfection, that it did one's heart
good to hear him. We never had any one, for
that matter, in this side of the country like him,
before or since, except James Gandsey, that is
own piper to Lord Headley — his honour's lord-
ship is the real good gentleman — and 'tis Mr.

1 See Weld's Killarney, 8vo ed. p. 228.

Gandsey's music that is the pride of Killarney lakes.   Well, as I was saying, Diarmid was Judy's grandfather, and he rented a small mountainy farm ; and he was walking about the fields one moonlight night, quite melancholy-like in himself for want of the *tobaccy ;* because, why, the river was flooded, and he could not get across to buy any, and Diarmid would rather go to bed without his supper than a whiff of the dudeen.   Well, your honour, just as he came to the old fort in the far field, what should he see ? — the Lord preserve us ! — but a large army of the good people, 'coutered for all the world just like the dragoons ! ' Are ye all ready ?' said a little fellow at their head dressed out like a general. ' No ;' said a little curmudgeon of a chap all dressed in red, from the crown of his cocked hat to the sole of his boot. ' No, general,' said he : ' if you don't get the Fir darrig a horse he must stay behind, and ye 'll lose the battle.''

" ' There's Diarmid Bawn,' said the general, pointing to Judy's grandfather, your honour, ' make a horse of him.'

" So with that master Fir darrig comes up to Diarmid, who, you may be sure, was in a mighty great fright ; but he determined, seeing there was no help for him, to put a bold face on the matter ; and so he began to cross himself, and to say some blessed words, that nothing bad could stand before.

" ' Is that what you 'd be after, you spalpeen ?' said the little red imp, at the same time grinning a horrible grin ; ' I 'm not the man to care a straw for either your words or your crossings.' So, without more to do, he gives poor Diarmid a rap with the flat side of his sword, and in a moment he was changed into a horse, with little Fir darrig stuck fast on his back.

" Away they all flew over the wide ocean, like so many wild geese, screaming and chattering all the time, till they came to Jamaica; and there they had a murdering fight with the good people of that country. Well, it was all very well with them, and they stuck to it manfully, and fought it out fairly, till one of the Jamaica men made a cut with his sword under Diarmid's left eye, and then, sir, your see, poor Diarmid lost his temper entirely, and he dashed into the very middle of them, with Fir darrig mounted upon his back, and he threw out his heels, and he whisked his tail about, and wheeled and turned round and round at such a rate, that he soon made a fair clearance of them, horse, foot, and dragoons. At last Diarmid's faction got the better, all through his means; and then they had such feasting and rejoicing, and gave Diarmid, who was the finest horse amongst them all, the best of every thing.

" ' Let every man take a hand of *tobaccy* for Diarmid Bawn,' said the general; and so they did; and away they flew, for 'twas getting near morning, to the old fort back again, and there they vanished like the mist from the mountain.

" When Diarmid looked about the sun was rising and he thought it was all a dream, till he saw a big rick of *tobaccy* in the old fort, and felt the blood running from his left eye: for sure enough he was wounded in the battle, and would have been *kilt* entirely, if it was n't for a gospel composed by Fat'..er Murphy that hung about his

neck ever since he had the scarlet fever ; and for
certain, it was enough to have given him another
scarlet fever to have had the little red man all
night on his back, whip and spur for the bare life.
However, there was the *tobaccy* heaped up in a
great heap by his side ; and he heard a voice, although he could see no one, telling him, ' That
'twas all his own, for his good behaviour in the
battle; and that whenever Fir darrig would want
a horse again he'd know where to find a clever
beast, as he never rode a better than Diarmid
Bawn.'   That's what he said, sir."

"Thank you, Pat," said the squire ; " it certainly is a wonderful story, and I am not surprised at Judy's alarm.   But now, as the storm
is over, and the moon shining brightly, I'll make
the best of my way home."   So saying, he dis-
robed himself of the blanket, put on his coat, and,
whistling his dogs, set off across the mountain ;
while Patrick stood at the door, bawling after
him, " May God and the blessed Virgin preserve
your honour, and keep ye from the good people ;
for 'twas of a moonlight night like this that Diarmid Bawn was made a horse of, for the Fir darrig to ride."

TEIGUE OF THE LEE

XXXI.

" I can't stop in the house — I won't stop in it for all the money that is buried in the old castle of Carrigrohan. If ever there was such a thing in the world ! — to be abused to my face night and day, and nobody to the fore doing it ! and then, if I'm angry, to be laughed at with a great roaring ho, ho, ho ! I won't stay in the house after to-night, if there was not another place in the country to put my head under." This angry soliloquy was pronounced in the hall of the old manor-house of Carrigrohan by John Sheehan. John was a new servant ; he had been only three days in the house, which had the character of being haunted, and in that short space of time he had been abused and laughed at, by a voice which sounded as if a man spoke with his head in a cask ; nor could he discover who was the speaker, or from whence the voice came. " I 'll not stop here," said John ; " and that ends the matter."

" Ho, ho, ho ! be quiet, John Sheehan, or else worse will happen to you."

John instantly ran to the hall window, as the words were evidently spoken by a person immediately outside, but no one was visible. He had scarcely placed his face at the pane of glass, when he heard another loud " Ho, ho, ho !" as if behind him in the hall; as quick as lightning he turned his head, but no living thing was to be seen.

"Ho, ho, ho, John!" shouted a voice that appeared to come from the lawn before the house; "do you think you'll see Teigue?—oh, never! as long as you live! so leave alone looking after him, and mind your business; there's plenty of company to dinner from Cork to be here to-day, and 'tis time you had the cloth laid."

"Lord bless us! there's more of it!—I'll never stay another day here," repeated John.

"Hold your tongue, and stay where you are quietly, and play no tricks on Mr. Pratt, as you did on Mr. Jervois about the spoons."

John Sheehan was confounded by this address from his invisible persecutor, but nevertheless he mustered courage enough to say—"Who are you?—come here, and let me see you, if you are a man;" but he received in reply only a laugh of unearthly derision, which was followed by a "Good-by—I'll watch you at dinner, John!"

"Lord between us and harm! this beats all! —I'll watch you at dinner!—maybe you will; —'tis the broad daylight, so 'tis no ghost; but this is a terrible place, and this is the last day I'll stay in it. How does he know about the spoons?—if he tells it, I'm a ruined man!— there was no living soul could tell it to him but Tim Barrett, and he's far enough off in the wilds of Botany Bay now, so how could he know it— I can't tell for the world! But what's that I see there at the corner of the wall!—'tis not a man!—oh, what a fool I am! 'tis only the old stump of a tree !— But this is a shocking place — I'll never stop in it, for I'll leave the house to-morrow; the very look of it is enough to frighten any one."

The mansion had certainly an air of desolation; it was situated in a lawn, which had nothing to break its uniform level, save a few tufts of nar-cissuses and a couple of old trees coeval with the building. The house stood at a short distance from the road, it was upwards of a century old, and Time was doing his work upon it; its walls were weather-stained in all colours, its roof show-ed various white patches, it had no look of com-fort; all was dim and dingy without, and within there was an air of gloom, of departed and de-parting greatness, which harmonised well with the exterior. It required all the exuberance of youth and of gaiety to remove the impression, almost amounting to awe, with which you trod the huge square hall, paced along the gallery which surrounded the hall, or explored the long rambling passages below stairs. The ball-room, as the large drawing-room was called, and several other apartments, were in a state of decay : the walls were stained with damp ; and I remember well the sensation of awe which I felt creeping over me when, boy as I was, and full of boyish life, and wild and ardent spirits, I descended to the vaults ; all without and within me became chilled beneath their dampness and gloom— their extent, too, terrified me ; nor could the merriment of my two schoolfellows, whose father, a respectable clergyman, rented the dwelling for a time, dispel the feelings of a romantic imagination until I once again ascended to the upper regions.

John had pretty well recovered himself as the dinner-hour approached, and the several guests arrived. They were all seated at table, and had begun to enjoy the excellent repast, when a voice was heard from the lawn : —

" Ho, ho, ho, Mr. Pratt, won't you give poor Teigue some dinner ? ho, ho, a fine company you have there, and plenty of every thing that's good ; sure you won't forget poor Teigue ? "

John dropped the glass he had in his hand.

" Who is that ? " said Mr. Pratt's brother, an officer of the artillery.

" That is Teigue," said Mr. Pratt, laughing, " whom you must often have heard me mention."

" And pray, Mr. Pratt," enquired another gentleman, " who *is* Teigue ? "

" That," he replied, " is more than I can tell. No one has ever been able to catch even a glimpse of him. I have been on the watch for a whole evening with three of my sons, yet, although his voice sometimes sounded almost in my ear, I could not see him. I fancied, indeed, that I saw a man in a white frieze jacket pass into the door from the garden to the lawn, but it could be only fancy, for I found the door locked, while the fellow, whoever he is, was laughing at our trouble. He visits us occasionally, and sometimes a long interval passes between his visits, as in the present case ; it is now nearly two years since we heard that hollow voice outside the window. He has never done any injury that we know of, and once when he broke a plate, he brought one back exactly like it."

" It is very extraordinary," said several of the company.

" But," remarked a gentleman to young Mr. Pratt, " your father said he broke a plate; how did he get it without your seeing him?"

" When he asks for some dinner, we put it outside the window and go away; whilst we watch he will not take it, but no sooner have we withdrawn than it is gone."

" How does he know that you are watching?"

" That's more than I can tell, but he either knows or suspects. One day my brothers Robert and James with myself were in our back parlour, which has a window into the garden, when he came outside and said, ' Ho, ho, ho! master James, and Robert, and Henry, give poor Teigue a glass of whiskey.' James went out of the room, filled a glass with whiskey, vinegar, and salt, and brought it to him. ' Here, Teigue,' said he, ' come for it now.' ' Well, put it down, then, on the step outside the window.' This was done, and we stood looking at it. ' There, now, go away,' he shouted. We retired, but still watched it. ' Ho, ho! you are watching Teigue; go out of the room, now, or I won't take it.' We went outside the door and returned, the glass was gone, and a moment after we heard him roaring and cursing frightfully. He took away the glass, but the next day the glass was on the stone step under the window, and there were crumbs of bread in the inside, as if he had put it in his pocket; from that time he was not heard till to-day."

"Oh," said the colonel, "I'll get a sight of him; you are not used to these things; an old soldier has the best chance; and as I shall finish my dinner with this wing, I'll be ready for him when he speaks next. — Mr. Bell, will you take a glass of wine with me?"

"Ho, ho! Mr. Bell," shouted Teigue. "Ho, ho! Mr. Bell, you were a quaker long ago. Ho, ho! Mr. Bell, you're a pretty boy;— a pretty quaker you were; and now you're no quaker, nor any thing else:— ho, ho! Mr. Bell. And there's Mr. Parkes: to be sure, Mr. Parkes looks mighty fine to-day, with his powdered head, and his grand silk stockings, and his bran new rakish-red waistcoat. — And there's Mr. Cole, — did you ever see such a fellow? a pretty company you've brought together, Mr. Pratt: kiln-dried quakers, butter-buying buckeens from Mallow-lane, and a drinking exciseman from the Coal-quay, to meet the great thundering artillery-general that is come out of the Indies, and is the biggest dust of them all."

"You scoundrel!" exclaimed the colonel: "I'll make you show yourself;" and snatching up his sword from a corner of the room, he sprang out of the window upon the lawn. In a moment a shout of laughter, so hollow, so unlike any human sound, made him stop, as well as Mr. Bell, who with a huge oak stick was close at the colonel's heels; others of the party followed on the lawn, and the remainder rose and went to the windows. "Come on, colonel," said Mr. Bell; "let us catch this impudent rascal."

"Ho, ho! Mr. Bell, here I am — here's Teigue

— why don't you catch him ? — Ho, ho ! colonel Pratt, what a pretty soldier you are to draw your sword upon poor Teigue, that never did any body harm."

" Let us see your face, you scoundrel," said the colonel.

" Ho, ho, ho ! — look at me — look at me : do you see the wind, colonel Pratt ? — you'll see Teigue as soon ; so go in and finish your dinner."

" If you're upon the earth I'll find you, you villain !" said the colonel, whilst the same unearthly shout of derision seemed to come from behind an angle of the building. " He's round that corner," said Mr. Bell — " run, run."

They followed the sound, which was continued at intervals along the garden wall, but could discover no human being ; at last both stopped to draw breath, and in an instant, almost at their ears, sounded the shout.

" Ho, ho, ho ! colonel Pratt, do you see Teigue now ? — do you hear him ? — Ho, ho, ho ! you're a fine colonel to follow the wind."

" Not that way, Mr. Bell—not that way ; come here," said the colonel.

" Ho, ho, ho ! what a fool you are ; do you think Teigue is going to show himself to you in the field, there ?   But, colonel, follow me if you can : — you a soldier ! — ho, ho, ho !"   The colonel was enraged — he followed the voice over hedge and ditch, alternately laughed at and taunted by the unseen object of his pursuit — (Mr. Bell, who was heavy, was soon thrown out), until at length, after being led a weary chase, he found himself at the top of the cliff, over that part of the river Lee which, from its great depth, and the blackness of its water, has received the name of Hell-hole. Here, on the edge of the cliff, stood the colonel out of breath, and mopping his forehead with his handkerchief, while the voice, which seemed close at his feet, exclaimed — " Now, colonel Pratt — now, if you're a soldier, here's a leap for you; — now look at Teigue — why don't you look at him? — Ho, ho, ho! Come along: you're warm, I'm sure, colonel Pratt, so come in and cool yourself; Teigue is going to have a swim!" The voice seemed as descending amongst the trailing ivy and brushwood which clothes this picturesque cliff nearly from top to bottom, yet it was impossible that any human being could have found footing. " Now, colonel, have you courage to take the leap? — Ho, ho, ho! what a pretty soldier you are. Good-by — I'll see you again in ten minutes above, at the house — look at your watch colonel: — there's a dive for you;" and a heavy plunge into the water was heard. The colonel stood still, but no sound followed, and he walked slowly back to the house, not quite half a mile from the Crag."

" Well, did you see Teigue?" said his brother, whilst his nephews, scarcely able to smother their laughter, stood by. — " Give me some wine," said the colonel. " I never was led such a dance in my life: the fellow carried me all round and round, till he brought me to the edge of the cliff, and then down he went into Hell-hole, telling me he'd be here in ten minutes: 'tis more than that now, but he's not come."

" Ho, ho, ho! colonel, is'nt he here? — Teigue

never told a lie in his life: but, Mr. Pratt, give me a drink and my dinner, and then good night to you all, for I'm tired; and that's the colonel's doing." A plate of food was ordered: it was placed by John, with fear and trembling, on the lawn under the window. Every one kept on the watch, and the plate remained undisturbed for some time.

" Ah! Mr. Pratt, will you starve poor Teigue? Make every one go away from the windows, and master Henry out of the tree, and master Richard off the garden wall."

The eyes of the company were turned to the tree and the garden wall; the two boys' attention was occupied in getting down: the visiters were looking at them; and " Ho, ho, ho! — good luck to you, Mr. Pratt! — 'tis a good dinner, and there's the plate, ladies and gentlemen—good-bye to you, colonel — good-bye, Mr. Bell! — good-bye to you all! " — brought their attention back, when they saw the empty plate lying on the grass; and Teigue's voice was heard no more for that evening. Many visits were afterwards paid by Teigue; but never was he seen, nor was any discovery ever made of his person or character.

NED SHEEHY'S EXCUSE.

XXXII.

Ned Sheehy was servant-man to Richard Gumbleton, esquire, of Mountbally, Gumbletonmore, in the north of the county of Cork; and a better servant than Ned was not to be found in that honest county, from Cape Clear to the Kilworth Mountains; for nobody—no, not his worst enemy—could say a word against him, only that he was rather given to drinking, idling, lying, and loitering, especially the last; for send Ned of a five minute message at nine o'clock in the morning, and you were a lucky man if you saw him before dinner. If there happened to be a public-house in the way, or even a little out of it, Ned was sure to mark it as dead as a pointer; and knowing every body, and every body liking him, it is not to be wondered at he had so much to say and to hear, that the time slipped away as if the sun somehow or other had knocked two hours into one.

But when he came home, he never was short of an excuse: he had, for that matter, five hundred ready upon the tip of his tongue; so much so, that I doubt if even the very reverend doctor Swift, for many years Dean of St. Patrick's, in Dublin, could match him in that particular, though his reverence had a pretty way of his own of writing things which brought him into very decent company. In fact, Ned would fret a saint, but then he was so good-humoured a fellow, and really so handy about a house, — for, as he said himself, he was as good as a lady's-maid, — that his master could not find it in his heart to part with him.

In your grand houses — not that I am saying that Richard Gumbleton, esquire, of Mountbally, Gumbletonmore, did not keep a good house, but a plain country gentleman, although he is second cousin to the last high-sheriff of the county, cannot have all the army of servants that the lord-lieutenant has in the castle of Dublin — I say, in your grand houses, you can have a servant for every kind of thing, but in Mountbally, Gumbletonmore, Ned was expected to please master and mistress ; or, as counsellor Curran said, — by the same token the counsellor was a little dark man — one day that he dined there, on his way to the Clonmel assizes — Ned was minister for the home and foreign departments.

But to make a long story short, Ned Sheehy was a good butler, and a right good one too, and as for a groom, let him alone with a horse : he could dress it, or ride it, or shoe it, or physic it, or do any thing with it but make it speak — he was a second whisperer ! — there was not his match in the barony, or the next one neither. A pack of hounds he could manage well, ay, and ride after them with the boldest man in the land. It was Ned who leaped the old bounds ditch at the turn of the boreen of the lands of Reenascreena, after the English captain pulled up on looking at it, and cried out it was " No go." Ned rode that day Brian Boro, Mr. Gumbleton's famous chestnut, and people call it Ned Sheehy's leap to this hour.

So, you see, it was hard to do without him: however, many a scolding he got; and although his master often said of an evening, " I'll turn off Ned," he always forgot to do so in the morning. These threats mended Ned not a bit; indeed, he was mending the other way, like bad fish in hot weather.

One cold winter's day, about three o'clock in the afternoon, Mr. Gumbleton said to him,

" Ned," said he, " go take Modderaroo down to black Falvey, the horse-doctor, and bid him look at her knees; for Doctor Jenkinson, who rode her home last night, has hurt her somehow. I suppose he thought a parson's horse ought to go upon its knees; but, indeed, it was I was the fool to give her to him at all, for he sits twenty stone if he sits a pound, and knows no more of riding, particularly after his third bottle, than I do of preaching. Now mind and be back in an hour at furthest, for I want to have the plate cleaned up properly for dinner, as sir Augustus O'Toole, you know, is to dine here to-day. — Don't loiter for your life."

" Is it I, sir?" says Ned. " Well, that beats any thing; as if I'd stop out a minute!" So, mounting Modderaroo, off he set.

Four, five, six o'clock came, and so did sir Augustus and lady O'Toole, and the four misses O'Toole, and Mr. O'Toole, and Mr. Edward O'Toole, and Mr. James O'Toole, which were all the young O'Tooles that were at home, but no Ned Sheehy appeared to clean the plate, or to lay the tablecloth, or even to put dinner on. It is needless to say how Mr. and Mrs. Dick Gumbleton fretted and fumed; but it was all to no use. They did their best, however, only it was a disgrace to see long Jem the stable-boy, and Bill the gossoon that used to go of errands, waiting, without any body to direct them, when there was a real baronet and his lady at table; for sir Augustus was none of your knights. But a good bottle of claret makes up for much, and it was not one only they had that night. However, it is not to be concealed that Mr. Dick Gumbleton went to bed very cross, and he awoke still crosser.

He heard that Ned had not made his appearance for the whole night; so he dressed himself in a great fret, and, taking his horsewhip in his hand, he said,

"There is no further use in tolerating this scoundrel: I'll go look for him, and if I find him, I'll cut the soul out of his vagabond body! I will by —— "

" Don't swear, Dick dear," said Mrs. Gumbleton (for she was always a mild woman, being daughter of fighting Tom Crofts, who shot a couple of gentlemen, friends of his, in the cool of the evening, after the Mallow races, one after the other), " don't swear, Dick dear," said she; " but do, my dear, oblige me by cutting the flesh off his bones, for he richly deserves it. I was quite ashamed of lady O'Toole, yesterday, I was, 'pon honour."

Out sallied Mr. Gumbleton; and he had not far to walk: for, not more than two hundred yards from the house, he found Ned lying fast asleep under a ditch (a hedge), and Modderaroo stand-ing by him, poor beast, shaking every limb. The loud snoring of Ned, who was lying with his head upon a stone as easy and as comfortable as if it had been a bed of down or a hop-bag, drew him to the spot, and Mr. Gumbleton at once perceived, from the disarray of Ned's face and person, that he had been engaged in some perilous adventure during the night. Ned appeared not to have des-cended in the most regular manner; for one of his shoes remained sticking in the stirrup, and his hat, having rolled down a little slope, was em-bedded in green mud. Mr. Gumbleton, however, did not give himself much trouble to make a cu-rious survey, but with a vigorous application of his thong soon banished sleep from the eyes of Ned Sheehy.

" Ned!" thundered his master in great indigna-tion, — and on this occasion it was not a word and blow, for with that one word came half a dozen: " Get up, you scoundrel," said he.

Ned roared lustily, and no wonder, for his mas-ter's hand was not one of the lightest; and he cried out, between sleeping and waking — " O, sir! — don't be angry, sir! — don't be angry, and I'll roast you easier — easy as a lamb!"

" Roast me easier, you vagabond!" said Mr. Gumbleton; " what do you mean? — I'll roast you, my lad. Where were you all night? — Mod-deraroo will never get over it. — Pack out of my service, you worthless villain, this moment; and, indeed, you may give God thanks that I don't get you transported."

" Thank God, master dear," said Ned, who

was now perfectly awakened — " it's yourself anyhow. There never was a gentleman in the whole county ever did so good a turn to a poor man as your honour has been after doing to me : the Lord reward you for that same. Oh ! but strike me again, and let me feel that it is yourself, master dear ; — may whisky be my poison — "

" It will be your poison, you good-for-nothing scoundrel," said Mr. Gumbleton.

" Well, then *may* whisky be my poison," said Ned, " if 'twas not I was — God help me ! — in the blackest of misfortunes, and they were before me, whichever way I turned 'twas no matter. Your honour sent me last night, sure enough, with Modderaroo to mister Falvey's — I don't deny it — why should I ? for reason enough I have to remember what happened."

" Ned, my man," said Mr. Gumbleton, " I'll listen to none of your excuses : just take the mare into the stable and yourself off, for I vow to — "

" Begging your honour's pardon," said Ned earnestly, " for interrupting your honour ; but, master, master ! make no vows — they are bad things : I never made but one in all my life, which was, to drink nothing at all for a year and a day, and 't is myself repinted of it for the clean twelvemonth after. But if your honour would only listen to reason : I'll just take in the poor baste and if your honour don't pardon me this one time may I never see another day's luck or grace."

" I know you, Ned," said Mr. Gumbleton. " Whatever your luck has been, you never had any grace to lose : but I don't intend discussing the matter with you. Take in the mare, sir."

Ned obeyed, and his master saw him to the stables. Here he reiterated his commands to quit, and Ned Sheehy's excuse for himself began. That it was heard uninterruptedly is more than I can affirm ; but as interruptions, like explanations, spoil a story, we must let Ned tell it his own way.

" No wonder your honour," said he, " should be a bit angry — grand company coming to the house and all, and no regular serving-man to wait, only long Jem ; so I dont blame your honour the least for being fretted like ; but when all's heard, you will see that no poor man is more to be pitied for last night than myself. Fin Mac Coul never went through more in his born days than I did, though he was a great *joint* (giant), and I only a man.

" I had not rode half a mile from the house, when it came on, as your honour must have perceived clearly, mighty dark all of a sudden, for all the world as if the sun had tumbled down plump out of the fine clear blue sky. It was not so late, being only four o'clock at the most, but it was as black as your honour's hat. Well, I didn't care much, seeing I knew the road as well as I knew the way to my mouth, whether I saw it or not, and I put the mare into a smart canter ; but just as I turned down by the corner of Terence Leahy's field — sure your honour ought to know the place well — just at the very spot the fox was killed when your honour came in first out of a whole field of a hundred and fifty gentlemen, and may be more, all of them brave riders."

(Mr. Gumbleton smiled.)

" Just then, there, I heard the low cry of the good people wafting upon the wind. ' How early you are at your work, my little fellows!' says I to myself; and, dark as it was, having no wish for such company, I thought it best to get out of their way; so I turned the horse a little up to the left, thinking to get down by the boreen, that is that way, and so round to Falvey's; but there I heard the voice plainer and plainer close behind, and I could hear these words :—

> ' Ned! Ned!
> By my cap so red!
> You 're as good, Ned,
> As a man that is dead.'

' A clean pair of spurs is all that's for it now,' said I; so off I set as hard as I could lick, and in my hurry knew no more where I was going than I do the road to the hill of Tarah. Away I galloped on for some time, until I came to the noise of a stream, roaring away by itself in the darkness. ' What river is this?' said I to myself — for there was nobody else to ask — 'I thought,' says I, 'I knew every inch of ground, and of water too, within twenty miles, and never the river surely is there in this direction.' So I stopped to look about; but I might have spared myself that trouble, for I could not see as much as my hand. I didn't know what to do; but I thought in myself, it's a queer river, surely, if somebody does not live near it; and I shouted out as loud as I could,

Murder! murder!—fire!—robbery!—any thing that would be natural in such a place — but not a sound did I hear except my own voice echoed back to me, like a hundred packs of hounds in full cry above and below, right and left.   This didn't do at all; so I dismounted, and guided myself along the stream, directed by the noise of the water, as cautious as if I was treading upon eggs, holding poor Modderaroo by the bridle, who shook, the poor brute, all over in a tremble, like my old grandmother, rest her soul anyhow! in the ague. Well, sir, the heart was sinking in me, and I was giving myself up, when, as good luck would have it, I saw a light.   'Maybe,' said I, ' my good fellow, you are only a jacky lanthorn, and want to bog me and Modderaroo.'   But I looked at the light hard, and I thought it was too *study* (steady) for a jacky lanthorn.   ' I'll try you,' says I — ' so here goes;'   and, walking as quick as a thief, I came towards it, being very near plumping into the river once or twice, and being stuck up to my middle, as your honour may perceive cleanly the marks of, two or three times in the *slob*.[1]   At last I made the light out, and it coming from a bit of a house by the roadside; so I went to the door and gave three kicks at it, as strong as I could.

" ' Open the door for Ned Sheehy,' said a voice inside.   Now, besides that I could not, for the life of me, make out how any one inside should know me before I spoke a word at all, I did not like the

Or *slaib*; mire on the sea strand or river's bank.— O'BRIEN.

sound of that voice, 'twas so hoarse and so hollow, just like a dead man's!—so I said nothing immediately. The same voice spoke again, and said, ' Why don't you open the door to Ned Sheehy ?' ' How pat my name is to you,' said I, without speaking out, ' on tip of your tongue, like butter;' and I was between two minds about staying or going, when what should the door do but open, and out came a man holding a candle in his hand, and he had upon him a face as white as a sheet.

" ' Why, then, Ned Sheehy,' says he, ' how grand you're grown, that you won't come in and see a friend, as you're passing by.'

" ' Pray, sir,' says I, looking at him — though that face of his was enough to dumbfounder any honest man like myself—' Pray, sir,' says I, ' may I make so bold as to ask if you are not Jack Myers that was drowned seven years ago, next Martinmas, in the ford of Ah-na-fourish ?'

" ' Suppose I was,' says he : ' has not a man a right to be drowned in the ford facing his own cabin-door any day of the week that he likes, from Sunday morning to Saturday night ?'

" ' I'm not denying that same, Mr. Myers, sir,' says I, ' if 'tis yourself is to the fore speaking to me.'

" ' Well,' says he, ' no more words about that matter now : sure you and I, Ned, were friends of old ; come in, and take a glass ; and here's a good fire before you, and nobody shall hurt or harm you, and I to the fore, and myself able to do it.'

" Now, your honour, though 'twas much to drink with a man that was drowned seven years before, in the ford of Ah-na-fourish, facing his own door, yet the glass was hard to be withstood — to say nothing of the fire that was blazing within — for the night was mortal cold. So tying Modderaroo to the hasp of the door — if I don't love the creature as I love my own life — I went in with Jack Myers.

" Civil enough he was — I 'll never say otherwise to my dying hour — for he handed me a stool by the fire, and bid me sit down and make myself comfortable. But his face, as I said before, was as white as the snow on the hills, and his two eyes fell dead on me, like the eyes of a cod without any life in them. Just as I was going to put the glass to my lips, a voice — 'twas the same that I heard bidding the door be opened — spoke out of a cupboard that was convenient to the left hand side of the chimney, and said, ' Have you any news for me, Ned Sheehy ?'

" ' The never a word, sir,' says I, making answer before I tasted the whisky, all out of civility; and, to speak the truth, never the least could I remember at that moment of what had happened to me, or how I got there; for I was quite bothered with the fright.

" ' Have you no news,' says the voice, ' Ned, to tell me, from Mountbally Gumbletonmore ; or from the Mill ; or about Moll Trantum that was married last week to Bryan Oge, and you at the wedding ?'

" ' No, sir,' says, I, ' never the word.'

" ' What brought you in here, Ned, then ?' says the voice. I could say nothing ; for, whatever other people might do, I never could frame an excuse; and I was loth to say it was on account of the glass and the fire, for that would be to speak the truth.

" ' Turn the scoundrel out,' says the voice; and at the sound of it, who would I see but Jack Myers making over to me with a lump of a stick in his hand, and it clenched on the stick so wicked. For certain, I did not stop to feel the weight of the blow; so, dropping the glass, and it full of the stuff too, I bolted out of the door, and never rested from running away, for as good, I believe, as twenty miles, till I found myself in a big wood.

" ' The Lord preserve me! what will become of me now!' says I. ' Oh, Ned Sheehy !' says I, speaking to myself, ' my man, your're in a pretty hobble ; and to leave poor Modderaroo after you !'   But the words were not well out of my mouth, when I heard the dismallest ullagoane in the world, enough to break any one's heart that was not broke before, with the grief entirely; and it was not long till I could plainly see four men coming towards me, with a great black coffin on their shoulders. ' I'd better get up in a tree,' says I, ' for they say 't is not lucky to meet a corpse: I'm in the way of misfortune to-night, if ever man was.'

" I could not help wondering how a *berrin* (funeral) should come there in the lone wood at that time of night, seeing it could not be far from the dead hour. But it was little good for me thinking, for they soon came under the very tree I was roosting in, and down they put the coffin, and began to make a fine fire under me. I'll be smothered alive now, thinks I, and that will be the end of me; but I was afraid to stir for the life, or to speak out to bid them just make their fire under some other tree, if it would be all the same thing to them. Presently they opened the coffin, and out they dragged as fine looking a man at you'd meet with in a day's walk.

" ' Where 's the spit ? ' says one.

" ' Here 't is,' says another, handing it over; and for certain they spitted him, and began to turn him before the fire.

" If they are not going to eat him, thinks I, like the *Hannibals* father Quinlan told us about in his *sarmint* last Sunday.

" ' Who 'll turn the spit while we go for the other ingredients ? ' says one of them that brought the coffin, and a big ugly-looking blackguard he was.

" ' Who 'd turn the spit but Ned Sheehy ? ' says another.

" Burn you ! thinks I, how should you know that I was here so handy to you up in the tree ?

" ' Come down, Ned Sheehy, and turn the spit,' says he.

" ' I 'm not here at all, sir,' says I, putting my hand over my face that he may not see me.

" ' That won't do for you, my man,' says he; ' you 'd better come down, or maybe I 'd make you.'

" ' I 'm coming, sir,' says I; for 't is always right to make a virtue of necessity. So down I came, and there they left me turning the spit in the middle of the wide wood.

" ' Don't scorch me, Ned Sheehy, you vaga-bond,' says the man on the spit.

" ' And my lord, sir, and ar'n't you dead, sir," says I, ' and your honour taken out of the coffin and all ? '

" ' I ar'n't,' says he.

" ' But surely you are, sir,' says I, ' for 't is to no use now for me denying that I saw your honour, and I up in the tree.'

" ' I ar'n't,' says he again, speaking quite short and snappish.

" So I said no more, until presently he called out to me to turn him easy, or that maybe 't would be the worse turn for myself.

" ' Will that do, sir ? ' says I, turning him as easy as I could.

" ' That 's too easy,' says he : so I turned him faster.

" ' That 's too fast,' says he; so finding that, turn him which way I would, I could not please him, I got into a bit of a fret at last, and desired him to turn himself, for a grumbling spalpeen as he was, if he liked it better.

" Away I ran, and away he came hopping, spit and all, after me, and he but half-roasted. ' Murder!' says I, shouting out; ' I 'm done for at long last — now or never !' — when all of a sudden, and 't was really wonderful, not knowing where I was rightly, I found myself at the door of the very little cabin by the roadside that I had bolted out of from Jack Myers; and there was Modderaroo standing hard by.

" ' Open the door for Ned Sheehy,' says the voice,—for 't was shut against me,—and the door flew open in an instant. In I ran, without stop or stay, thinking it better to be beat by Jack

Myers, he being an old friend of mine, than to be spitted like a Michaelmas goose by a man that I knew nothing about, either of him or his family, one or the other.

" ' Have you any news for me ? ' says the voice, putting just the same question to me that it did before.

" ' Yes, sir,' says I, ' and plenty.'   So I mentioned all that had happened to me in the big wood, and how I got up in the tree, and how I was made come down again, and put to turning the spit, roasting the gentleman, and how I could not please him, turn him fast or easy, although I tried my best, and how he ran after me at last, spit and all.

" ' If you had told me this before, you would not have been turned out in the cold,' said the voice.

" ' And how could I tell it to you, sir,' says I, ' before it happened ? '

" ' No matter,' says he, ' you may sleep now till morning on that bundle of hay in the corner there, and only I was your friend, you 'd have been *kilt* entirely.'   So down I lay, but I was dreaming, dreaming all the rest of the night, and when you, master dear, woke me with that blessed blow, I thought 't was the man on the spit had hold of me, and could hardly believe my eyes when I found myself in your honour's presence, and poor Modderaroo safe and sound by my side ; but how I came there is more than I can say, if 't was not Jack Myers, although he did make the offer to strike me, or some one among the good people that befriended me."

"It is all a drunken dream, you scoundrel," said Mr. Gumbleton; "have I not had fifty such excuses from you?"

"But never one, your honour, that really happened before," said Ned, with unblushing front. "Howsomever, since your honour fancies 't is drinking I was, I'd rather never drink again to the world's end, than lose so good a master as yourself, and if I'm forgiven this once, and g et another trial ——"

"Well," said Mr. Gumbleton, "you may, for this once, go into Mountbally Gumbletonmore again; let me see that you keep your promise as to not drinking, or mind the consequences; and, above all, let me hear no more of the good people, for I don't believe a single word about them, whatever I may do of bad ones."

So saying, Mr. Gumbleton turned on his heel, and Ned's countenance relaxed into its usual expression.

"Now I would not be after saying about the good people what the master said last," exclaimed Peggy, the maid, who was within hearing, and who, by the way, had an eye after Ned: "I would not be after saying such a thing; the good people, maybe, will make him feel the *differ* (difference) to his cost."

Nor was Peggy wrong, for, whether Ned Sheehy dreamt of the Fir Darrig or not, within a fortnight after, two of Mr. Gumbleton's cows, the best milkers in the parish, ran dry, and before the week was out Modderaroo was lying dead in the stone quarry.

T

THE LUCKY GUEST.

XXXIII.

The kitchen of some country houses in Ireland presents in no ways a bad modern translation of the ancient feudal hall. Traces of clanship still linger round its hearth in the numerous dependants on "the master's" bounty. Nurses, foster-brothers, and other hangers on, are there as matter of right, while the strolling piper, full of mirth and music, the benighted traveller, even the passing beggar, are received with a hearty welcome, and each contributes planxty, song, or superstitious tale, towards the evening's amusement.

An assembly, such as has been described, had collected round the kitchen fire of Ballyrahen-house, at the foot of the Galtee mountains, when, as is ever the case, one tale of wonder called forth another; and with the advance of the evening each succeeding story was received with deep and deeper attention. The history of Cough na Looba's dance with the black friar at Rahill, and the fearful tradition of *Coum an 'ir morriv* (the dead man's hollow), were listened to in breathless silence. A pause followed the last relation, and all eyes rested on the narrator, an old nurse who occupied the post of honour, that next the fireside. She was seated in that peculiar position which the Irish name "*Currigguib*," a position generally assumed by a veteran and determined story-teller. Her haunches resting upon the ground, and her feet bundled under the body; her arms folded across and supported by her knees, and the outstretched chin of her hooded head pressing on the upper arm; which compact arrangement nearly reduced the whole figure into a perfect triangle.

Unmoved by the general gaze, Bridget Doyle made no change of attitude, while she gravely asserted the truth of the marvellous tale concerning the Dead Man's Hollow; her strongly marked countenance at the time receiving what painters term a fine chiaro obscuro effect from the fire-light.

"I have told you," she said, "what happened to my own people, the Butlers and the Doyles, in the old times; but here is little Ellen Connell from the county Cork, who can speak to what happened under her own father and mother's roof — the Lord be good to them!"

Ellen, a young and blooming girl of about sixteen, was employed in the dairy at Ballyrahen. She was the picture of health and rustic beauty; and at this hint from nurse Doyle, a deep blush mantled over her countenance; yet, although "unaccustomed to public speaking," she, without further hesitation or excuse, proceeded as follows:—

"It was one May eve, about thirteen years ago, and that is, as every body knows, the airiest day in all the twelve months. It is the day above all other days," said Ellen, with her large dark eyes cast down on the ground, and drawing a deep sigh, "when the young boys and the young girls go looking after the *Drutheen*, to learn from it rightly the name of their sweethearts.

"My father, and my mother, and my two brothers, with two or three of the neighbours, were sitting round the turf fire, and were talking of one thing or another. My mother was hushoing my little sister, striving to quieten her, for she was cutting her teeth at the time, and was mighty uneasy through the means of them. The day, which was threatening all along, now that it was coming on to dusk, began to rain, and the rain increased and fell fast and faster, as if it was pouring through a sieve out of the wide heavens ; and when the rain stopped for a bit there was a wind which kept up such a whistling and racket, that you would have thought the sky and the earth were coming together. It blew and it blew as if it had a mind to blow the roof off the cabin, and that would not have been very hard for it to do, as the thatch was quite loose in two or three places. Then the rain began again, and you could hear it spitting and hissing in the fire, as it came down through the big *chimbley*.

"'God bless us,' says my mother, 'but 't is a dreadful night to be at sea,' says she, 'and God be praised that we have a roof, bad as it is, to shelter us.'

"I don't, to be sure, recollect all this, mistress Doyle, but only as my brothers told it to me, and other people, and often have I heard it ; for I was so little then, that they say I could just go under the table without tipping my head. Anyway, it was in the very height of the pelting and whistling that we heard something speak outside the door. My father and all of us listened, but there was no more noise at that time. We waited a little longer, and then we plainly heard a sound like an old man's voice, asking to be let in, but mighty feeble and weak. Tim bounced up, without a word, to ask us whether we'd like to let the old man, or whoever he was, in — having always a heart as soft as a mealy potato before the voice of sorrow. When Tim pulled back the bolt that did the door, in marched a little bit of a shrivelled, weather-beaten creature, about two feet and a half high.

" We were all watching to see who'd come in, for there was a wall between us and the door; but when the sound of the undoing of the bolt stopped, we heard Tim give a sort of a screech, and instantly he bolted in to us. He had hardly time to say a word, or we either, when the little gentleman shuffled in after him, without a God save all here, or by your leave, or any other sort of thing that any decent body might say. We all, of one accord, scrambled over to the furthest end of the room, where we were, old and young, every one trying who'd get nearest the wall, and farthest from him. All the eyes of our body were stuck upon him, but he didn't mind us no more than that frying-pan there does now. He walked over to the fire, and squatting himself down like a frog, took the pipe that my father dropped from his mouth in the hurry, put it into his own, and then began to smoke so hearty, that he soon filled the room of it.

" We had plenty of time to observe him, and

my brothers say that he wore a sugar-loaf hat that was as red as blood : he had a face as yellow as a kite's claw, and as long as to-day and to-morrow put together, with a mouth all screwed and puckered up like a washer-woman's hand, little blue eyes, and rather a highish nose ; his hair was quite grey and lengthy, appearing under his hat, and flowing over the cape of a long scarlet coat, which almost trailed the ground behind him, and the ends of which he took up and planked on his knees to dry, as he sat facing the fire. He had smart corduroy breeches, and woollen stockings drawn up over the knees, so as to hide the kneebuckles, if he had the pride to have them ; but, at any rate, if he hadn't them in his knees he had buckles in his shoes, out before his spindle legs. When we came to ourselves a little we thought to escape from the room, but no one would go first, nor no one would stay last ; so we huddled ourselves together and made a dart out of the room. My little gentleman never minded any thing of the scrambling, nor hardly stirred himself, sitting quite at his ease before the fire. The neighbours, the very instant minute they got to the door, although it still continued pelting rain, cut gutter as if Oliver Cromwell himself was at their heels ; and no blame to them for that, anyhow. It was my father, and my mother, and my brothers, and myself, a little hop-of-my-thumb midge as I was then, that were left to see what would come out of this strange visit ; so we all went quietly to the *labbig**, scarcely daring to throw an eye at

* *Labbig* — bed, from *Leaba*. — Vide O'BRIEN and O'REILLY.

him as we passed the door. Never the wink of sleep could they sleep that live-long night, though, to be sure, I slept like a top, not knowing better, while they were talking and thinking of the little man.

" When they got up in the morning every thing was as quiet and as tidy about the place as if nothing had happened, for all that the chairs and stools were tumbled here, there, and everywhere, when we saw the lad enter. Now, indeed, I forget whether he came next night or not, but anyway, that was the first time we ever laid eye upon him. This I know for certain, that, about a month after that he came regularly every night, and used to give us a signal to be on the move, for 't was plain he did not like to be observed. This sign was always made about eleven o'clock; and then, if we 'd look towards the door, there was a little hairy arm thrust in through the key-hole, which would not have been big enough, only there was a fresh hole made near the first one, and the bit of stick between them had been broken away, and so 't was just fitting for the little arm.

" The Fir darrig continued his visits, never missing a night, as long as we attended to the signal; smoking always out of the pipe he made his own of, and warming himself till day dawned before the fire, and then going no one living knows where : but there was not the least mark of him to be found in the morning ; and 't is as true, nurse Doyle, and honest people, as you are all here sitting before me and by the side of me, that the family continued thriving, and my father and brothers rising in the world while ever he came to us. When we observed this, we used always look for the very moment to see when the arm would come, and then we'd instantly fly off with ourselves to our rest. But before we found the luck, we used sometimes sit still and not mind the arm, especially when a neighbour would be with my father, or that two or three or four of them would have a drop among them, and then they did not care for all the arms, hairy or not, that ever were seen. No one, however, dared to speak to it or of it insolently, except, indeed, one night that Davy Kennane — but he was drunk — walked over and hit it a rap on the back of the wrist; the hand was snatched off like lightning; but every one knows that Davy did not live a month after this happened, though he was only about ten days sick. The like of such tricks are ticklish things to do.

" As sure as the red man would put in his arm for a sign through the hole in the door, and that we did not go and open it to him, so sure some mishap befel the cattle: the cows were elf-stoned, or overlooked, or something or another went wrong with them. One night my brother Dan refused to go at the signal, and the next day, as he was cutting turf in Crogh-na-drimina bog, within a mile and a half of the house, a stone was thrown at him which broke fairly, with the force, into two halves. Now, if that had happened to hit him he'd be at this hour as dead as my great great-grandfather. It came whack-slap against the spade he had in his hand, and split at once in two pieces. He took them up and fitted them together and they made a perfect heart. Some way or the other he lost it since, but he still has the one which was shot at the spotted milch cow, before the little man came near us. Many and many a time I saw that same; 'tis just the shape of the ace of hearts on the cards, only it is of a dark-red colour, and polished up like the grate that is in the grand parlour within. When this did not kill the cow on the spot, she swelled up; but if you took and put the elf-stone under her udder, and milked her upon it to the last stroking, and then made her drink the milk, it would cure her, and she would thrive with you ever after.

" But, as I said, we were getting on well enough as long as we minded the door and watched for the hairy arm, which we did sharp enough when we found it was bringing luck to us, and we were now as glad to see the little red gentleman, and as ready to open the door to him, as we used to dread his coming at first and be frightened of him. But at long last we throve so well that the landlord — God forgive him — took notice of us, and envied us, and asked my father how he came by the penny he had, and wanted him to take more ground at a rack-rent that was more than any Christian ought to pay to another, seeing there was no making it. When my father — and small blame to him for that — refused to lease the ground, he turned us off the bit of land we had, and out of the house and all, and left us in a wide and wicked world, where my father, for he was a soft innocent man, was not up to the roguery and the trickery that was practised upon him. He was taken this way by one and that way by another, and he treating them that were working his downfall. And he used to take bite and sup with them, and they with him, free enough as long as the money lasted; but when that was gone, and he had not as much ground, that he could call his own, as would sod a lark, they soon shabbed him off. The landlord died not long after; and he now knows whether he acted right or wrong in taking the house from over our heads.

"It is a bad thing for the heart to be cast down, so we took another cabin, and looked out with great desire for the Fir darrig to come to us. But ten o'clock came and no arm, although we cut a hole in the door just the *moral* (model) of the other. Eleven o'clock! — twelve o'clock! — no, not a sign of him: and every night we watched, but all would not do. We then travelled to the other house, and we rooted up the hearth, for the landlord asked so great a rent for it from the poor people that no one could take it; and we carried away the very door off the hinges, and we brought every thing with us that we thought the little man was in any respect partial to, but he did not come, and we never saw him again.

"My father and my mother, and my young sister, are since dead, and my two brothers, who could tell all about this better than myself, are both of them gone out with Ingram in his last voyage to the Cape of Good Hope, leaving me behind without kith or kin."

Here young Ellen's voice became choked with sorrow, and bursting into tears, she hid her face in her apron.

Fɪʀ Dᴀʀʀɪɢ, correctly written Feaṅ Deaṅʒ, means the red man, and is a member of the fairy community of Ireland, who bears a strong resemblance to the Shakspearian Puck, or Robin Goodfellow. Like that merry goblin, his delight is in mischief and mockery; and this Irish spirit is doubtless the same as the Scottish *Red Cap;* which a writer in the Quarterly Review (No. XLIV. p. 358.), tracing national analogies, asserts is the Robin Hood of England, and the Saxon spirit Hudkin or Hodeken, so called from the hoodakin or little hood wherein he appeared,—a spirit similar to the Spanish Duende. The Fir Darrig has also some traits of resemblance in common with the Scotch Brownie, the German Kobold (particularly the celebrated one, Hinzelman), the English Hobgoblin (Milton's " Lubber Fiend "), and the Follet of Gervase of Tilbury, who says of the Folletos, " Verba utique humano more audiuntur et effigies non comparent. De istis pleraque miracula memini me in vita abbreviata et miraculis beatissimi Antonii reperisse."—*Otia Imperialia.*

The red dress and strange flexibility of voice possessed by the Fir Darrig form his peculiar characteristics; the latter, according to Irish tale-tellers, is like Fuaiṁ na dton, the sound of the waves; and again it is compared to Ceol na naiṅʒeal, the music of angels; Ceileabaṅ na néaṅ, the warbling of birds, &c.; and the usual address to this fairy is, Na beaṅ ḟoċmoid Fuiṅ, do not mock us. His entire dress, when he is seen, is invariably described as crimson; whereas, Irish fairies generally appear in hata dub, culaiʒ ʒlaṙ, rtocaiʒ baṅa, aʒuṙ bṙoʒa deaṅʒa; a black hat, a green suit, white stockings, and red shoes.

FAIRY LEGENDS.

TREASURE LEGENDS.

"Bell, book, and candle, shall not drive me back
When gold and silver becks me to come on."
King John.

"This is fairy gold, boy, and 't will prove so."
Winter's Tale

TREASURE LEGENDS.

DREAMING TIM JARVIS.

XXXIV.

Timothy Jarvis was a decent, honest, quiet, hard-working man, as every body knows that knows Balledehob.

Now Balledehob is a small place, about forty miles west of Cork. It is situated on the summit of a hill, and yet it is in a deep valley; for on all sides there are lofty mountains that rise one above another in barren grandeur, and seem to look down with scorn upon the little busy village which they surround with their idle and unproductive magnificence. Man and beast have alike deserted them to the dominion of the eagle, who soars majestically over them. On the highest of those mountains there is a small, and as is commonly believed, unfathomable lake, the only inhabitant of which is a huge serpent, who has been sometimes seen to stretch its enormous head above the waters, and frequently is heard to utter a noise which shakes the very rocks to their foundation.

But, as I was saying, every body knew Tim Jarvis to be a decent, honest, quiet, hard-working man, who was thriving enough to be able to give his daughter Nelly a fortune of ten pounds; and Tim himself would have been snug enough besides, but that he loved the drop sometimes. However, he was seldom backward on rent day. His ground was never distrained but twice, and both times through a small bit of a mistake; and his landlord had never but once to say to him — "Tim Jarvis, you're all behind, Tim, like the cow's tail." Now it so happened that, being heavy in himself, through the drink, Tim took to sleeping, and the sleep set Tim dreaming, and he dreamed all night, and night after night, about crocks full of gold and other precious stones; so much so, that Norah Jarvis his wife could get no good of him by day, and have little comfort with him by night. The grey dawn of the morning would see Tim digging away in a bog-hole, maybe, or rooting under some old stone walls like a pig. At last he dreamt that he found a mighty great crock of gold and silver — and where do you think? Every step of the way upon London-bridge, itself! Twice Tim dreamt it, and three times Tim dreamt the same thing; and at last he made up his mind to transport himself, and go over to London, in Pat Mahoney's coaster — and so he did!

Well, he got there, and found the bridge without much difficulty. Every day he walked up and down looking for the crock of gold, but never the find did he find it. One day, however, as he was looking over the bridge into the water,

a man, or something like a man, with great black
whiskers, like a Hessian, and a black cloak that
reached down to the ground, taps him on the
shoulder, and says he —" Tim Jarvis, do you see
me?"

" Surely I do, sir," said Tim; wondering that
any body should know him in the strange place.

" Tim," says he, " what is it brings you here
in foreign parts, so far away from your own cabin
by the mine of grey copper at Balledehob?"

" Please your honour," says Tim, " I'm come
to seek my fortune."

" You're a fool for your pains, Tim, if that's
all," remarked the stranger in the black cloak;
" this is a big place to seek one's fortune in, to
be sure, but it's not so easy to find it."

Now, Tim, after debating a long time with
himself, and considering, in the first place, that it
might be the stranger who was to find the crock
of gold for him; and in the next, that the stranger
might direct him where to find it, came to the
resolution of telling him all.

" There's many a one like me comes here
seeking their fortunes," said Tim.

" True," said the stranger.

" But," continued Tim, looking up, " the body
and bones of the cause for myself leaving the
woman, and Nelly, and the boys, and travelling
so far, is to look for a crock of gold that I'm
told is lying somewhere hereabouts."

" And who told you that, Tim?"

" Why then, sir, that's what I can't tell myself rightly — only I dreamt it."

" Ho, ho! is that all, Tim!" said the stranger,

laughing; "I had a dream myself; and I dreamed that I found a crock of gold, in the Fort field, on Jerry Driscoll's ground at Balledehob; and by the same token, the pit where it lay was close to a large furze bush, all full of yellow blossom."

Tim knew Jerry Driscoll's ground well; and, moreover, he knew the Fort field as well as he knew his own potato garden; he was certain, too, of the very furze bush at the north end of it — so, swearing a bitter big oath, says he —

"By all the crosses in a yard of check, I always thought there was money in that same field!"

The moment he rapped out the oath the stranger disappeared, and Tim Jarvis, wondering at all that had happened to him, made the best of his way back to Ireland. Norah, as may well be supposed, had no very warm welcome for her runaway husband — the dreaming blackguard, as she called him — and so soon as she set eyes upon him, all the blood of her body in one minute was into her knuckles to be at him; but Tim, after his long journey, looked so cheerful and so happy-like, that she could not find it in her heart to give him the first blow! He managed to pacify his wife by two or three broad hints about a new cloak and a pair of shoes, that, to speak honestly, were much wanting for her to go to chapel in; and decent clothes for Nelly to go to the patron with her sweetheart, and brogues for the boys, and some corduroy for himself. "It was n't for nothing," says Tim, "I went to foreign parts all the ways; and you 'll see what 'll come out of it — mind my words."

A few days afterwards Tim sold his cabin and his garden, and bought the fort field of Jerry Driscoll, that had nothing in it, but was full of thistles, and old stones, and blackberry bushes; and all the neighbours — as well they might — thought he was cracked!

The first night that Tim could summon courage to begin his work, he walked off to the field with his spade upon his shoulder; and away he dug all night by the side of the furze bush, till he came to a big stone. He struck his spade against it, and he heard a hollow sound; but as the morning had begun to dawn, and the neighbours would be going out to their work, Tim, not wishing to have the thing talked about, went home to the little hovel, where Norah and the children were huddled together under a heap of straw; for he had sold every thing he had in the world to purchase Driscoll's field, though it was said to be " the back-bone of the world, picked by the devil."

It is impossible to describe the epithets and reproaches bestowed by the poor woman on her unlucky husband for bringing her into such a way. Epithets and reproaches which Tim had but one mode of answering, as thus: — " Norah, did you see e'er a cow you 'd like?"—or, " Norah, dear, has n't Poll Deasy a feather-bed to sell?" — or, " Norah, honey, would n't you like your silver buckles as big as Mrs. Doyle's?"

As soon as night came Tim stood beside the furze bush, spade in hand. The moment he jumped down into the pit he heard a strange rumbling noise under him, and so, putting his ear against the great stone, he listened, and over-heard a discourse that made the hair on his head stand up like bulrushes, and every limb tremble.

" How shall we bother Tim ?" said one voice.

" Take him to the mountain, to be sure, and make him a toothful for the *ould sarpint ;* 't is long since he has had a good meal," said another voice.

Tim shook like a potato-blossom in a storm.

" No," said a third voice ; " plunge him in the bog, neck and heels."

Tim was a dead man, barring the breath.[1]

" Stop !" said a fourth ; but Tim heard no more, for Tim was dead entirely. In about an hour, however, the life came back into him, and he crept home to Norah.

When the next night arrived, the hopes of the crock of gold got the better of his fears, and taking care to arm himself with a bottle of po-theen, away he went to the field. Jumping into the pit, he took a little sup from the bottle to keep his heart up — he then took a big one — and then with desperate wrench, he wrenched up the stone. All at once, up rushed a blast of wind, wild and fierce, and down fell Tim — down, down, and down he went — until he thumped upon what seemed to be, for all the world, like a floor of sharp pins, which made him bellow out

<hr>

[1] " I' non morì, e non rimasi vivo :
    Pensa oramai per te, s' hai fior d' ingegno
    Qual io divenni d' uno e d' altro privo."
                    DANTE, *Inferno,* canto 34.

in earnest. Then he heard a whisk and a hurra, and instantly voices beyond number cried out —

> "Welcome, Tim Jarvis, dear!
> Welcome, down here!"

Though Tim's teeth chattered like magpies with the fright, he continued to make answer — "I'm he-he-har-ti-ly ob-ob-liged to-to you all, gen-gen-tlemen, fo-for your civility to-to a poor stranger like myself." But though he had heard all the voices about him, he could see nothing, the place was so dark and so lonesome in itself for want of the light. Then something pulled Tim by the hair of his head, and dragged him, he did not know how far, but he knew he was going faster than the wind, for he heard it behind him, trying to keep up with him, and it could not. On, on, on, he went, till all at once, and suddenly, he was stopped, and somebody came up to him, and said, "Well, Tim Jarvis, and how do you like your ride?"

"Mighty well! I thank your honour," said Tim; "and 'twas a good beast I rode, surely!"

There was a great laugh at Tim's answer; and then there was a whispering, and a great cugger mugger, and coshering; and at last a pretty little bit of a voice said, "Shut your eyes, and you'll see, Tim."

"By my word, then," said Tim, "that is the queer way of seeing; but I'm not the man to gainsay you, so I'll do as you bid me, any how." Presently he felt a small warm hand rubbed over his eyes with an ointment, and in the next minute he saw himself in the middle of thousands of little men and women, not half so high as his brogue, that were pelting one another with golden guineas and lily-white thirteens[1], as if they were so much dirt. The finest dressed and the biggest of them all went up to Tim, and says he, " Tim Jarvis, because you are a decent, honest, quiet, civil, well-spoken man," says he, " and know how to behave yourself in strange company, we've altered our minds about you, and will find a neighbour of yours that will do just as well to give to the old serpent."

" Oh, then, long life to you, sir!" said Tim, " and there's no doubt of that."

" But what will you say, Tim," enquired the little fellow, " if we fill your pockets with these yellow boys? What will you say, Tim, and what will you do with them?"

" Your honour's honour, and your honour's glory," answered Tim, " I'll not be able to say my prayers for one month with thanking you — and indeed I've enough to do with them. I'd make a grand lady, you see, at once of Norah — she has been a good wife to me. We'll have a nice bit of pork for dinner; and, maybe, I'd have a glass, or maybe two glasses; or sometimes, if 'twas with a friend, or acquaintance, or gossip, you know, three glasses every day; and I'd build a new cabin; and I'd have a fresh egg every morning, myself, for my breakfast; and I'd snap my fingers at the 'squire, and beat his hounds, if they'd come coursing through my fields; and I'd

---

1 An English shilling was thirteen pence, Irish currency.

have a new plough; and Norah, your honour, would have a new cloak, and the boys would have shoes and stockings as well as Biddy Leary's brats — that's my sister what was — and Nelly would marry Bill Long of Affadown; and, your honour, I'd have some corduroy for myself to make breeches, and a cow, and a beautiful coat with shining buttons, and a horse to ride, or may-be two. I'd have every thing," said Tim, " in life, good or bad, that is to be got for love or money — hurra-whoop! — and that's what I'd do."

" Take care, Tim," said the little fellow, " your money would not go faster than it came, with your hurra-whoop."

But Tim heeded not this speech: heaps of gold were around him, and he filled and filled away as hard he could, his coat and his waist-coat and his breeches pockets; and he thought himself very clever, moreover, because he stuffed some of the guineas into his brogues. When the little people perceived this, they cried out — " Go home, Tim Jarvis, go home, and think yourself a lucky man."

" I hope, gentlemen," said he, " we won't part for good and all; but may-be ye'll ask me to see you again, and to give you a fair and square ac-count of what I've done with your money."

To this there was no answer, only another shout — " Go home, Tim Jarvis — go home — fair play is a jewel; but shut your eyes, or ye'll never see the light of day again."

Tim shut his eyes, knowing now that was the way to see clearly; and away he was whisked as before — away, away he went till he again stopped all of a sudden.

He rubbed his eyes with his two thumbs — and where was he?   Where, but in the very pit in the field that was Jer Driscoll's, and his wife Norah above with a big stick ready to beat " her dreaming blackguard."   Tim roared out to the woman to leave the life in him, and put his hands in his pockets to show her the gold; but he pulled out nothing only a handful of small stones mixed with yellow furze blossoms.   The bush was under him, and the great flag-stone that he had wrenched up, as he thought, was lying, as if it was never stirred, by his side: the whiskey bottle was drained to the last drop; and the pit was just as his spade had made it.

Tim Jarvis, vexed, disappointed, and almost heart-broken, followed his wife home: and, strange to say, from that night he left off drinking, and dreaming, and delving in bog-holes, and rooting in old caves.   He took again to his hard working habits, and was soon able to buy back his little cabin and former potato-garden, and to get all the enjoyment he anticipated from the fairy gold.

Give Tim one or, at most, two glasses of whis-key punch (and neither friend, acquaintance, nor gossip can make him take more), and he will re-late the story to you much better than you have it here.   Indeed, it is worth going to Balledehob to hear him tell it.   He always pledges himself to the truth of every word with his fore-fingers crossed; and when he comes to speak of the loss of his guineas, he never fails to console himself by adding — " If they stayed with me I wouldn't have luck with them, sir; and father O'Shea told me 'twas as well for me they were changed, for if they hadn't, they'd have burned holes in my pocket, and got out that way."

I shall never forget his solemn countenance, and the deep tones of his warning voice, when he concluded his tale, by telling me, that the next day after his ride with the fairies, Mick Dowling was missing, and he believed him to be given to the *sarpint* in his place, as he had never been heard of since. " The blessing of the saints be between all good men and harm," was the concluding sentence of Tim Jarvis's narrative, as he flung the remaining drops from his glass upon the green sward.

RENT-DAY.

XXXV.

" Oh ullagone, ullagone ! this is a wide world, but what will we do in it, or where will we go ? " muttered Bill Doody, as he sat on a rock by the Lake of Killarney.   " What will we do ? to-morrow's rent-day, and Tim the Driver swears if we don't pay up our rent, he'll cant every *ha'perth* we have ; and then, sure enough, there's Judy and myself, and the poor little *grawls* [1] will be turned out to starve on the high road, for the never a halfpenny of rent have I ! — Oh hone, that ever I should live to see this day !"

Thus did Bill Doody bemoan his hard fate, pouring his sorrows to the reckless waves of the most beautiful of lakes, which seemed to mock his misery as they rejoiced beneath the cloudless sky of a May morning.   That lake, glittering in sun-shine, sprinkled with fairy isles of rock and ver-dure, and bounded by giant hills of ever-varying hues, might, with its magic beauty, charm all sadness but despair ; for alas,

> " How ill the scene that offers rest
> And heart that cannot rest agree ! "

Yet Bill Doody was not so desolate as he sup-

---

[1] Children.

posed; there was one listening to him he little thought of, and help was at hand from a quarter he could not have expected.

"What's the matter with you, my poor man?" said a tall portly looking gentleman, at the same time stepping out of a furze-brake. Now Bill was seated on a rock that commanded the view of a large field. Nothing in the field could be concealed from him, except this furze-brake, which grew in a hollow near the margin of the lake. He was, therefore, not a little surprised at the gentleman's sudden appearance, and began to question whether the personage before him belonged to this world or not. He, however, soon mustered courage sufficient to tell him how his crops had failed, how some bad member had charmed away his butter, and how Tim the Driver threatened to turn him out of the farm if he didn't pay up every penny of the rent by twelve o'clock next day.

"A sad story indeed," said the stranger; "but surely, if you represented the case to your landlord's agent, he won't have the heart to turn you out."

"Heart, your honour! where would an agent get a heart!" exclaimed Bill. "I see your honour does not know him: besides, he has an eye on the farm this long time for a fosterer of his own; so I expect no mercy at all at all, only to be turned out."

"Take this, my poor fellow, take this," said the stranger, pouring a purse full of gold into Bill's old hat, which in his grief he had flung on the ground. "Pay the fellow your rent, but I'll take care it shall do him no good. I remember the time when things went otherwise in this country, when I would have hung up such a fellow in the twinkling of an eye!"

These words were lost upon Bill, who was insensible to every thing but the sight of the gold, and before he could unfix his gaze, and lift up his head to pour out his hundred thousand blessings, the stranger was gone. The bewildered peasant looked around in search of his benefactor, and at last he thought he saw him riding on a white horse a long way off on the lake.

" O'Donoghue, O'Donoghue!" shouted Bill; " the good, the blessed O'Donoghue!" and he ran capering like a madman to show Judy the gold, and to rejoice her heart with the prospect of wealth and happiness.

The next day Bill proceeded to the agent's; not sneakingly, with his hat in his hand, his eyes fixed on the ground, and his knees bending under him; but bold and upright, like a man conscious of his independence.

" Why don't you take off your hat, fellow; don't you know you are speaking to a magistrate?" said the agent.

" I know I'm not speaking to the king, sir," said Bill; " and I never takes off my hat but to them I can respect and love. The Eye that sees all knows I've no right either to respect or love an agent!"

" You scoundrel!" retorted the man in office, biting his lips with rage at such an unusual and unexpected opposition, " I'll teach you how to be insolent again — I have the power, remember."

" To the cost of the country, I know you have," said Bill, who still remained with his head as firmly covered as if he was the lord Kingsale himself.

" But, come," said the magistrate; " have you got the money for me ? — this is rent-day. If there's one penny of it wanting, or the running gale that's due, prepare to turn out before night, for you shall not remain another hour in possession."

" There is your rent," said Bill, with an unmoved expression of tone and countenance; " you'd better count it, and give me a receipt in full for the running gale and all."

The agent gave a look of amazement at the gold; for it was gold — real guineas! and not bits of dirty ragged small notes, that are only fit to light one's pipe with. However willing the agent may have been to ruin, as he thought, the unfortunate tenant, he took up the gold, and handed the receipt to Bill, who strutted off with it as proud as a cat of her whiskers.

The agent going to his desk shortly after, was confounded at beholding a heap of gingerbread cakes instead of the money he had deposited there. He raved and swore, but all to no purpose; the gold had become gingerbread cakes, just marked like the guineas, with the king's head, and Bill had the receipt in his pocket; so he saw there was no use in saying any thing about the affair, as he would only get laughed at for his pains.

From that hour Bill Doody grew rich; all his undertakings prospered; and he often blesses the day that he met with O'Donoghue, the great prince that lives down under the lake of Killarney.

Like the butterfly, the spirit of Donoghue closely hovers over the perfume of the hills and flowers it loves; while, as the reflection of a star in the waters of a pure lake, to those who look not above, that glorious spirit is believed to dwell beneath.

LINN-NA-PAYSHTHA.

XXXVI.

TRAVELLERS go to Leinster to see Dublin and the Dargle; to Ulster, to see the Giant's Causeway, and, perhaps, to do penance at Lough Dearg; to Munster, to see Killarney, the beautiful city of Cork, and half a dozen other fine things; but whoever thinks of the fourth province? — whoever thinks of going —

> — " westward, where Dick Martin *ruled*
> The houseless wilds of Cunnemara?"

The Ulster-man's ancient denunciation " to Hell or to Connaught," has possibly led to the supposition that this is a sort of infernal place above ground — a kind of terrestrial Pandemonium — in short, that Connaught is little better than hell, or hell little worse than Connaught; but let any one only go there for a month, and, as the natives say, " I'll warrant he'll soon see the differ, and learn to understand that it is mighty like the rest o' green Erin, only something poorer;" and yet it might be thought that in this particular " worse would be needless;" but so it is.

" My gracious me," said the landlady of the Inn at Sligo, " I wonder a gentleman of your *teest* and *curosity* would think of leaving Ireland without making a *tower* (tour) of Connaught, if it was nothing more than spending a day at Hazlewood, and up the lake, and on to the *ould* abbey at Friarstown, and the castle at Dromahair."

Polly M'Bride, my kind hostess, might not in this remonstrance have been altogether disinterested; but her advice prevailed, and the dawn of the following morning found me in a boat on the unruffled surface of Lough Gill. Arrived at the head of that splendid sheet of water, covered with rich and wooded islands with their ruined buildings, and bounded by towering mountains, noble plantations, grassy slopes, and precipitous rocks, which give beauty, and, in some places, sublimity to its shores, I proceeded at once up the wide river which forms its principal tributary. The " ould abbey " is chiefly remarkable for having been built at a period nearer to the Reformation than any other ecclesiastical edifice of the same class. Full within view of it, and at the distance of half a mile, stands the shattered remnant of Breffni's princely hall. I strode forward with the enthusiasm of an antiquary, and the high-beating heart of a patriotic Irishman. I felt myself on classic ground, immortalised by the lays of Swift and of Moore. I pushed my way into the hallowed precincts of the grand and venerable edifice. I entered its chambers, and, oh my countrymen, I found them converted into the domicile of pigs, cows, and poultry! But the exterior of " O'Rourke's old hall," grey, frowning, and ivy-covered, is well enough; it stands on a beetling precipice, round which a noble river wheels its course.   The opposite bank is a very steep ascent, thickly wooded, and rising to a height of at least seventy feet; and, for a quarter of a mile, this beautiful copse follows the course of the river.

The first individual I encountered was an old cowherd; nor was I unfortunate in my cicerone, for he assured me there were plenty of old stories about strange things that used to be in the place; " but," continued he, " for my own share, I never met any thing worse nor myself.   If it bees ould stories that your honour's after, the story about Linn-na-Payshtha and Poul-maw-Gullyawn is the only thing about this place that's worth one jack-straw.   Does your honour see that great big black hole in the river yonder below?"   He pointed my attention to a part of the river about fifty yards from the old hall, where a long island occupied the centre of the wide current, the water at one side running shallow, and at the other assuming every appearance of unfathomable depth.   The spacious pool, dark and still, wore a deathlike quietude of surface.   It looked as if the speckled trout would shun its murky pre-cincts — as if even the daring pike would shrink from so gloomy a dwelling-place.   " That's Linn-na-Payshtha, sir," resumed my guide, " and Poul-maw-Gullyawn is just the very *moral* of it, only that it's round, and not in a river, but stand-ing out in the middle of a green field, about a short quarter of a mile from this.   Well, 'tis as good as fourscore years — I often *hard* my father, God be merciful to him! tell the story — since Manus O'Rourke, a great buckeen, a cock-fighting, drinking blackguard that was long ago, went to sleep one night and had a dream about Linn-na-Payshtha. This Manus, the dirty spalpeen, there was no ho with him; he thought to ride rough-shod over his betters through the whole country, though he was not one of the real stock of the O'Rourkes. Well, this fellow had a dream that if he dived in Linn-na-Payshtha at twelve o'clock of a Hollow-eve night, he'd find more gold than would make a man of him and his wife, while grass grew or water ran. The next night he had the same dream, and sure enough if he had it the second night, it came to him the third in the same form. Manus, well becomes him, never told mankind or womankind, but swore to himself, by all the books that ever were shut or open, that, any how, he would go to the bottom of the big hole. What did he care for the Payshtha-more that was lying there to keep guard on the gold and silver of the old ancient family that was buried there in the wars, packed up in the brewing-pan? Sure he was as good an O'Rourke as the best of them, taking care to forget that his grandmother's father was a cow-boy to the earl O'Donnel. At long last Hollow-eve comes, and sly and silent master Manus creeps to bed early, and just at midnight steals down to the river side. When he came to the bank his mind misgave him, and he wheeled up to Frank M'Clure's — the old Frank that was then at that time — and got a bottle of whisky, and took it with him, and 'tis unknown how much of it he drank. He walked across to the island, and down he went gallantly to the bottom like a stone.

Sure enough the Payshtha was there afore him, lying like a great big conger eel, seven yards long, and as thick as a bull in the body, with a mane upon his neck like a horse. The Payshtha-more reared himself up; and, looking at the poor man as if he'd eat him, says he, in good English,

" ' Arrah, then, Manus,' says he, ' what brought you here? It would have been better for you to have blown your brains out at once with a pistol, and have made a quiet end of your-self, than to have come down here for me to deal with you.'

" ' Oh, plase your honour,' says Manus, ' I beg my life :' and there he stood shaking like a dog in a wet sack.

" ' Well, as you have some blood of the O'Rourkes in you, I forgive you this once; but, by this and by that, if ever I see you, or any one belonging to you, coming about this place again, I'll hang a quarter of you on every tree in the wood.'

" ' Go home,' says the Payshtha — ' go home, Manus,' says he; ' and if you can't make better use of your time, get drunk; but don't come here, bothering me. Yet, stop! since you are here, and have ventured to come, I'll show you some-thing that you'll remember till you go to your grave, and ever after, while you live.'

" With that, my dear, he opens an iron door in the bed of the river, and never the drop of water ran into it; and there Manus sees a long dry cave, or under-ground cellar like, and the Payshtha drags him in, and shuts the door. It wasn't long before the baste began to get smaller, and smaller, and smaller; and at last he grew as little as a taughn of twelve years old; and there he was, a brownish little man, about four feet high."

" ' Plase your honour,' says Manus, ' if I might make so bold, maybe you are one of the good people?'

" ' Maybe I am, and maybe I am not; but, anyhow, all you have to understand is this, that I'm bound to look after the Thiernas [1] of Breffni, and take care of them through every generation; and that my present business is to watch this cave, and what's in it, till the old stock is reigning over this country once more.'

" ' Maybe you are a sort of a banshee?'

" ' I am not, you fool,' said the little man. ' The banshee is a woman. My business is to live in the form you first saw me in, guarding this spot. And now hold your tongue, and look about you.'

" Manus rubbed his eyes, and looked right and left, before and behind; and there was the vessels of gold and the vessels of silver, the dishes, and the plates, and the cups, and the punch-bowls, and the tankards: there was the golden mether, too, that every Thierna at his wedding used to drink out of to the kerne in real usquebaugh. There was all the money that ever was saved in the family since they got a grant of this manor, in the days of the Firbolgs, down to the time of their *outer* ruination. He then brought Manus on with him to where there was arms for three

---

* *Tighearna*—a lord.   Vide O'BRIEN.

hundred men; and the sword set with diamonds, and the golden helmet of the O'Rourke; and he showed him the staff made out of an elephant's tooth, and set with rubies and gold, that the Thierna used to hold while he sat in his great hall, giving justice and the laws of the Brehons to all his clan. The first room in the cave, ye see, had the money and the plate, the second room had the arms, and the third had the books, papers, parchments, title-deeds, wills, and every thing else of the sort belonging to the family.

" ' And now, Manus,' says the little man, ' ye seen the whole o' this, and go your ways; but never come to this place any more, or allow any one else. I must keep watch and ward till the Sassanach is druv out of Ireland, and the Thiernas o' Breffni in their glory again.' The little man then stopped for a while and looked up in Manus's face, and says to him in a great passion, ' Arrah! bad luck to ye, Manus, why don't ye go about your business?'

" ' How can I? — sure you must show me the way out,' says Manus, making answer. The little man then pointed forward with his finger.

" ' Can't we go out the way we came?' says Manus.

" ' No, you must go out at the other end — that's the rule o' this place. Ye came in at Linn-na-Payshtha, and ye must go out at Poul-maw-Gullyawn: ye came down like a stone to the bottom of one hole, and ye must spring up like a cork to the top of the other.' With that the little man gave him one *hoise*, and all that Manus remembers was the roar of the water in his ears; and sure enough he was found the next morning, high and dry, fast asleep, with the empty bottle beside him, but far enough from the place he thought he landed, for it was just below yonder on the island that his wife found him. My father, God be merciful to him! heard Manus swear to every word of the story."

As there are few things which excite human desire throughout all nations more than wealth, the legends concerning the concealment, discovery, and circulation of money, are, as may be expected, widely extended; yet in all the circumstances, which admit of so much fanciful embellishment, there every-where exists a striking similarity.

Like the golden apples of the Hesperides, treasure is guarded by a dragon or serpent. Vide Creuzer, Religions de l'Antiquité, traduction de Guigniaut, i. 248. Paris, 1825. Stories of its discovery in consequence of dreams or spiritual agency are so numerous, that, if collected, they would fill many volumes, yet they vary little in detail beyond the actors and locality. Vide Grimm's Deutsche Sagen, i. 290. Thiele's Danske Folkesagn, i. 112. ii. 24. Kirke's Secret Commonwealth, p. 12. &c.

The circulation of money bestowed by the fairies or supernatural personages, like that of counterfeit coin, is seldom extensive. See story, in the Arabian Nights, of the old rogue whose fine looking money turned to leaves. When Waldemar, Holgar, and Grœn Jette, in Danish tradition, bestow money upon the boors whom they meet, their gift sometimes turns to fire, sometimes to pebbles, and sometimes is so hot, that the receiver drops it from his hand, when the gold, or what appeared to be so, sinks into the ground.

In poor Ireland, the wretched peasant contents himself by soliloquising—"Money is the devil, they say; and God is good that He keeps it from us."

FAIRY LEGENDS.

ROCKS AND STONES.

" Forms in silence frown'd,
Shapeless and nameless; and to mine eye
Sometimes they rolled off cloudily,
Wedding themselves with gloom — or grew
Gigantic to my troubled view,
And seem'd to gather round me."

BANIM's *Celt's Paradise*